A GENTLEMAN OF QUESTIONABLE JUDGMENT

THE LORD JULIAN MYSTERIES—BOOK NINE

GRACE BURROWES

GRACE BURROWES PUBLISHING

Cover art by Cracked Light Studio

DEDICATION

To Sweetness J Horse, mare beyond compare, and to all the Sweeties and their brothers.

I did not know you were a daughter of the turf until the day you died, but I knew you were a princess from the moment I saw you take Precious Cargo over the first of many jumps.

CHAPTER ONE

"In spring," Clarence Tenneby said, "a young man's thoughts turn to horse racing. You know how it is, my lord. The grass is greener, the breeze freshens, and one longs to feel the very earth shake with the pounding hooves of a dozen eager steeds galloping for the finish line. The crowds roar their enthusiasm for favorites and forlorn hopes alike, and everybody has a fine time."

Tenneby beamed at an elegant bay filly as if she were the belle of the ball, not the belle of Caldicott Hall's horse barn. He fished a quarter apple from a pocket and fed the beast a treat without asking my permission. Matilda was rising three. She'd started light training in harness the previous summer, and had recently moved on to first steps under saddle. She was a favorite with the grooms and a hopeless flirt when it came to apples.

"Do say you'll join us, Lord Julian," Tenneby went on, ambling down the barn aisle. "From what I heard last year, you could do with some fresh air and sunshine."

A year ago, I'd still been very much recovering from an ill-advised outing to Waterloo. I'd had no business struggling back into uniform to join that battle, but one did not ignore the commands of conscience.

One longed to ignore Clarence Tenneby, with his cherubic, beamish features, guileless blue eyes, and red locks styled a la Brutus. Based on what little I knew of him, Tenneby had been the boy last picked to join the schoolyard teams and the first to be pranked. He'd borne it all good-naturedly, according to the reports from those in his form. Through the vagaries of inheritance and fate, he was now in line for an earldom.

More than one younger son was likely regretting his treatment of Tenneby all those years ago.

"I appreciate the invitation, Tenneby, truly I do, but spring is a busy time on any country estate, and Caldicott Hall is no exception. With His Grace traveling on the Continent, I am expected to keep a hand in here." More to the point, after recently enduring more than a fortnight in Hampshire, I looked forward to spending the next weeks and months *at home*. London was in the midst of its annual social whirl, while I thrived on the peace and quiet of the countryside.

"One must keep a hand in, of course," Tenneby said, pausing outside the stall of my personal mount, Atlas, "but plowing is nearly complete, and it's too soon for haying. Do say you'll nip along to Berkshire and join us."

The only place I wanted to nip along to was the Hall's spacious, peaceful library, where I could pen my next epistle to my darling Hyperia.

"I must regretfully decline," I said as Atlas hung his dark head over the half door of his stall. "Hello, Lord Layabout." I held out a hand, which he delicately sniffed before turning a curious eye on Tenneby.

"The famous Atlas, I take it. Dalhousie was much taken with him. Elegance and power in equal generous measures, according to the marquess. A shame the beast was gelded."

My sojourn to Hampshire had been at the request of the Marquess of Dalhousie. At some point in my visit to Dalhousie

Manor, his lordship had mentioned Tenneby. The recollection roused in me a sense of vague unease, but then, my experiences in uniform had left me suspicious by nature.

"This is indeed Atlas." I scratched a hairy ear. "Bought him on the Peninsula. Iberian sire, draft dam. Sweet-natured, exquisitely trained. Unbelievable stamina and will beggar his dignity for a carrot." My horse was dear to me, and if that added to my reputation as an eccentric, so be it. I wore blue-tinted spectacles when out of doors to protect my weak eyes from bright sunshine, and my past included a dubious period of captivity in French hands.

The unkindest of the gossips labeled me a traitor, which I was not, but those who'd called me half unhinged by my ordeal were sadly close to the mark. With time, the support of my familiars, and a concerted effort on my part, I now estimated myself to be between one-quarter and one-eighth unhinged.

On good days, I presented as absolutely sound, and I had been having a notably good day before Tenneby's phaeton had come tooling up to the Hall's front door.

"Dalhousie said you let him ride Atlas." Tenneby produced another apple quarter, and Atlas turned a limpid gaze on the new object of all his affections. "I was and am most envious. We don't import enough Iberian bloodstock, in my opinion. That quality of hidden fire is underappreciated hereabouts. Back when Good King Hal married Catherine of Aragon, we brought in Iberian horses by the boatload, didn't we? Now we must have our Thoroughbreds, and I am foremost among the breed's admirers. Why hide the fire when you can send it blazing around a racecourse, eh?"

Lest Tenneby start regaling me with bloodlines and turf tales, I led my guest to the next stall. That we were wandering the stable aisle as opposed to gracing the formal parlor was only to be expected. Tenneby was horse mad and, more specifically, a member of the turf fraternity—the subset of the horse-mad throng devoted passionately to racing. When any other guest would have asked for a tour of the portrait gallery, Tenneby had begged to see the stables.

On a pretty spring day, I was willing to oblige him, and yet, his impromptu call also struck me as odd. I'd been well ahead of him at school. He'd not served in uniform. We were hardly loyal correspondents. He, along with half the peerage, had condoled me by post on the death of the previous Duke of Waltham, my late father.

And now, years later, here was Tenneby, unannounced and offering invitations to a private race meeting in Berkshire. Most odd. I was on very few guest lists and much preferred it that way.

"Surely you can spare me a few days, my lord? All the best people will be there. Berkshire is a quick hop out from Town, much easier to get to than Newmarket, you'll agree."

The distance was about the same in either direction. Newmarket lay to the east of London, in the direction of Suffolk, while Tenneby's destination lay to the west, a day's journey of sixty-five miles or so by coach, if weather and roads cooperated.

"Tenneby, I am flattered, but what you call 'all the best people' are, in general, parties I would rather avoid. As far as many of them are concerned, I am responsible for Lord Harry's death, if not for Napoleon's entire occupation of Spain. I keep myself to myself as best I can, and we're all much happier that way."

Mention of my late brother was a bit unsporting, even ruthless, as Harry himself had occasionally been ruthless.

A glint of mulishness flashed in Tenneby's eyes. "I suspected you'd be reluctant, but how will you ever live down the gossip if you simply hide in the shires? That just makes you look more guilty. His lordship died while loyally serving his country, and no more need be said on the matter."

Apparently, only blunt speech would do. "I have nothing to prove to those people, Tenneby, and I hope you don't either."

He studied the gray gelding lipping at his hay in the loose-box before us. "So you would think, what with me being Uncle Temmie's heir and all, but that has only made the whispers worse."

I knew I would regret asking. Knew it, knew it, and knew it again. "What whispers?"

"Nice quarters on that one. Perfect shoulder angle. He was likely a grand jumper in his day. Dalhousie didn't tell you?"

The gray had indeed been a grand jumper, one of Harry's winnings at the card table. I hadn't much use for the gelding myself, but my brother Arthur, the current duke, wouldn't part with him.

"Dalhousie had much on his mind when I visited him in Hampshire." The marquess had been preoccupied by feuding family and multiple murder attempts, to hear him tell it.

"He neglected to mention that I was robbed of victory at Epsom several years past?"

That inkling of suspicion I'd been ignoring flared into a frisson of foreboding. "Dalhousie referred in passing to race results that weren't what you'd hoped for." Tenneby had refused to pay a marker for one thousand pounds owed to Dalhousie as a result of Tenneby's horse losing. Perhaps it was one thousand guineas. The turf set bought and sold horses in guineas rather than pounds, for reasons unknown to saner mortals.

"The race was rigged, my lord. My colt, Excalibur, should have romped away with the purse, but he barely staggered past the finish line. Poor lad ought to have won the day, and the shame of it nearly killed him."

Horses did not die of shame—wise creatures—but I nearly had. Shame, sorrow, melancholia, and exhaustion of the spirit. That experience stopped me from dismissing Tenneby's indignation out of hand, because surely the horse's *owner* had felt profoundly humiliated.

"Dalhousie offered no particulars." I did recall that Tenneby refused to pay the wagered amount because he was that convinced the race had been thrown.

"Decent of him," Tenneby said. "The truth is, I made a fool of myself, demanding a rematch, accusing grooms, jockeys, and stewards of every imaginable offense. They all made allowances—up to a point—but nobody took me seriously. People don't. Take me seriously. Even when I'm the earl, they won't, meaning no disrespect to

Uncle Temmie. They wouldn't if I were made king. I'm turf mad, a bumbler, though I do run an occasional winner. Blind hogs and acorns. You've doubtless heard the talk."

The gray sent us a sidewise look and took another bite of his hay.

I needed to stop Tenneby before he leaped the next figurative fence. "I do not hear the talk. I mind my own patch and ignore those who seek only to gossip. I suggest you do the same. We can return to the Hall by way of the yearling pasture if you'd like to see our younger stock."

He gave me another half glower. The self-declared bumbler well knew he was being cozened. "Tentative Tenneby, they used to call me, because I was always so deferential and unprepossessing. You try being chubby, not too bright, and a plain mister sent along to public school with baby dukes and princes. It's not my fault Papa was rich, and he was right in the end to see me properly educated. I'm the earl's heir now, and those baby dukes will have to take notice of me in the Lords."

To speak of inheriting a title was ill-mannered. I made allowances because I, too, had inhabited the margins at public school. Arthur, as the future duke and a naturally conscientious scholar, had seen smooth sailing in his academic ventures. Harry, the spare and a born charmer, had fared easily while earning mediocre marks.

Along I came, Lord Julian, nicknamed Extra in reference to being an extra spare. I was by turns engrossed by languages and indifferent to philosophy, keen on natural history, and disdainful of oratory. Headmaster had despaired of my wasted potential. I'd despaired of sunny matutinal eternities endured in musty classrooms.

"Tenneby, we are no longer schoolboys. Let the past go." I headed out of the barn into the bright midday air. I got a stab of agony in the eyeballs for my haste and quickly donned my blue spectacles.

"You wear those because of the war," Tenneby said. "You never minded bright light before."

"I saw a powder wagon explode from too close a vantage point. I nearly went blind for a time." A terrifying and humbling experience.

"Now about your race meeting. I wish you every success, but I fail to see how my attendance would in any way aid your cause. Would you like some luncheon, or prefer to be on your way?"

He appeared entirely unoffended by my transparent attempt to send him packing. "Those same boys, the baby dukes and lordlings, all love the turf. One of them cheated me out of twenty-eight thousand pounds three years ago, and I want you on hand to ensure it doesn't happen again. Say you'll come, and I will make it worth your while."

More desperation. Any fellow with pretensions to status did not discuss money or its near equivalents. "Tenneby, you are overset. If I were to attend the race meeting, I'd do so purely for enjoyment, not to antagonize half the peerage and their turf-obsessed heirs."

"The best stallion England has ever seen is running in my colors, and if the ruddy earldom isn't to be bankrupted by Christmas, that horse had better win. You disdain to help me because you don't want to offend a lot of peacocks and highborn wastrels. Your timidity will allow a scoundrel to triumph over honest sportsmen once more."

Every officer in the British army was instructed to ensure that his underlings felt as if the outcome of the entire war turned on their steadfast loyalty, their marksmanship, their stamina on yet another forced march. The argument was compelling and effective, but I'd ceased to be swayed by it five minutes into my first battle.

And I was not timid. "Wagering is no way to raise funds, Tenneby. Whatever else might have been said about you, you were considered to have good judgment." The same could not be said of me. "Antagonizing one's social superiors is always ill-advised." Though sometimes necessary, as I'd found in my various investigations.

Tenneby tromped along beside me as I made for the yearling pasture. "I am being sensible now by recruiting you to attend this meeting, my lord. With you on hand as my guest, nobody will try any underhanded business. All I ask is that Excalibur run a fair race.

Given your reputation for untangling mischief, he'll get the chance to win that he deserves."

An appeal to vanity should have been the worst insult of all, and yet, I was tempted. The job Tenneby described was not an investigation per se—no mysteries to untangle—but rather, the *prevention* of mischief. I could have a look around, perhaps walk the racecourse of a morning or two... but no.

One former reconnaissance officer against the collective capacity of the turf crowd for getting up to tricks was bad odds indeed. Highly qualified and experienced race stewards were hard put to achieve that end, and I was nobody to take on the job at a private meeting.

"Tenneby, I appreciate that you believe yourself to have been the victim of a crime for which nobody was held accountable. I grasp how that predisposes one to extra caution and to distrust of one's fellows. Your concerns are valid, but I am not the party best situated to address them. I know nothing about horse racing and care even less for the sport. Now, shall you stay to lunch, or will you take advantage of this fine weather to continue to your next destination?"

He halted and made a visual inspection of the Hall's lovely stables, a gray granite facility in the shape of a horseshoe two stories high. I'd all but grown up in the stable yard, and when I'd first mustered out, I'd spent hours in the barn simply grooming Atlas.

I loved the Hall, and the jewel in the Caldicott domestic crown was, to me, the stable.

"You won't come, then?" Tenneby said, tapping his hat more firmly onto his head.

"I can't see how my attendance would address the need for security that you describe."

"So be it. I will be on my way, then, and thank you for hearing me out. Miss West will doubtless be disappointed that you declined my invitation, but she'll rub along well enough without your escort. A lady with that much poise and charm is never at a loss for a gallant or two."

Hyperia was attending the race meeting? My own dear Perry?

Ladies did attend the public race meetings, though they were carefully kept away from the blacklegs and bookmakers and from the women on hand to ply a very old trade indeed.

Tenneby caught the eye of a groom and waved an arm in a gesture that requested that his phaeton be brought around. "A pleasure to have taken the tour, my lord. That gray is going to waste, though. He's pining for a good steeplechase, and on this, I do account myself something of an expert."

Bother the gray. Hyperia hadn't said a word to me about attending any race meeting. "Tenneby, when, precisely, is this race meeting, and where exactly will it be held?"

Tenneby's dilemma—a shortage of cash to go with an anticipated abundance of social standing—had become increasingly common. For the past century or so, England had been at war, with the last twenty years seeing a tremendous effort expended to defeat the Corsican menace.

Or—to echo the sentiments of cynical officers—to reopen Continental markets to British trade.

Fortunes had nonetheless been amassed as a result of all that wartime patriotism, or rather, all that determination to defend a worldwide mercantile empire. Many of those fortunes had been made by enterprising commoners keen to take advantage of the industrial advances the war effort had inspired. The aristocracy, by contrast, had for the most part kept its nose out of trade and had expected to be spared the postwar crash that had yet to come right.

A doomed expectation, as it turned out.

For the members of the peerage still earning wealth mostly from the land, a series of bad harvests, terrible winters, and rising competition from overseas markets put many a titled family in dun territory. From wool, to wheat, to wood, former enemies, allies, and even former colonies were producing more, better, and faster than Merry Olde could.

The Caldicotts had been lucky, in that our dukes tended to pragmatism. Grandpapa, Papa, and now Arthur had diversified the family holdings to the extent that the Hall was self-sufficient and even profitable most years, and the family wealth was securely invested in all manner of endeavors.

These musings accompanied me as I made a social call on the day following Tenneby's visit.

"Where did Tenneby's father earn his fortune?" I asked.

I'd found Lady Ophelia Oliphant sketching in her orchard, the space awash in pink, red, and white blooms. We walked beneath an outer row of damsons, their fragrance gilding a peaceful and damnably sunny afternoon.

"Not wool," Lady Ophelia said, strolling arm in arm with me. "Guns, I think. The gun barrels used in tropical surrounds rust almost as soon as they arrive, so the need is endless. Or was endless. Hector Tenneby was the sensible sort, as younger sons ought to be. He lived modestly, had his sons well educated and his older daughters well dowered. The youngest girl—Emmaline? No. Evelyn. She's said to be only modestly fixed. That wife of his..."

I'd paid this visit in part because Lady Ophelia was a living appendix to *DeBrett's Guide to the Peerage*. She knew the titled families by heart, as most wellborn ladies did. She also knew the untitled cousins, the remittance men, the tippling aunties who'd been sent on extended travel after their first Season, only to return in much less wanton spirits a year later.

Her ladyship, being my godmother, also knew *me*. "What of Mrs. Tenneby?" I asked.

"Not Mrs. Tenneby, Julian. Heaven forgive you that slip. Lady Chloe, born Lady Chloe Dearborn. Hector Tenneby married up, but then, he could afford to. Lady Chloe's family made the usual trade."

"A daughter's happiness in exchange for a suitor's wealth?"

"You needn't sound so disapproving. Lady Chloe was kept in

comfort and style for all of her days. A bit too much comfort, would be my guess. She had a penchant for wagering. My theory is that she gambled as revenge for a broken heart, but that is pure speculation."

Lady Ophelia's speculations were to be accorded considerable deference. She was a contemporary of my mother and in great good looks, given her mature years. I'd taken some time to realize that she had convinced all and sundry that she was merely an aging belle, ingenuous, voluble, and happy to waft from one social gathering to the next.

Godmama, in fact, missed little, forgot nothing, and kept a catalog of scandals at her mental fingertips. I had my suspicions regarding Lady Ophelia's past, but she'd for the most part respected my privacy, and thus I returned the courtesy.

I paused with her ladyship at a corner of the orchard. "Tenneby told me the earldom is approaching dun territory. Is it possible that Lady Chloe borrowed from her brother-in-law the earl?"

"Of course," Godmama replied. "Though 'borrowed' puts too fine a point on it. The earl would have covered his sister-in-law's debts rather than see the family embarrassed by her excesses, and now her son is set to inherit the resulting mess. Old Temerity must see a certain justice in that."

"Temerity?"

She resumed our progress. "The Tenneby family holds the Earldom of Temmington. Somewhere along the way, the present earl acquired the *nom de guerre* Temerity, though it's meant to be ironic. Just as Sally Jersey's incessant chattering has earned her the sobriquet Silence, the present Lord Temmington is self-effacing, retiring, and cordial to a fault. Always equivocating and explaining, poor fellow. The nephew has a bit of the same quality."

As a schoolboy, perhaps, but my encounter with Clarence Tenneby the previous day suggested a quantity of resentment lurked beneath the self-effacing manners—resentment and determination.

"I am reluctant to attend this race meeting," I said as a breeze stirred the branches above and sent a shower of blossoms down onto our heads and shoulders. "No good can come of it."

Lady Ophelia stopped walking again, removed my hat from my head, and brushed the fallen petals from the crown and brim. "Have you agreed to go?"

My own dear mother would not have presumed on my person to such an extent, though Hyperia would have. Hyperia, whom I missed desperately.

"I have agreed to consider the invitation." I accepted the return of my hat and replaced it on my head. "Tenneby swears on the grave of the sainted Eclipse that he was cheated out of winning at Epsom three years ago. One of the lesser races, but the sums changing hands on the outcome were enormous."

"Aren't they always? Is that what makes you hesitate to take on Tenneby's investigation?"

"My reservations are myriad, Godmama. Tenneby claims he isn't asking me to sort out what went wrong three years ago, which is fortunate, because that trail has doubtless been obliterated by now. He wants me on hand as a tacit deterrent."

"Not exactly flattering to be cast as a glorified bullyboy, is it?"

"Damned near insulting, but also... recognition of a sort. I have solved a few of Society's more vexing puzzles." And I'd enjoyed doing so, to be honest. "I fear Tenneby overestimates the extent to which I could deter anybody from anything, though. In military circles, I'm the next thing to a pariah, and in social circles..."

"You *are* a pariah, and worse than that, you're a pariah engaged to be married. One cannot even plead your bachelorhood with the hostesses looking to make up the numbers."

I was also a ducal heir, but as Godmama had said, I'd chosen my prospective bride, and thus I was no longer of interest to even the matchmakers. Was I still of interest to my dear Hyperia?

"What's the worst that could happen?" Godmama linked her arm through mine, and we resumed walking.

"Good question. I could attend, suffer the usual slurs and indignities, and be completely ineffective as Tenneby is once again fleeced of his last groat." The absolute worst thing would be if Hyperia publicly snubbed me because she resented my presence. A gentleman would never break off an engagement, but Hyperia and I had encountered some headwinds in Hampshire, and I was less confident of her esteem than I'd been previously.

"You're convinced Tenneby was fleeced three years ago?"

"He's convinced. He simply can't prove it."

"I'm the Queen of England. I simply can't prove it, but you believe him."

I mentally rummaged around among hunches, intuitions, observations, and inklings. "Clarence Tenneby has always been an ideal victim. Basically sweet-natured, avoids confrontation, has enough standing to circulate among his betters, and even more standing since his cousin fell at Waterloo. Bullying Tenneby can be done under the guise of humor, teasing, bonhomie, pranks. From pranks to schemes is a short step, and, in fact, Tenneby has done nothing about the loss three years ago, except grumble."

Grumble loudly and refuse to honor the larger markers, probably because he needed the funds elsewhere.

"You never could abide a bully. Your headmasters referred to you as solitary, but that wasn't the whole story, was it?"

"I am solitary by nature, and as a reconnaissance officer, appreciation for my own company was an asset."

Lady Ophelia brushed a stray petal from the sleeve of her cloak. "You weren't Arthur or Harry, a very great failing, but you made your peace with it. Tenneby wasn't as wise as you, and now he's to be an earl. I suppose it's natural that he'd want to get back some of his own before the title befalls him. Stand on his own two common gentlemanly feet, so to speak. From a certain perspective, he's brave to even try."

"You're saying I should go." Godmama wasn't entirely wrong to cast Tenneby's stubbornness in an honorable, even heroic, light. "I know nothing about horse racing, except that it has ruined lives and marriages and left men who were in good health at breakfast dead before sunset."

"Rather like war, isn't it? So much good and bad fortune turning on last night's rainy weather. Not a very inviting prospect to one with your history."

We'd made a complete circuit of the orchard and come back to her ladyship's blanket, basket, and easel. From a distance, Godmama still had the slender, lithe grace of youth. The spring sunshine told another tale, in fine lines about her eyes and mouth and silver threads at her temples.

Tempus fugit. "Hyperia will be there," I said. "I suspect that's what gave Tenneby the notion to recruit me." That, and the Marquess of Dalhousie's enthusiastic satisfaction with services rendered.

"Ah. Well, then. You had best not go after all."

"Why?"

She patted my cheek, which annoyed me exceedingly. "Because then you might have to resume repairing the damage with dear Hyperia that your outing to Hampshire caused. You might have to court your intended as she wishes to be courted and not only as you prefer to court her. What a dreary prospect."

"Godmama, tread lightly."

She raised her eyebrows in what might have been genuine surprise. "If you're that unsure of Hyperia's affections, then you must attend this race meeting, Julian. Sort matters out. You and Hyperia have been engaged only since the Yuletide holidays, and breaking it off now would hardly cause a scandal. She's a plain miss and on the shelf, et cetera and so forth. You're... *you*. If she's no longer enamored of you, better to find that out now, isn't it?"

Better to never find that out at all.

"I'll go, but not to interrogate Hyperia about her intentions. She is articulate, intelligent, and more than capable of knowing and speaking her mind." She was also unfailingly kind, at least to me, and that bothered me. Kindness and pity were close kin.

"Then why go?" Lady Ophelia asked, enthroning herself on a stool before her easel. "You will be surrounded by loud, drunken fools taking unpardonable risks and treating it all as if it's a lark."

Much like the army. "Tenneby claims his stallion is unbeatable, but the last time he made that claim, he ended up an impoverished laughingstock. He needs..."

Her ladyship took up a pencil. "Yes?"

"He needs allies." More to the point, he'd asked for my help, at great cost to his pride. I respected him for that, enough that I would try my best to assist him.

And the less said about my own pride, the better.

CHAPTER TWO

"A race meeting is like a grand party that goes on for days," Atticus said, kicking his heels against the traveling coach's backward-facing bench. "There's races, and wagers, and drinking, and more wagers, and more races, and the fastest horses you ever did see. Eclipse could run better'n fifty miles an hour!"

I sent a reproving look toward my tiger's boots, to no avail. "Not for any great distance, he couldn't. Who has been filling your head with these tales?"

"Old Fergus and the grooms. Half of 'em was jockeys, or their brothers and uncles was jockeys. Fergus saw Eclipse beat Bucephalus at Newmarket. He were just a lad then—Fergus, not Eclipse. Said you never seen nothing like that horse and never will."

The great Eclipse had been forced into retirement at stud because he had literally beaten all comers. Nobody would bet against him. His style of running had been peculiar—nose low—but he'd had both speed and the will to win. In the years since his death in 1789 at the age of twenty-four, his progeny had exhibited those same traits, though not in the glorious abundance their sire had known.

And now, my tiger, a mere lad, was being bamboozled with legends and fairy tales.

"Atticus, I'm glad the prospect of this meeting pleases you, but heed me: Racing is serious business. Huge sums are wagered, and exorbitant expenses go into maintaining a racing stable. I am attending at Tenneby's request because he anticipates foul play. Keep your wits about you."

The boy's heels went mercifully still. "Foul play? Like tampering with the horses?"

"Possibly, or with the course, or with the stewards, or with God knows what. Tenneby doesn't know why his horse ran so poorly three years ago. For all we know, it wasn't even his colt on the course, but rather, another animal that closely resembled his, substituted at the last minute."

Atticus's mouth formed into a perfect O. "That's bleedin' cheating."

"Language, lad. You will hear some virtuosic swearing at this gathering, but a gentleman minds his tongue."

Atticus scowled, and I chided myself for raising a tender subject.

Atticus was not a gentleman. He was a boy of about nine or ten years whom I'd plucked from the staff of a Kentish manor to be my tiger. At the time, I'd had little use for a tiger, but my sensibilities had been offended by the neglect of a keen young mind. Atticus, who'd begun life in a London poorhouse, also had a feral sort of honor that I understood and trusted. He'd made himself useful in my investigations, though I was trying to coax him into spending more time on book learning and less time gossiping with the grooms.

"Fergus rode his first race when he were twelve," Atticus said. "Boys don't weigh much."

No, no, no, and no. "And how old was Fergus when he broke his collarbone for the first time?"

Atticus gifted me with another scowl. "Jockeys are tough. A fall here or there doesn't bother them."

Boys were not tough, though society insisted they appear to be.

"If anybody says he'll pay you to ride a half-broken Thoroughbred youngster, you *decline*, Atticus. Tell them your unreasonable, block-headed, clod-pated employer forbids it. I don't care if you're approached for a morning gallop, a canter on the Downs, or a match race."

The scowl became a glower. "Why? You say I'm a natural in the saddle."

I'd begun Atticus's education by teaching him to ride, a skill many grooms acquired, but not all. From there, assisted by Hyperia, I'd embarked on the ongoing struggle to make the boy literate. His diction was also a work in progress, going half Cockney when he was excited or worried and turning up nearly proper when he was in more confident spirits.

"You are a natural equestrian, but today's Thoroughbred is not a creature trained for a mannerly hack. Those who breed racehorses are interested in only one quality—speed. Your hero Eclipse had a dangerously foul temper, and that temper has been bred into many of his progeny, along with his speed. These horses are schooled from a young age to run their hearts out. You don't steer them so much as you hang on for dear life and pray to cross the finish line this side of your celestial reward."

Atticus pushed a mop of dark hair away from his eyes. "Fergus says there's nothing like winning a hard race."

Fergus was overdue for a very pointed lecture. He'd dazzled Harry and me with the same blather, leaving Arthur to explain the finer and more dangerous details of race riding to us.

"Ask Fergus why he limps, my boy. Ask him why he can predict foul weather by the throbbing in his shoulder. Ask him why, if being a jockey was the pinnacle of all his joys, he gave it up before he turned twenty."

"Twenty is old."

Ah, youth and the blessed ignorance attendant thereto. "He was tired of starving himself, Atticus, and of breaking bones so some rich toff could make a packet without taking any risks, while the jockey was left to limp home with a few quid in his pocket—when he could walk at all." Fergus hadn't admitted to that denouement until I'd been much older—nearly twenty myself.

"I could do it," Atticus said, little chin jutting. "I could make it across the finish line and maybe even win. Fergus says it's half luck and half skill—yours and the horse's."

I understood a child's skepticism toward adult authority. From Atticus's perspective, I was elderly (though not yet thirty years of age), prone to a profound type of intermittent forgetfulness, cursed with weak eyes, and out of favor with Society. What did I know about anything? I'd turned the very same distrust on most of my governesses, tutors, and teachers, until they'd proven their competence.

I could lecture Atticus, exhort, forbid, and threaten, but those tactics had never worked on me as a boy. They hadn't worked on Atticus when I'd thought to leave him in the schoolroom during the investigation in Hampshire.

Instead, he'd disobeyed direct orders and stowed away on the baggage coach and then provided material assistance in my efforts to resolve the Marquess of Dalhousie's difficulties.

Subtle tactics were in order.

"If you'd like to try riding racehorses, I'll arrange for you to go along on some training gallops. You can rely on Fergus's dubiously fond recollections, or you can make up your own mind. The choice is yours. Just know that anybody who hires you to ride won't give a ruddy damn whether you break your head or lose a hand, while I do give a damn, as do Miss West, His Grace, and Lady Ophelia."

The chin dipped. "You'd let me do practice gallops?"

He could ride, but he had no idea the degree of speed and power a fit Thoroughbred brought to the undertaking. "On the flat."

He nodded, suggesting that even his overdeveloped equestrian confidence was daunted by the prospect of the enormous hedges, yawning ditches, muddy banks, and water hazards typical of any steeplechase course.

"Are we agreed, Atticus? You will tell me if you'd like to ride a few gallops, and I'll arrange it, but you will not accept any rides offered by strangers."

He nodded.

I stuck out my hand because I meant business, and I wanted him to know it. We shook, the first time that male ritual had been observed between us, and I—foolishly—felt marginally less fretful on his behalf. Atticus was brave but not reckless, proud but not arrogant. A few heart-pounding excursions—and maybe even a tumble or two onto spring grass—and he could weigh risks and rewards on the basis of firsthand evidence.

Though as to that, the fields in the surrounds of Tenneby's estate looked sorely overdue for some rain.

As the coach turned between the gateposts of Tenneby's family seat, I was already chastising myself for the bargain I'd struck with Atticus. I could ensure that he rode only on good ground, that the other training riders didn't cut him off, use their whips on his face or on his horse. I could limit the risks so the practice gallops were only incrementally more dangerous than the risks he took every time he climbed into the saddle.

But Hyperia would hate the whole notion of letting a boy ride a Thoroughbred racer. Every day, in all sorts of weather, boys did exactly that at training stables, but Atticus was *my* boy to guide and protect. If anything happened to him, Hyperia would hold me responsible.

As I'd hold myself responsible.

"You're looking glum, guv," Atticus said. "Place seems pretty enough to me."

The coach was navigating a sweeping turn of the drive doubtless intended to give visitors a lovely first impression of Tenneby Acres. The façade was uniform golden sandstone rising to three neoclassical stories, complete with pediment, frieze, and perfectly symmetrical front steps marching down from a wide front terrace.

Pots of yellow, white, and red tulips graced not only the terrace, but the first-floor window boxes. A bright green door as well as bright green shutters echoed the verdure of the surrounding park.

I was abruptly homesick for the Hall, a larger and more staid version of the same style. "Tenneby is blessed in his dwelling."

"I hope he's blessed in his kitchen too. I'm starving."

"We follow the usual arrangement, Atticus. You dine in the servants' hall and sleep in my dressing closet." Safer for him that way.

"I can sleep in the footmen's dormitory, guv, or bunk in with the grooms." Said with a certain, calculated casualness. As an aspiring jockey, Atticus naturally expected himself to hold his own with the stable yard's enlisted men. Thank heavens he did not aspire to a career in pugilism—yet.

"I have no doubt you would manage accommodations among the grooms splendidly and even turn them to good use when gathering intelligence, but how am I to obtain your reports, Atticus? If you attach yourself exclusively to the stable, my only excuse for crossing your path is to visit my horse. Atlas will spend most of the next two weeks loafing in a paddock. How will you communicate with me then?"

"We could meet in the carriage house."

"And be overheard by every trysting couple ever to enjoy a liaison."

Atticus looked to be considering the novel possibility that commodious coaches had a purpose other than travel. "That's stupid."

Awkward, certainly, and often stuffy. "You will content yourself with the cot in my dressing closet and exert yourself to look after my effects when you aren't looking after Atlas. Miss West will be glad to know you're keeping an eye on me."

Low tactics again, to invoke Hyperia's name, but effective tactics, as I well knew.

"Miss West will like to know how my reading is coming. I'm much better than I was."

"Do us proud, lad, or she will have stern words for all concerned."

The coach rolled to a halt, and the footman opened the door and let down the steps.

"Does Miss West know we'll be here?" Atticus asked as I gathered up my top hat and gloves.

"I did try to alert her, but even if our presence is a surprise, I'm sure she'll be exceedingly pleased to see us." On that enormous bouncer, I stepped down from the coach.

As it happened, Hyperia emerged from the house in the next instant. With the instincts of a man very much in love, I grasped—from the swish of her skirts, from the quality of her stride—that my darling was anything but pleased to see me.

"Julian." Hyperia curtseyed to a depth proper for greeting a duke's son.

I bowed with similar punctilio. "Hyperia. A pleasure." Mostly. She was in great good looks, the afternoon sun finding every fiery highlight in her chestnut hair, the spring breeze putting roses in her cheeks. That she'd come out of doors without a bonnet, though, was proof of singular agitation.

The undiscerning eye of Society considered my intended only passably pretty, and Hyperia worked hard to keep it so. She was shortish, curvy, and green-eyed—three strikes—and she chose demure fashions and subdued colors. Her hair was never tortured into the elaborate styles favored by Mayfair's diamonds, and she was accomplished at flattery that avoided flirtation.

Hyperia hid the lights of her intelligence and beauty under every bushel basket, shawl, and bonnet available. She threatened no one and missed nothing. That she had consented to marry me, with all my quirks and flaws, went squarely into the category of *too good to be true.*

"I did not know you'd be here," she said, coming straight to the point, another of her many gifts.

To explain, apologize, or dissemble? What sort of reply did she want? I was all at sea, despite having had mile after jouncing mile to plan my entrance. Worse yet, we were in full view of any guest or servant lingering by a window. The groom heading the horses could hear our every word, as could John Coachman, to say nothing of Atticus, lurking in the coach.

I affected a puzzled expression. "Shall I leave?" She would not send me away, not with half the turf crowd already on the premises.

"Of course not. I simply... Well, you have never expressed an interest in horse racing."

Neither had she. "Tenneby invited me at the urging of the Marquess of Dalhousie. For me to ignore the invitation altogether would have been unmannerly."

I was being somewhat honest. Lord Dalhousie had promised to speak well of me in polite circles. One did not tell a marquess bent on gentlemanly goodwill to keep his handsome gob shut, though I wished he had.

"Then you won't be staying long?"

Hyperia was not only annoyed, maybe not even annoyed, but *worried*. Well, well, well. "Might we continue this discussion elsewhere? I'm sure John Coachman would like to get the horses out of harness, and I know I could do with some lemonade."

Atticus, the little schemer, was apparently determined to accompany the coach around to the stable block, where he'd doubtless begin ingratiating himself with any groom who rode in the practice gallops.

"Did you come alone?" Hyperia asked.

"I brought Atticus, lest he once again disobey orders and bring himself. He's looking forward to impressing you with his literary accomplishments."

I waved to John Coachman, and he directed the horses to walk on. I was traveling light—no baggage coach would come lumbering up the drive three hours hence—and my trunks would be unloaded at the porter's entrance.

"Then Lady Ophelia isn't with you?" Hyperia asked, which

struck me as odd. Godmama often acted as Hyperia's chaperone, and the two were close correspondents.

"Her ladyship is enjoying a rural respite between rounds in Town. Hyperia, I truly am in need of something to drink. Cook packed us a generous hamper, but Atticus makes locusts look lack-adaisical when it comes to food and drink." I also wanted to get out of the bright sunshine and off what amounted to an open-air stage.

I had questions for Hyperia, just as she had been questioning me.

"Come along," she said, leading the way through the open front door. "Not all of the guests have arrived. Tenneby is kept very busy settling in horses, greeting guests, and, I gather, settling his own nerves. He'll greet you shortly, I'm sure."

I did not care one sweaty saddle pad whether Tenneby bothered himself to do the pretty.

I followed Hyperia into a lovely foyer rising to two stories. The theme was pink marble pilasters, white marble flooring, robust ferns, and abundant sunlight admitted by soaring two-story windows. A gorgeous staircase—more white marble—swept in a graceful curve up to the next story. The banisters beneath the handrail were carved to depict twining ivy.

The earldom might well be in dun territory now, but at some point, the Tennebys had enjoyed abundant means.

"The winter parlor has been turned into an all-day buffet," Hyperia said. "Saves the staff having to answer a dozen bells every hour. Seems a bit expedient to me, but Tenneby's sister hasn't much experience as a hostess, and he really shouldn't have asked that of her anyway."

"Tenneby's sister?" He'd not mentioned a sister to me, which might well have been an innocent oversight, though Godmama had said one sister remained unmarried. In Tenneby's horse-mad mind, sisters likely ranked below the boot-boy. Prettier, perhaps, but not half so useful as the boot-boy when a man came home after a muddy morning on horseback.

"Evelyn Tenneby. She was presented four Seasons ago, courtesy of some auntie, but she did not take. I'm here ostensibly at her invitation."

We passed down a corridor notable for spotless carpets, an absence of cobwebs, and an abundance of horse portraits. *Gray Squirrel at the St. Ledger. Pegasus at the Macaroni Stakes. Potoooooooo at the 1200 Guineas Stakes.*

All were in the spare, balanced style of the late George Stubbs. I peered closer at a particularly fine rendering. "This *is* a Stubbs, not merely in his style."

"Why would anybody name a horse Potoo?" Hyperia asked.

Pot-Eight-Os. Potatoes, though the joke is said to have originated in a stable boy's poor spelling on a feed bucket."

Hyperia left off studying the painting to study me. "How do you know that?"

"Harry was turf mad for a time."

Mention of my brother had Hyperia resuming our progress down the corridor. "I was surprised he didn't join a cavalry regiment," she said.

"I was relieved. Wellington hated the cavalry, and for good reason. They were forever pursuing havoc when they should have been pursuing victory. They had a penchant for reckless dashes behind enemy lines when they should have been regrouping."

"Don't say that too loudly. Half the men here might be former cavalry."

Splendid. The more military sorts on hand, the more snide comments and veiled insults I was likely to endure. I had sent word of the meet to one former military connection, though, who would make an admirable addition to the gathering.

"The food is in here." Hyperia led the way into a sunny little parlor—more horse portraits—that also boasted comfortably upholstered chairs and a sofa, a southern exposure, and thick if slightly worn carpets. The sideboard offered bread made with white flour, a cold collation of meats and cheeses, a number of condiments, along with biscuits, savory and sweet tarts, and whole oranges. A pair of punchbowls occupied what looked like a card table.

"Join me," I said, filling a glass from the smaller punchbowl. "Tell me all the latest news." The recipe was cidery, with citrus notes and warm spices. The heated version would have been more palatable, but I was thirsty and not about to try my luck with the offerings in the larger bowl.

"I haven't much news," Hyperia said, putting some tarts on a plate. "What do you hear from His Grace?"

A safe place to start. "Arthur has left Greece and is racketing about Italy. He says Banter is in alt, the wine is hearty, and he misses the Hall." Arthur and I were six years apart, and more significantly, he had been raised to step into the ducal role. I had been raised as an extra spare, with Harry occupying the middle ground of next heir.

Arthur and I got on well, now that we were adults. I still felt as if my only surviving brother was in some regards an unknown quantity, and he doubtless felt the same about me. Familial ties, the shared loss of Harry, and a congruence of values drew us together. When I'd truly needed to rely on Arthur, he'd come through without hesitation.

That he would leave the Hall in my hands while he traveled on the Continent with his dear Banter both flattered and unnerved me.

"When will the duke come home?" Hyperia asked, taking a seat on one of the comfortable chairs by the window.

"I make it a point not to ask him, Perry. He has been so dutiful for so long, while Harry and I did as we pleased. Arthur deserves his holiday."

I fashioned myself a sandwich of ham, cheese, and mustard, piled tarts on the side of my plate, and took the chair closest to Hyperia's.

"Is this outing a holiday for you?" Hyperia asked, sipping her drink.

"More like a duty wedged between planting and haying. What about for you?" Why was I fencing with her? Hyperia and I had been through much together, and she had been loyal to me when I'd been too morose to be loyal to myself.

"Same."

An awkward silence ensued. I took a bite of my sandwich—the bread was slightly stale—and Hyperia nibbled a tart. What duty could she possibly be fulfilling at a race-meeting-cum-house-party?

I set down my plate. "Tenneby all but begged me to attend, Perry. He claims he was cheated out of twenty-eight thousand pounds at Epsom three years ago, and he's worried more mischief will arise at this gathering."

Hyperia finished her tart. "Was it hard for you to tell me that, Julian?"

Julian. When in charity with me, she called me Jules. "A bit awkward, wading into business matters when I long to take you in my arms, but not difficult." My besetting sin, according to Hyperia, was an unwillingness to trust her. She did not doubt my love or loyalty, but in some way a wiser man would understand, she felt slighted by my tendency toward self-reliance.

I further blundered in her eyes by occasionally turning up protective of her in situations she deemed herself capable of managing without my aid. I was learning to restrain such impulses, to think before drawing my figurative sword, but the impulse itself refused to die.

She was mine to love, and that meant mine to protect. Nothing I had read in Mrs. Wollstonecraft's polemics had convinced me otherwise.

"When were you planning on telling me that you'd jaunted off to Berkshire?" Hyperia asked.

"I put a letter in the post to your London address. I wrote it the day after I agreed to attend." *What are you doing here, Hyperia?* The question went unasked, perhaps because my conscience was troubled by my evasiveness, perhaps because whacking a hornet's nest had ever been ill-advised.

"Your hair is getting darker," Hyperia said, gaze upon my locks. "Near your part, you've turned strawberry blond."

After I'd endured months of torment in French hands, losing

Harry, and finding myself at large in bitter cold spring weather on the slopes of the Pyrenees, my hair had turned white. Had I been asked as a youth, I would have confidently asserted that I wasn't vain about my (then) reddish-brown hair. Hair was hair, better to have some, probably, than none, but such developments were beyond a person's control.

Turn my tresses as white as an ermine's coat, and I missed those nondescript brown locks sorely. To my great relief, color was reasserting itself in the new growth, though hair white at the bottom, flaxen in the middle, and blond at the top added to my credentials as an eccentric.

"Did you bring Atlas?" Hyperia asked, choosing another tart.

I'd told her that I longed to embrace her, and she'd reciprocated by asking after my horse. What on earth was afoot? "He came by easy stages, and I will check on him before supper. How is Healy faring with his plays?"

Hyperia choked on her tart. I patted her back.

She waved me off. "Healy might put in an appearance here," she said, sipping her punch. "I'm sure he will, in fact. He says creativity benefits from a periodic change of air, and one doesn't argue with one's brother over a topic on which he is a self-appointed expert."

Said with a touch of sororal asperity, which I found shamefully reassuring. Hyperia loved her brother, but Healy viewed himself as the head of the family despite having at best a shaky grasp of his own affairs. He'd lit upon writing plays as a means of earning coin without sacrificing his status as a gentleman, though none of his works had yet been produced.

Neither of his works, rather. As far as I knew, he'd completed one play and was perpetually toiling away on another.

We finished our snacks without further sallies into small talk. Hyperia explained to me which apartment had the pleasure of housing her, and a housekeeper arrived to escort me to my quarters.

Hyperia would have bustled off to some unknown destination,

but before the housekeeper could kidnap me, I put a hand on Perry's sleeve.

"I have missed you terribly," I said, "and I am overjoyed to see you. Will you hack out with me tomorrow morning?"

She took my hand and squeezed my fingers. "Gladly. I'll see you at supper too. Rest as well as you can before then, Jules. This promises to be a lively gathering."

Jules. Hyperia had called me Jules. Leaning on that slender reed of reassurance, I let the housekeeper take me captive. She didn't show me to my rooms, though. A footman accosted us at the foot of the gleaming staircase.

"A lad from the stable is asking for you, my lord. Says you're needed double time, and he was most insistent."

"Small, dark-haired, tends to Cockney when agitated?"

"That's him, sir. He was ready to storm the footmen's steps and search the house for you."

I made my excuses to the housekeeper and took the path to the stable. Raised voices led me to the open end of a large U-shaped stable yard. Around the perimeter, horses gazed out of open half doors. Some were munching hay. Some were watching, ears pricked, as one large groom shoved at the chest of a much smaller fellow. Between the stall doors, potted tulips bloomed in cheery yellows, whites, and reds, very likely echoing Tenneby's racing colors.

"Trying to cheat, you was," the shover bellowed. "Mr. Tenneby will hear about this."

The shovee, though at least six inches shorter than his assailant, spat on his palms and balled his fists. "Mr. Tenneby will hear that his head lad is a rude jackanapes who don't know shit from shamrocks, and so says Paddy Denton."

Paddy apparently had supporters, and his diction identified him as a son of the Emerald Isle. If the larger fellow was Tenneby's head lad, he would have backers as well. Murmurs began as the crowd formed itself into the inevitable human ring in the middle of which all the best pugilism occurred.

Also much of the worst folly.

I elbowed my way past a pair of gawking grooms and into the center of the circle. "Gentlemen, let's not be hasty. Surely this is all just a misunderstanding?"

Paddy Denton and Tenneby's head lad turned equally hostile glowers on me. I was a toff—clothing, hygiene, and speech confirmed my status—and I was meddling with both stable yard justice *and* a whacking good row.

What had I expected? Atticus's head was filled with a victorious outing to the Grand National, Hyperia was barely speaking to me, and now every groom and jockey on the premises would happily do me an injury.

Fast work, even for me.

CHAPTER THREE

"Says W8." Paddy Denton handed me a piece of paper and pointed past my shoulder. "That's the west side of the yard, unless the sun has taken a notion to travel backward in the sky, and I can count to eight without even taking off me boots." His chin jutted in a manner reminiscent of a righteous Atticus.

The stalls were numbered, a number plate affixed to the bottom half of each of the double doors. The indicated stall already had an occupant, a sleek gray who watched the proceedings with calm interest.

"He were trying to switch the horses, sir," the head lad countered in all his English certainty. "Denton's filly is a dapple gray, same as Maybelle there. Both rising four, both standing about sixteen hands. Easiest thing in the world to trade 'em out while the rest of us is busy setting fair for the night."

Denton spread his stance. "I'll have you know, Josiah Woglemuth, that the stall was assigned by Mr. Tenneby himself. Furthermore, you great, beef-witted ignoramus, I've no wish to steal your wretched skinny nag when our filly will leave yours swishing flies at the starting line."

"That filly," Woglemuth said, pointing to the gray in the stall, "will be a flat streak on the horizon while your spavined, speckled mule is still passing its first fart of the day."

Atticus had wiggled to the front of the crowd, and when he should have been worried, he was clearly enjoying the insults.

"That will do," I said. "Nobody was trying to exchange the horses. Denton, your horse can be stabled in stall 8*M*—M for mares, I presume. Woglemuth, if you'd get your lads back to work, we can all put this confusion behind us." I passed Woglemuth the slip of paper.

He turned it upside down then right side up, then upside down again. "Blimey. Who'd a thought?"

Denton snatched back the note. "Your filly is still as slow as black treacle on an icicle, but she has a pretty head."

Woglemuth nodded. "Your Cleo has a nice arse, which our Maybelle will never have a chance to admire on course. Back to work, lads."

Denton collected his filly, who did have a fine set of quarters, and led her over to the open door of another stall labeled with an 8, but on the northern side of the stable yard.

"They coulda killed each other," Atticus said, sidling up to me. "Coulda come to blows in the next second. Who would have ridden Cleopatra if Denton had got his head busted?"

Not you, young man. "That's Patrick Denton, formerly Sergeant Patrick Denton?"

"Dunno about formerly anything, but he's groom and jockey for Cleopatra and a couple colts. Lord Wickley owns all three. He's an earl. You could tell him I'm to ride morning gallops, couldn't you, guv?"

"Oh, possibly, except I've never met his lordship, and you are not to think about riding a morning gallop until you have my permission to take on a specific mount. Furthermore, I will be present on such occasions until further notice."

"But you'll meet everybody at supper tonight, and you could ask Lord Wickley then. Denton might not want to ride all three."

"If Denton is the groom for all three, he's very likely riding them daily, in succession, and perhaps several others as well. He is also mucking, feeding, rugging up, turning out, watering, keeping their gear in good repair, and race riding. He's a very busy man."

"He does that for all three of 'em?"

"On the Sabbath, he'll be excused from riding. Every other day, he'll be up at the crack of doom, in all sorts of weather, riding for miles on end."

If I'd hoped to daunt Atticus's ambitions, I'd failed. He'd clearly decided that a jockey's life was to be coveted above all other callings. So much for my efforts to give him a gentleman's education.

"I can watch, though, can't I? I can watch the gallops."

"Don't make a pest of yourself, but yes, you can watch if you keep your eyes and ears open. Denton might give his string tomorrow off if they're just arriving today." Likely not, though. They'd get an easy ride, but not a day off, and the decision would be Lord Wickley's rather than Denton's.

"Did you tell Miss West I've been workin' on me letters?"

"I did, and she is looking forward to confirming my report first-hand. Where has our Atlas been stabled?"

Atlas was *my* Atlas and always would be, but in recent weeks, Atticus had graduated to hacking out on my gelding on the days when I was not available to ride. On the one hand, I knew the boy's equitation would get a tremendous boost riding such a highly trained and generous-spirited animal.

On the other, I resented the duty to share Atlas with anybody, ever. He'd been a comrade in arms in Spain and the Low Countries, as nobody else had been, and I was pathetically jealous of his loyalty.

Utter nonsense on my part, of course.

"Atlas is in a saddle horse row," Atticus said, striding across the stable yard. "Their stalls look out the back. The racehorses are all on the inside rows so the grooms can keep a better eye on 'em. Colts to one side, mares to the north, geldings sprinkled about as may be. Coach horses have another barn closer to the carriage house. Forge is to the south, downwind of everything else because of the off-chance of a spark."

"You've done some reconnoitering, young man."

We passed into the dim and aromatic confines of the barn. "Isn't that why you brung me?"

Well, yes, and also because the boy would have been miserable at the Hall, toiling away in the schoolroom with neither myself nor Atlas on hand to add interest to his days. My nephew, Leander, was younger than Atticus, and the two did not seem to have formed an alliance.

"I *brought* you because I cannot trust you to bide where I tell you to."

The stalls were mostly full, the horses at their afternoon hay. Some would be turned out overnight, though the time of year meant caution had to be exercised. Spring grass was notoriously rich, just as autumn grass might be deep and beautiful, but lacked much in the way of nutrition. Most horses were allowed only a few hours at grass this early in the season, with longer and longer periods of turnout as the weather moderated.

Though in the absence of rain, Tenneby's pastures were far from lush.

"He looks happy," Atticus said as we reached Atlas's stall, and indeed, the horse was contentedly munching a fragrant pile of hay. A mound of fresh droppings graced a corner of his abode—Atlas was a tidy soul—and the consistency of the manure assured me that all was well with his digestion.

"Can you get him out for a hand-walk and some hand-grazing at sunset?" I asked.

"Why not turn him out for the night?"

"Because for the past four days, he's had little grass, and Tenneby's pastures have come in, despite apparently dry weather. Atlas will gorge himself at the same time we're asking him to drink water that's not quite what he's used to at home. That's two steps in the direction of an avoidable colic. I'll hack him out in the morning and then ask that he be given a couple hours at grass, preferably by himself or with two or three pasture mates. By the time you're done observing the gallops, Atlas should be ready to come in."

Atticus watched as the gelding sniffed the water in his bucket but disdained to drink. "Do you always think like this, guv? Fourteen what-ifs and what-abouts all piled on top of each other?"

"One tries to consider all the available evidence before choosing a course of action."

Atticus pushed away from the door. "Izat how you're courting Miss Hyperia? Considering evidence and courses of action?"

Well... yes. "How do you advise me to proceed?"

Atticus gave me a pitying look, which from a boy young enough to be my son was lowering indeed. "You court her however she wants you to."

He scampered off on some errand known only to him, and I was still watching Atlas in hopes he'd drink some water when a voice to my right caused Atlas to cease eating his hay and once again have a look out his half door.

"I'm told it was you who deprived Denton of his little pre-race bout of fisticuffs. Proper little Papist that he is, he rides better when he's in a temper. I would have preferred to see my jockey good and riled. I trust you'll let matters run their course if you should come across a similar disagreement among the peasantry again?"

"Lord Wickley?" I asked, surveying a fair-haired dandy turned out in the first stare of equestrian fashion. His cravat was pristine, his boots spotless, and his spurs gleaming. He was perhaps two inches shorter than my six foot two and perfectly proportioned for the lesser height. I'd put his age at about six-and-twenty.

Too old to be forgiven the airs and attitudes of an arrogant sprout.

"And you'd be Lord Julian." He looked me up and down with the same expression he likely turned on foundered ponies. "You doubtless believed yourself to be keeping peace among the heathen, but meddling is meddling, I'm sure you'll agree. No apology necessary— this time. Until supper."

He did not so much as touch a finger to his hat brim, but rather, strode away as if he was expected urgently at a royal levee.

"A right charmer that one," Josiah Woglemuth muttered from across the barn aisle. He ceased raking the dirt floor and checked the latch on the nearest stall. "I shouldn't speak ill of my betters, but Mr. Tenneby warned me about the earl. Paddy Denton rides for him, and whatever else might be true, his lordship ought not to speak ill of his own jockey."

"Agreed. You'll keep an eye on my Atlas?"

"Aye, and the boy. Lad's mad keen for horses. You can see that straight off."

"He's not to be race riding, Woglemuth. Atticus is still new to the saddle, and I don't want his broken neck on my conscience."

"Nor mine. No call to use jockeys that young, and Mr. Tenneby wouldn't stand for it neither."

Mr. Tenneby had been playing least in sight since my arrival. I doubted he knew if children were being put in the saddle on the practice gallops.

"Do you really think Denton would try to switch fillies on you?"

Woglemuth studied the regular swirling pattern he'd raked into the aisle's dirt floor. "I saw what I saw. He was leading our Maybelle out of her stall, and his Cleo was tied up to the nearest hitching ring. Would have been the work of a moment, and those two horses could be twins."

"You've marked a hoof?" A horse's hoof was made of the same substance as hair or fingernails. A sharp object scratched along the outer hoof wall or even on the tough sole would leave a mark but cause no sensation. Some cavalry units branded their horses on the hooves rather than on the hide.

He nodded. "I have my little system of marks. Mind, Paddy Denton has a reputation for riding a clean race, but Mr. Tenneby has reasons for distrusting some of the other owners. You'd best ask him about that if you want the details."

"I will do exactly that." I left the stable aware of a gnawing hunger, despite the snack I'd stolen with Hyperia. I also battled a sense of foreboding. The simplest explanation for this bout of slanging in the stable yard was that Wickley had set his groom up for confusion, knowing that fisticuffs would likely result.

But would Denton truly ride a better race for having been beaten to flinders by a man twice his size? Or had Denton been determined to distract all and sundry from his failed attempt to switch the fillies? Was Wickley in such a bad humor because I'd meddled—his word—or because the exchange of horses had been foiled?

I'd lay the situation at the feet of my host and see what Tenneby made of the business—assuming I could find my host.

"Lord Julian, where have you been hiding?" Clarence Tenneby bustled to my side as soon as I joined the predinner crowd. Folding doors had been drawn back to turn the music room and the first informal parlor into one space, and still the assemblage was crowded.

"I've been getting my bearings," I said, returning his smile, though heaven defend me if I were ever seen to beam in public as Tenneby was beaming now. "Tenneby Acres is lovely."

"Ain't it, though? A proper jewel. Come admire the view from the terrace. Not quite a balmy evening, but a breath of fresh air will do us good."

Tenneby's effusive greeting was doubtless partly for show. Ladies who'd ignored me before gave me a second appraisal. Gentlemen regarded me over their glasses of champagne with veiled calculation. Was I in the market for a horse? Looking to win an easy fortune wagering?

Or was I once again poking my lordly beak into polite society's less savory corners?

The brisk evening air was a welcome change from the stuffy parlors.

"Let's admire the stars from the garden," Tenneby said. He

moved like a chubby toddler, watching where he put his feet on the steps, a slight hunch to his posture. "Beautiful night, ain't it?"

Overhead and to the east, stars were appearing against a darkening firmament. To the west, the last streaks of indigo and gray were fading to black. The scent on the breeze was grassy with a hint of turned earth. A peaceful combination, one any military picket on night watch learned to appreciate.

"The weather is certainly pleasant," I said, though we need not have come outside to exchange that small talk. "I'll need a guest list, Tenneby, and some time to review it with you. I've already made Lord Wickley's acquaintance."

"That one... He all but demanded to be included. Informed me that he'd be happy to grace my 'little gathering' with his presence because Newmarket had grown so tedious. His horses break down on the harder turf over in Suffolk is the problem. This year's dry spring is proving too much for them, so here he is, his equine darlings pampered like kings and queens at my expense. And if Wickley is underfoot, I could hardly refuse hospitality to his archrival Lord Pierpont, could I?"

"A vexing contretemps, I'm sure." About which I could condole Tenneby all evening and still not quiet his laments. "I will also need to know who on your guest list was present at Epsom three years ago."

A gust of laughter wafted from the house.

"You think somebody will try the same scheme?"

"You are apparently concerned that they will. Assuming you were cheated, the method was effective. You haven't discovered the means responsible for your bad luck, and somebody else was significantly enriched."

"Half the turf was enriched at my expense. Uncle will cut me off without a farthing if I can't produce better results this time, though we haven't actually that many farthings left."

Uncle would be Lord Temmington. "He fancies racehorses?"

"No, he does not, not any more, though he used to. He doesn't fancy his oldest nephew much either, I'll have you know. When it comes to my uncle, I'm torn between humoring an old campaigner who's set in his ways and having a pointed discussion with a full-grown colt who needs reminding about his manners."

"Might I share with you some advice my older brother imparted to me?" I ought to keep my mouth shut, but Harry had—on some occasions—been right.

"Please. My sister says I've bitten off more than I can chew with this meeting, but she's gloomy by nature. Calls it practical, but practicality isn't the same as perpetually predicting my ruin."

"Sisters can be a challenge, but we do love them. With regard to your uncle, approach him as you would a green horse. Your posture will tell him as much about you as your tone of voice, and only when both have his attention will he focus on your actual words."

The hum of conversation from the house was gradually growing louder.

"Head up, look him in the eye, look where you're going, go where you're looking, that sort of thing?"

"Exactly, no sudden moves and plenty of patience, but no doubt about your objective." Not much difference from commanding new recruits, truth be known. "Comport yourself at all times with bodily confidence, as if you know what you're about."

"Even when I don't." Tenneby's teeth gleamed in the shadows. "Simple enough with a horse. Second nature, in fact. One wants to be deferential with an elder, though, particularly *the earl.* Uncle Temmie can be difficult, though few would believe that."

"Respect him, of course, but let him know that you respect yourself as well. Saves a lot of discussion."

"One can but try. I'd best be getting back to my other guests. I'll have the lists for you in the morning."

"Before you go, did you hear of the squabble in the stable yard this afternoon?"

Tenneby nodded. "Paddy Denton has a temper, though he doesn't take it out on horses. He and Woglemuth came to reasonable, albeit mistaken, conclusions, and I understand no blows were exchanged."

"This time. Wickley as much as told me he'd engineered the confusion in hopes that Denton would start a brawl. He claimed his jockey rides a better race when holding a bit of a grudge."

"Or his jockey rides a better race when he's mounted on my Maybelle rather than Wickley's plodding Cleo. Woglemuth would have sorted the matter out before anybody was at the starting line, but I see your point."

Woglemuth *might* have sorted the matter out, though racing days were prodigiously busy, with horses moving everywhere, crowds on hand, and last-minute substitutions for jockeys being necessitated by injuries.

"Woglemuth seems an estimable sort," I said.

"Nobody's fool, and a horseman to his bones. Come in with me, and I'll introduce you around."

Tenneby was so spontaneously gracious, so *innocent*. "Best not. Bruit it about that I'm here because Miss West is here, and you tolerate my presence only because you don't want to offend the lady."

"Tolerate your presence...? Oh, I see. Muddy the waters, lay a false scent. Very clever. Miss West is lovely."

"We are engaged to be married, though we have made no formal announcement." Why not? Not all engagements were made public in the newspapers—very few, in fact—but I was a ducal heir, and as dubious as my reputation was in some circles, the matchmakers would appreciate official notice that I'd made my choice.

"My sister likes your Miss West. Says she's quite sensible. When the lady asked for an invitation, Evvie was only too pleased to accommodate her."

Hyperia had *asked* to be invited? Without letting me know? "What of Healy West—is he expected as well?"

"He is indeed. He's bought his first colt and claims beginner's luck is with him. Says that horse will leave everything in the dust. St. George by name. Doesn't want to overface the colt with a first outing at Newmarket, so I suggested St. George test the waters in a smaller, friendlier crowd."

Bad news, but also a relief. Doubtless, Hyperia was on hand to limit the damage her brother's newfound venture caused—though, why not tell me that?

"Keep an eye on West, will you? He is prone to believing his every whim is divinely inspired, and his next scheme will be the one that wins him a nabob's fortune."

Tenneby started for the steps, then stopped, squared his shoulders, and lifted his gaze from the ground to the glittering windows of the manor house.

"West will fit right in with the turf crowd, my lord. One has to be a bit of a fool to thrive in our world, a bit of a dreamer. The trick is to be able to afford the dream. Haven't quite figured that part out yet, but I have high hopes."

No doubt, twenty-eight thousand sorely missed pounds would have helped a great deal. "You go in first. I'll follow in a few minutes. Please do not introduce me around. Continue to treat me as something of an avoidable nuisance, but do get me those lists."

He saluted with two fingers and strode up to the house as if he were being introduced to a young equine sale prospect for the first time. Confident, steady steps, his shoulders back, and only a slight stumble as he crossed the threshold into his home.

"Healy has bought a racehorse," I said, taking a seat next to Hyperia. "Is that why you've joined the gathering?" We occupied a padded bench in the music room, an impromptu glee having been organized to entertain guests after the buffet supper.

Hyperia had arrived late to the predinner gathering, been all but accosted by Lord Pierpont, and enjoyed his obnoxiously handsome company for the duration of the meal. Wickley had escorted her to the music room, and had not Evelyn Tenneby been glued to the earl's other arm, I'd likely still be admiring my intended from afar.

"You heard about St. George?" Hyperia muttered. "I fear for my brother's sanity, Julian. Truly, I do."

"Have you seen the colt run?"

A footman came around with a tray of cheddar and sliced oranges. I filled a small plate and passed it to Hyperia.

"I have seen the colt," Hyperia said quietly. "I haven't seen him run. He's all knees and ribs, Julian, and he cost a fortune."

Bad news. Healy West had no fortune to spend. "If St. George is fast, nothing else matters, provided he's sound. He might well be a good investment."

She considered a pale slice of cheese. "Are you defending my blockheaded brother?"

"Looking on the bright side. Then too, if Healy's latest project means I get to spend the next two weeks with you, perhaps I owe him my thanks."

Hyperia put the cheese back on the plate, uneaten. "When I say the horse cost a fortune, Julian, I am not exaggerating. Healy knew better, he ignored my advice, and I suspect he'll be made a laughing-stock before the race meeting ends. A bankrupt laughingstock."

"Gambling debts are not enforceable by the courts, my dear. They are strictly debts of honor, payable on no particular schedule other than as soon as possible. Do I take it your brother no longer aspires to become the next Richard Sheridan, playwright extraordinaire?"

Hyperia fiddled with her bracelet, a circlet of plain gold links. "The one play he's written is quite good. I suspect the second effort suffers by comparison, and thus he hasn't finished it. I'm speculating. He won't tell me what's amiss, and if I ask more than once how the writing is coming, he scolds me for nagging."

Her words held a small revelation for me: Hyperia had recently castigated me for keeping from her certain elements of my past that I found upsetting.

Memories accosted me seemingly without provocation or on the merest hint of inspiration. A bird hopping about near a fountain would bring back the horrors of Ciudad Rodrigo. Gunfire set my belly roiling. Thunder was a different sort of torment. Hot chocolate served with a pinch of cinnamon sent me back to frigid Spanish winters in dimly lit cantinas.

All of these burdens and many more, I tried to carry in silence, in hopes they would abate, or at least not escalate. Hyperia insisted that hoarding my misery perpetuated the pain, and thus I had begun to make an effort to share with her recollections of my worst moments.

I still had nightmares. I still dreaded certain dates on the calendar. I still hated storms and found talking about the whole business exceedingly tedious, but I had tried to comply with Hyperia's request.

"Is Healy your legal guardian?" I asked.

"No, but he's in authority over my funds. If I am unmarried at age thirty, the funds come to me more or less directly, or the trust does."

"And the man in authority over your funds refuses to keep you apprised of his activities. He won't answer your questions, he won't explain himself to you, and yet, he will profess to anybody listening that he loves and esteems you." Hyperia had nearly shown me the door for lesser offenses. "How have you not planted him a facer?"

She blinked at the plate of fruit and cheese. "I want to kick him, Jules. I want to take all his funds away and dole them out only as I see fit. I want to refuse him a key to our own front door."

"You had a key made, I hope?"

She nodded. "Healy has become secretive again. I don't think he's being blackmailed, but he's... making questionable decisions."

"Do you want my assistance, Hyperia?" I asked the question as casually as I could, but every part of me was wondering why in blazes she hadn't simply summoned me, laid the problem at my feet, and directed me to get to the bottom of it. This was the woman who'd insisted that my burdens were also hers to carry, for pity's sake.

"I haven't the right to trouble you with more of Healy's mischief."

"Now that surprises me, because I have it on the best authority—unassailable, expert authority—that when two people plight their troth, they take on the honor, duty, and privilege of sharing their troubles. I'll sort him out, Hyperia, just say the word."

I was making a promise rather than boasting.

"I do love you," she said very softly. "Let's see if Healy and his St. George even show up. For all I know, he's hared off to Newmarket, where he's hard at work digging himself into a hole of scandal so deep, I will have to cry off our engagement."

"I love you too, Hyperia West. Depend upon that as you depend upon the sun to rise in the east. We'll have no talk of crying off, unless you find the prospect of marriage to me untenable."

"Never," she said, with more seriousness than the moment warranted. "Tell me how Atticus is faring with *Tom Jones*."

"He's finished the whole book and pronounced it ridiculous, which it is." On one level. On another, polite society had never been so savagely lampooned. "What shall I give him next?"

We chatted pleasantly between offerings from a quartet, octet, and then quintet of male voices, all very charming and lighthearted. When the gathering broke up, I claimed the right to light Hyperia up to her quarters before either Wickley or Pierpont could elbow their way to her side.

I waited until we were halfway up the white staircase before I posed a question that had been nagging at me. "Perry, is there a reason why we haven't announced our engagement publicly?"

"No reason," she said, "except that an announcement leads to questions about a date, and I don't suppose we'll set a date until His Grace is back from his travels."

She could set any date in the next five years, and I'd agree to it regardless of Arthur's whereabouts. "His Grace will want to be present, I'm sure."

"Why do you ask, Jules?"

"Tenneby requested my presence at this gathering because he is certain that three years ago, at Epsom, he was fleeced of a fortune.

My presence is supposed to deter troublemakers, or so Tenneby hopes. I refused to involve myself until he told me you'd be present." How had he known to dangle that lure, when he was no great social lion, nor in the confidence of the hostesses?

"I do know Evelyn from school, though she was years behind me. She might have heard from Lady Ophelia or one of her cronies that I'm engaged to you. My rooms are down this corridor."

We turned right, the same direction in which my quarters lay. "I will be keeping an eye on the horse racing in any case, Hyperia. I'd appreciate it if you'd do likewise." I avoided the words *assist me*, because increasingly, Hyperia's contributions to my investigations were not assistance so much as they were the critical insights that solved the whole puzzle.

I should tell her that, but not in a corridor frequented by other guests and punctuated by shadowed alcoves.

"Wickley and Pierpont own rival stables, don't they?" Hyperia said. "I did wonder why they paid me any notice. This gathering needs more unattached females."

Who would in all likelihood be ignored in favor of four-footed company. "You're still up for a morning hack tomorrow?"

"I am, let's say an hour after daybreak. I've warned the stable I'll need a guest horse."

"Atticus will be overjoyed to see you, though his delight is nothing compared to mine." I dared to press a kiss to her cheek and parted from her outside her door.

Airing her brother's folly had relieved some of the tension between us, but not all. I had avoided asking how Hyperia had journeyed here or who was acting as her chaperone. If she'd traveled unaccompanied and was present without an older female to see to the proprieties, then something more serious than Healy's latest folly was in play.

Hyperia and I had known each other since childhood, and I'd taken our compatibility for granted. When I'd gone off to war, I'd adhered to the required protocol and specifically instructed her to neither wait for my return nor wear the willow for me in case of my demise. She'd waited anyway and in every way had exerted herself to aid my various recoveries.

She brought a woman's perspective to the business of investigating and was able to make intuitive leaps while I collected facts and observations like some butterfly enthusiast patrolling an unfamiliar meadow.

I loved Hyperia, and I wanted to share the rest of my life with her, but now found myself in the miserable position of knowing she was right: If we could not confide in each other, if we could not trust each other, our marriage—if we ever wed—would be a disappointing arrangement all around.

CHAPTER FOUR

"Lord Julian, does one ask on what basis you are honored to escort Miss West to her bedroom door?"

Lord Pierpont in all his Byronic splendor leavened his question with a smile that put me in mind of the lizards so ubiquitous in Spain. He'd fallen in step with me as I'd proceeded to my quarters, suggesting his lordship had been lurking in an alcove.

"The lady and I are engaged to be married. I'm sure you will congratulate me on my good fortune."

He frowned. "Does Wickley know she's spoken for? How about we don't tell him? Let him make a cake of himself, as he is always wont to do."

And thus inflict on Hyperia insincere attentions from a strutting ass. How gentlemanly. "Miss West discloses our situation to whomever she pleases. We'll set a date when His Grace of Waltham returns from the Continent."

Pierpont tossed his head, which made the curl in the center of his brow flop. "Ah. You're here for a bit of pre-marital mischief with your intended, then? I was hoping I could prevail on you for some snoopery."

I was tired. I was concerned for Hyperia. I was concerned for Tenneby's race meeting, which had nearly seen its first brawl even before all the guests had assembled. I was worried about Atticus and his recent passion for becoming a jockey prodigy, and my patience for popinjays was at low ebb.

I took a leaf from my ducal brother's book. "Pierpont, my memory is dodgy at times, so please remind me: Have we been introduced?"

He chortled merrily. "Upon my word, Caldicott, one would never expect you to be a high stickler. We gentlemen of the turf are egalitarian sorts. But very well. Lord Pierpont Chandler at your service, charmed and delighted, and best wishes on your engagement to Miss West." He bowed, twirling his wrist elaborately. "Now you."

"Lord Julian Caldicott, pleased to make your acquaintance." Though I wasn't pleased at all, and by rights a third party known to us both should have made the introductions.

"You foiled *Wickedly's* little scheme, I'm told. He fancies himself a creature of bold initiatives—wicked smart, to hear him tell it. Trying to swap out mares in broad daylight is exactly his style, as is making a complete hash of the business. I would have thought Paddy Denton above such nonsense, but the fellow must eat, I suppose."

"Nobody was trying to swap out mares, my lord. Your informant was in error. If you don't mind, I'll bid you good night. The day has been long."

"Surely you don't mean to turn in now, Caldicott? It's not even midnight. I am genuinely shocked that a fellow who can't be that much older than I am is seeking his bed at such an hour."

I was centuries his elder in experience. "I am genuinely tired and committed to an early morning hack. If you will excuse me?"

"Ah, I understand. He who goes to bed early doesn't necessarily stay in that bed or occupy it alone. Am I right?"

My fatigue resulted in the sort of slow-wittedness that could do double service as forbearance. This courtesy twit had just insulted both me and my intended. *Again.*

"You are foxed," I said, doing my best to imitate Arthur's ducal froideur. "One does not take offense at the maunderings of an inebriate. Good night, my lord." I put my fingers on my door latch only to find that Pierpont had put his paw on my arm.

Not done. Such presumption was the outside of too much. My adventures in captivity had left me particularly ill-disposed toward the casual touch of strangers.

Pierpont withdrew his hand when I stared at him.

"Now, Caldicott, don't be like that. You're new to race meetings, I take it. We don't stand on ceremony—well, not much, especially at the private meets. I mean you no disrespect. In fact, I'm favoring you with a small, confidential request."

No request from Pierpont was any sort of favor to me.

I opened my sitting room door and gestured Pierpont through. "Be brief." I closed the door behind him, relieved to note that somebody had built up the fire. I took a taper from the spill-jar and lit a few candles, the better to watch Pierpont as he unburdened himself.

"It's like this, Caldicott. Horse races are supposed to be a test of the skill of the jockeys and speed of the horses."

"Are they truly? One had no idea." I blew out the taper and tossed it on the fire. "Do go on."

"Sometimes other factors are brought to bear."

If this was Pierpont bent on brevity, heaven spare me from his loquacious moods. "Like horse-swapping, nobbling the competition, getting a jockey too drunk to remain upright. Those sorts of factors." I'd also heard of kidnapping jockeys, tampering with jumps on steeplechase courses, and drugging horses with a dose of somnifera.

"How do you know of these tactics? I've never seen you at a meet. Lord Harry took an interest for a time, but you were described as the bookish brother."

"Cavalry officers are full of stories, and I heard them all." I'd also seen a few impromptu race meets in Spain. Over short distances, the Iberian steed could almost always best his English Thoroughbred cousin. Over distances of several miles, the conditioned Thoroughbred could maintain a faster pace. Somebody somewhere was doubtless crossing the two strains in hopes of getting both more speed and more stamina in the resulting equine.

"Well, I've heard a few stories about you too, Caldicott. Tenneby might think you're here to court your sweetheart, but I'd like you to keep an eye on the larger picture."

Matthew 6:24. *No man can serve two masters: for either he will hate the one, and love the other; or else he will hold to the one, and despise the other. Ye cannot serve God and mammon.*

"I am no longer a reconnaissance officer, Pierpont, and Tenneby is hosting a race meet, not a war."

"He's hosting both, does he but know it. You saw Lord Wickedly's opening salvo this afternoon, and you will notice, though he was present at the stable at the time, he left Denton to manage the situation unaided. He was *lurking*, letting his minions carry out his plan."

"And you know this because...?" Pierpont had clearly been lurking as well. A pair of truant schoolboys, each trying to spy on the competition's cricket practice.

"I make it a point to be kept well informed, and that's where you come in. All I'm asking is that you keep an eye on Wickley. He knew I planned to attend this meet, and the next thing I hear, he's cozened an invitation for himself. Newmarket is too crowded anymore. For young stock on a first outing, a venue like this is perfect, and my Minerva is a *most* promising prospect. Freya is coming along nicely as well, despite being a late foal. Wickley would never cheat outright— he is honorable, in his way—but he bears watching, my lord. You've seen that for yourself."

"I have seen nothing of the sort, and I have little experience of racing, as you note. Tenneby doubtless has stewards arranged for the competition days, and you must apply to them with any concerns. Good night, Lord Pierpont."

I opened the door to the corridor, letting in a rush of cooler air that made the candles flicker. Pierpont lingered by the hearth, treating me to what was doubtless supposed to be a brooding stare.

He looked, in fact, like a second former winding up for a pout because Headmaster hadn't liked his answer.

"You have a reputation, Caldicott. Nobody likes you, and they certainly don't admire you, but they respect your abilities. You pay attention. You notice details. I am asking you to keep a keen eye on the proceedings, is all."

He would not leave until I either tossed him out bodily or tossed him a crumb. "If I notice anything untoward, I will mention my concerns to Tenneby, who is the host and organizer for this affair."

"Excellent." He tossed his curl again. "And you'll want to watch Tenneby's sister while you're on hand. Evelyn has her brother twisted around her finger, but she's much given to stratagems and schemes, mark me on that. Fancies herself wearing the Wickley tiara, if you take my meaning."

Oh, of course. No farce was complete without a scheming hoyden. "Good night, sir."

"You needn't be rude. I was just leaving."

He sashayed out, doubtless off to gamble the night away in the library. I closed the door and wished I'd never left the Hall.

Well, not quite. I was delighted to be in Hyperia's vicinity, and if I had to endure this silly race meeting to earn that boon, then endure it, I would.

Lord Wickley's scent preceded him in the cool early morning mists. He reeked of cigars and the foul breath that resulted from hours spent consuming spirits. If he expected to surprise me by appearing at my elbow on the path to the stable, he was in for a disappointment. Then too, his tread was heavy, as if he preferred the earth to shake at his passing.

"A word to the wise, Caldicott."

I kept walking. "Lord Wickley, good morning. If wisdom is the topic of the moment, then the goddess Athena herself would suggest you have a good soaking bath before joining polite company for breakfast. Chewing a bale or two of parsley wouldn't go amiss either. Excellent for freshening the breath."

"The ladies will have to titter along without me at breakfast, alas. Nothing like a night of cards to get a gathering off on the right foot. I won, of course."

A gentleman did not boast of his good fortune. "Then somebody else lost and will be looking to get back his own." Not Tenneby, I hoped. Cheating at cards was too easy, and if Wickley would attempt to switch horses, he'd certainly try his hand at manipulating a deck of cards.

If.

"I'm passing along a bit of advice by way of belated appreciation for your efforts yesterday afternoon. You meant no harm. You were simply trying to keep the lads focused on their work rather than distracted by some impromptu pugilism."

"I'm told injured jockeys don't ride as well, and Woglemuth could certainly have landed a few blows on your man Denton."

"Paddy's damned quick. He could have given a good account of himself, but that's beside the point."

The point was, I was looking forward to my ride with Hyperia, and I did not want Wickley imposing his pungent company on the lady for even a moment. If he had any pretensions to decorum, he wouldn't want any woman to see him in his current condition either.

I stopped just short of the bend in the path that would have put the stable in sight. "I'm listening, Wickley, and an apology would suffice. 'My lord, I was unpardonably arrogant. No insult intended.' Then I say, 'None taken.' You offer your hand, we shake manfully, and you decamp to wash the stink of hedonism from your person. It isn't complicated." If fate were just, Wickley would fall asleep in the tub, take a chill, and come down with an ague.

I raised an eyebrow as I'd seen Arthur do on countless occasions, but the effect wasn't immediate compliance with my wishes. Wickley instead looked both bewildered and frustrated.

"Well, all that aside," he said, "I'm suggesting you keep your distance from Evelyn Tenneby. She's a taking little thing, I grant you, but she has airs above her station, and compromising a ducal scion would fit with her plans marvelously."

"Do you insult a lady, Wickley?" I kept the question casual. I wasn't about to step onto the field of honor because Pierpont and Wickley were enamored of the same unlucky female.

"One cannot blame the women for scheming, can one? Their whole lives depend on their ability to please, tease, and wheedle—and drop the occasional foal, too, of course. I'm merely observing that unless you want Tenneby for an in-law, you will avoid shadowed alcoves and tipsy maidens."

I made a pointed inspection of my pocket watch. "I am engaged to be married to a dear and delightful woman who has my entire loyalty, Wickley. Your warning isn't needed."

He absorbed this news while scratching the stubble on his chin. "Not Miss West? Please say she hasn't broken my heart for all time by settling for the likes of *you*?"

"A little brokenheartedness can have marvelous benefits, as can a hot bath. Good day, my lord."

I sauntered off, but Wickley trotted to catch up with me. "Don't tell Pierpoint-less that Miss West is spoken for. Let it be our little secret. She can tell him herself when she's of a mind to."

"I suspect he already knows, Wickley, and before you take up more of my time with your helpful advice—we won't call it meddling —I will most assuredly be watching the proceedings on the race-courses with great interest. I have not been to an informal meet previously, and Healy West, my future brother-in-law, will have a runner among the colts. I'm keen to see how he fares and how this whole business goes forth. Are we finished now?"

Wickley slowed. "If you note anything of a puzzling nature, my lord, I am at your service to answer questions and offer explanations. I was practically brought up on the back of a Thoroughbred and am considered a skilled whip. In my earliest youth, I was quite the

talented jockey, though alas, my aristocratic stature renders me
uncompetitive against smaller men. You may bring all of your queries
to me, and I will see you properly educated in the sport of kings."

He bowed and took himself off in a cloud of malodorous self-
importance.

Hyperia stepped around the bend in the path. "Good heavens.
Lord Wickley positively reeks. What on earth was he about?"

Hyperia brought the scent of roses with her everywhere, and
never had that aroma been more welcome. "I'm not sure what his aim
was, to be honest. Pierpont and Wickley have both warned me to
avoid Evelyn Tenneby, though the lady strikes me as pleasant
company and in no hurry to marry. Both men have also asked me
indirectly to monitor the race meet for potential wrongdoing."

Hyperia linked her arm through mine and escorted me in the
direction of the stable. "Then we are left to wonder: Was each man's
effusive request for your vigilance the first step in ensuring that you
overlook him when the time comes to suspect somebody? Or are they
both, like Tenneby, hoping that your presence will ensure unfailing
good sportsmanship?"

"I never fancied myself as a governess to a lot of turf-mad
coxcombs, Perry, but they will gamble fortunes on the outcome of a
single match, and that recklessness has consequences." Servants let
go without severance, tradesmen bilked of their goods, creditors left
with nothing when the debtor decamped for the Continent, as Beau
Brummel himself had recently done.

His debts of honor were said to total in the hundreds of thousands of pounds.

"And to think," Hyperia said quietly, "my own brother is enamored of this madness. You see why I had to attend?"

I did not see why she had to attend without telling me what she
was about and without my company at her side. Raising those
concerns would, however, disturb the goodwill with which we were
beginning our day.

"Perry, if you want to tell Healy that I asked you to join me here, then I will support that notion. I would have asked, had I thought you'd find any enjoyment in the gathering at all."

She hugged me there on the path, and my concern notched up toward alarm. What on earth was amiss with my darling that she did not believe she could enlist my aid or rely on my support?

"We know one thing," Hyperia said, continuing on toward the stable as if throwing her arms around me was nothing out of the ordinary. "Tenneby, Pierpont, and Wickley have all tasked you with keeping the cheats and swindlers from ruining this meet."

"The probability is thus very great," I continued the syllogism, "that somebody has planned spectacularly bad behavior. Therefore, we'd both best keep a sharp lookout."

"And a close eye on those three."

"Might we also keep a close eye on each other?" I said in an effort to lighten the moment. "I'd like that very much."

"You are trying to make me blush. For shame, Jules."

Hyperia strode ahead, to where Atticus was hand-walking Atlas around the perimeter of the stable yard. She hugged my horse around his sturdy neck, then hugged the boy tightly, inspiring him to grin and blush, and inspiring me to fall in love with my intended all over again.

CHAPTER FIVE

"Today is in the nature of an exhibition run," Tenneby said, passing me a list of names. "A chance for the horses to stretch their legs over a new course. Nobody will be pushing for a big victory. It's a stakes race but with a very modest pot."

Stakes, meaning one paid to run, and the fees made up a majority of the winnings.

Mine host had found me in the stable yard after my frustratingly pleasant hack with Hyperia. She and I had discussed the unseasonably dry weather—comfortable but worrisome. Then we'd moved on to the latest letters from Arthur—His Grace was a gifted travel writer, of all things. We'd also covered Atticus's aptitude for reading, though he was, we agreed, very bright generally. Mundane, innocuous topics, and normally, I would have delighted in airing even those with my intended.

Except that she was keeping items of significance from me, which was perhaps divine justice. I'd kept my own counsel on many occasions, and I could not count the number of times Hyperia had been forced to ask me, *What are you thinking, Jules?* Or, *What has put that look on your face?* Or, *What are you pondering?*

I'd thus small-talked and cantered along the edge of today's race-course with her and then watched her swan off to change for breakfast.

Leaving me with Tenneby and his list. "Why is almost every name on your list followed by an X?" I asked. A good dozen names in the first group—those who'd been present at Epsom three years ago—with a second group mostly unmarked.

"Coincidence. One doesn't take an interest in racing and then walk away from it in the ordinary course. One buys a horse, a colt usually, then another—a filly for a lark. Then one sells the colt only to see it mature into a blazingly fast 'chaser, or worse, see its progeny win every flat race they enter. One buys the full brother to the first horse and breeds the filly to him, just as she's rising five and developing the ability to jump the moon.

"So it goes," he went on, "and for every time you vow to quit, you vow once more to run a champion one way or another. We are a fraternity, and our membership varies little. The same fellows who were at Epsom three years ago are well represented at my informal gathering."

Pure coincidence, of course. Could Tenneby be setting a trap?

I considered the names. For every plain mister on the list, there was a courtesy lord or peer. Who among them was so desperate for a champion that he'd cheat?

"Are you a feuding fraternity, Tenneby? You describe a lot of hail-fellows-well-met, but you were fleeced, and nobody has assisted you to hold the responsible party or parties accountable."

"An aberration, and because I have no proof, my accusations were politely ignored. For the most part, we commiserate with each other, we encourage each other. We wish one another best of luck with all sincerity. Maybe it's a bit like military life. You're all in it together, and if somebody isn't in it, they will never understand. Makes for camaraderie."

Military training was also designed to leave a soldier feeling privileged to serve and above the civilian in God's eyes. Harry had noted that God's comment on the matter was to regularly see soldiers of all stripes cut down in their thousands on the battlefields. Not his idea of any sort of privilege at all.

"I take your meaning," I said. "It's a club. You either belong, or you don't." I did not and hoped to spend the rest of my days in that happy state. "Every single one of these fellows at the top had runners at Epsom three years ago?"

"Not all. Twickford scratched—horse came up lame on the morning of the race—though his gelding came back the next year to distinguish himself over shorter distances. Danner hadn't any entries, but he was involved in the betting. The fellows with the X's were *present* at Epsom, you understand? Underfoot. Capable of tampering with a horse or bribing a jockey, though I have no reason to suspect any of them."

"Thus you suspect all of them. What actually happened at Epsom, Tenneby?" I should have asked this question sooner, but my orders did not extend to righting the injustices of the past.

"Damnedest thing," Tenneby said, gesturing me onto the path that led to the house. "My colt, Excalibur, four years old at the time, was the fastest creature on four legs that year, bar none. His blood-lines go back to the Godolphin Arabian on the dam side and the Darley Arabian on the sire's. Sound familiar?"

"No."

"*Eclipse*, man. How can you not know the breeding of the greatest horse of all time?"

"My education has been sadly lacking, apparently. What of your colt?"

"I hadn't raced him all that often. The odds tend to come down if your horse is a sure thing, and my boy was a very sure thing. The jockeys always rode to win, but we never let Excalibur win by much. Three lengths was the rule, no more. In any case, he came up against a respectable field at Epsom, and the odds given for him were ten to one. Before the field had topped the hill, he had his three lengths. Around the turn they galloped, and my boy was still going away from the pack, romping along, until halfway down the final straight, he simply... ran out of puff. The field passed him as if he were standing still, and he was so demoralized by that performance I haven't raced him since."

The best racehorses had a will to win, a compulsion to gallop to the front of the field and stay there, come fire, flood, or falling stars. One didn't have to be turf mad to admire and respect that will.

"Horses tire, Tenneby. It sounds as if the distance was simply too much for him." The house came into view, and I realized I was both hungry and thirsty. I would not have to change before breakfast, but I did want to tidy up.

"The course is a mile and a half, Caldicott. That's nothing to a horse like Excalibur. He was in a four-years-and-up race and used to doing three- and four-mile courses. I'd started him over fences to preserve him from boredom, and the jockeys claimed that simply made him faster and stronger. He should have won."

I wanted to argue that horses had off days. They played too hard in the pasture, they took a bad step that didn't quite lame them, or pulled a muscle that wouldn't have bothered a hack, but tormented a Thoroughbred on race day. Except that Harry had dragged me to a meet at Epsom, and I knew the lay of the course, which was an enormous up-and-down horseshoe.

None of my excuses explained why Excalibur had led off *uphill* at a blazing pace, run even stronger out of the turn, and faltered only on the *downhill* portion of the track, with the finish in sight.

"What did the jockey say about this defeat?"

"He was in tears. Worried Excalibur was colicking and might have to be put down before ever having stood at stud. He had no explanation, and he knew that horse well. I watched the race, and I am confident my jockey was riding honestly. He even used his stick twice, to no avail. I can only conclude somebody tampered with my horse, but I know not how or when."

We'd reached the back terrace, a sunny flagstone expanse that looked out over a rolling park. "You've taken measures to safeguard your runners?"

"Of course, every owner does, but I took measures at Epsom. The feed was kept under lock and key, the bedding inspected before being spread. Only my grooms were permitted to handle the horse and his gear, or even to muck his stall. I am not the brightest fellow, Caldicott, I know that, but within the confines of horse racing, I am careful and well informed. I look after my runners."

Tenneby struck me as at least as perspicacious as Wickley or Pierpont, though that was admittedly not saying much.

"I'll keep a sharp lookout, Tenneby, and my tiger is doing the same in the stable. He's quite young and easily ignored, which works to his advantage. Miss West is my eyes and ears among the ladies, who often know more than we give them credit for."

Tenneby smiled. "My sister says the same. She quite likes you, by the way."

Famous. "You might warn her that both Pierpont and Wickley have taken a fancy to her, or so they'd have me think."

"Neither one is fit to glance at her hems, despite owning some fine horseflesh. In this life, there is no justice. I'm off to review today's race card and meet with my stewards. Good day to you, my lord."

He bowed smartly and marched off with as much spring in his step as a matchmaker who had spotted an undefended ducal bachelor among the potted palms at Almack's.

I folded Tenneby's list into an inside pocket of my riding jacket and would have made straight for my rooms but for an odd figure in a Bath chair parked at a corner of the terrace. He sat facing the park, unmoving, a wizened little fellow of venerable mien. His attire was at least twenty years out of fashion—brocade coat, lavishly embroidered waistcoat, pale silk hose. His white hair was queued back, and the hat on the balustrade before him was a black tricorn.

The voice in my head warned me that the elderly could be punctilious about etiquette, but this was an informal race meet. High sticklers need not apply.

"Lord Temmington." I bowed before the old fellow. "Lord Julian Caldicott, pleased to make your acquaintance."

He peered up at me with that twisting angle of the neck common to chickens and the aged. "Waltham's youngest boy, ain't ye? The old duke, that is. You're supposed to be a sensible sort. Survived the war, didn't ye? What the hell are ye doing at Clary's little horse party? Damnedest nonsense you ever did see, though some of the fillies are quite fetching."

I did not know if he referred to horses or women, but presumed to take the seat beside his. Children and the elderly were both acutely observant, of necessity. I assumed horses and dogs were, too, but I hadn't the luxury of interviewing them.

"My lord considers this race meeting nonsense, and yet, it's your larders providing the feasts, your stables housing the runners. Why agree to host such an expensive gathering when your nephew assures me that the earldom might soon be in want of coin?"

The earl said nothing for a moment, then turned stiffly in his seat and gestured to a footman lurking in the shade of a balcony.

"The lad and I will have a tray out here, Jones, and see that the food arrives hot."

"Very good, my lord." The footman bowed and departed.

"If they're Welsh, they're Jones," the earl said. "Scots are all MacDonalds—my first countess was a MacDonald—and the English ones are Millers. Same goes for the maids. My niece says I'm daft, but the staff answers when summoned."

"Just as all coachmen are John Coachman?"

"Precisely, and Evvie wouldn't dare tell Society that's a daft practice, would she? How is your mother? Quite a looker, if I recall. Too young for me, but nobody's fool. Always an attractive quality in a lady."

"Her Grace is thriving. She has a grandson to dote on now." I took a risk disclosing that much.

"Lord Harry's get," the old man said, nodding. "You're doing the right thing by the lad and by his father's memory. A throwback, was Lord Harry. He would have had an easier time of it in my day. We didn't set as much store by decorum and consequence. A fellow could get on if he was smart and hardworking, and his children could do better than he did. Nowadays, we pretend money stinks if it was got by trade, and heaven help our Evvie. Neither title nor fortune—yet—and she's no great beauty."

"No fortune at all?"

"I've done what I could for her, but it's less than I'd wish. Her papa's funds were running out as Evelyn came of age. Clary will look after her portion conscientiously, but..." He trailed off as the footman reappeared and set a heaping tray on the balustrade.

"Shall I pour out, my lord?" he asked.

"Go back to napping in the shade. All these guests doubtless have you lot run off your feet."

"Very good, my lord."

The morning was sunny and mild rather than hot. Another lovely spring day, and perfect weather for running a race. The park before us glowed with the vibrant green unique to early spring, which raised the question of how many more such mornings the earl would see.

His clothing, while clean and exquisitely fashioned, hung loosely on his gaunt frame, and his cheeks were sunken. I could yet see a resemblance to Tenneby in the eyes and chin and hear an echo of Tenneby's speech in the earl's words.

"Make yourself useful, boy."

I surveyed the tray. "Tea or chocolate?"

"Damned Jones. He thinks to fatten me up with the chocolate and rum buns. I'd best have the chocolate, or he'll give me wounded looks that would shame an angel. The porridge is for me."

I passed over a bowl and spoon, the porridge having been fortified with melted butter, honey, sugar, and grated apple, the whole topped with a dollop of whipped cream, a sprinkling of crushed walnuts, and a dash of cinnamon.

The cook at least, abetted by the footman, was determined to take excellent care of the old boy. "Tell me about the race meet, my lord. I've never been to a private gathering of this nature."

"It's like Mayfair with a mane and a tail. The talk is all of breeding, conformation, earnings, and progeny, but the subject is horses rather than heiresses, honorables, or heirs. Damned lot of nonsense, but it's diverting if you approach it in the right spirit."

"Does Tenneby approach it in the right spirit?" I set the earl's chocolate on the balustrade. "Best take a few bites of that porridge before it gets cold, sir. The Welsh guard has us under surveillance."

"Huh." The earl spooned up some breakfast. "Needs more honey. You ask about Clary and his approach to racing. He has the right spirit—horses and staff first, everything else comes after—but he's the odd man out. Never thought to hold a title, expected to inherit a thriving business, but peace has been awful for business, so they tell me. The title's bankrupt. Was when I inherited it, and selling off tenancies only goes so far."

"We're at the forlorn hope stage?"

I sipped my tea when what I wanted was a cool tankard of cider or lemonade. The very air was dry, but because it wasn't also hot, the low humidity was comfortable.

"Forlorn hope indeed. Clary suggested this race-meet notion, and at first I was appalled. You never saw such a crowd for emptying a man's cellars as the racing enthusiasts. Sailors are teetotalers by comparison, and that's nothing compared to what it costs to host the horseflesh."

I made myself a sandwich of cheese omelet and ham on toast. "You know a lot about this."

"Clary comes by the horse madness honestly. The Tennebys have always been great equestrians. I took an interest in horse racing back in the day."

"Your grandson was cavalry," I said, then wished the words back. His grandson was cavalry no more.

"Wellington never learned how to deploy his mounted forces. He blamed them for not following orders, but when a whole column doesn't follow the same orders, perhaps the orders are at fault. I hope Waterloo at least taught His Grace that much. Young Cranston is buried in the family plot. My countesses and his parents keep him company there. I will, too, soon." Said with great complaisance between bites of porridge.

A lot of loss, for both Tenneby and his uncle. "My condolences, sir. Why sink a fortune into hosting this meet if funds are limited?"

The earl gazed out upon the rolling beauty of his park, set aside his porridge, and sighed. "This is what Clary can do, you see? He cannot resurrect his family's mercantile interests, not with the title dangling two inches above his head. He's too honest to offer for a lady simply because she has a fortune and he's to be an earl. Too soft-hearted, some might say, but what sort of marriage would that be for him or the lady? He has only this estate and a few tenancies left to work with and his keen knowledge of horse racing. He's doing what he can, and I felt honor-bound to let him try."

"But he's been fleeced out of a sure thing before," I said. "Are you not setting him up to be made a fool of all over again? A bigger fool than ever?"

"Clary takes after his papa. Lutrell was the proverbial choirboy, all smiles, enjoyed his tucker, and liked by all, but Lutrell never forgot a face, could do sums in his head like a walking abacus, and could turn gossip at the club into sound business with more discernment than any man I've known. He warned us all that peace would be the ruin of the City. My second countess called Lutrell a pleasant plodder, and he was that, but he was also hardworking, careful, and thorough. Clary could pull off some upsets, my lord. He knows the pedigrees. He knows the horses. Give him a fair race, and he and his runners are the equal of any of these peacocks."

"And if he loses? What of all the Joneses, MacDonalds, and

Millers? What of Miss Evelyn and yourself? Visiting with your countesses will be a more complicated undertaking when some cit has rented this place for the next twenty years, especially when his payments don't cover the mortgage."

My questions were rude, given that Temmington was my elder and my host of record.

He sent me a sidewise glance. "Clary told you the family finances were in poor health. I made sure he would, and he keeps his promises. That isn't your fault, young man. You keep the racing aboveboard, and the rest will sort itself out."

"I am only one person, my lord, and you have forgotten more about horse racing than I will ever know. A dozen contenders have brought runners to this meet, and half of them will resent me on sight. What exactly do you expect me to do when they know how to cheat, and Tenneby himself, an expert in the field who took every precaution, could not catch them at it?"

The earl took up his porridge, though it had to be cold by now. "I expect you to *try*, sir. You know what it is to be treated unfairly, to be cast out. What you lack in subject-matter knowledge you will make up for in diligence. Your presence alone should put the miscreants on alert, if any miscreants there are."

I finished my tea when I wanted to stomp off in high dudgeon. I should not have come to this gathering. Tenneby's finances were not dodgy, they were approaching disastrous. An entire household would be thrown into dun territory if the races were rigged. Tenneby's children—assuming anybody would marry a bankrupt earl—would be laughed at behind their backs, and it would all be my fault.

I was in over my head and sinking fast. I was about to start making excuses for my inevitable failure when a tall, dark-haired man came up the terrace steps, something about his gait catching my eye.

I knew him, and before my mind could sort out from where, or who he was, my heart was telling me that I was glad to see him.

"Excuse me, my lord," I said, rising. "I must greet that fellow. Breakfast is much appreciated." I hurried across the terrace in time to confront the new arrival. "Devlin St. Just, you are a sight for literally sore eyes. As usual, the cavalry has left it to the last minute. Greet your host and then take a walk with me."

Colonel Devlin St. Just was no longer the laughing, robust dispatch rider who'd galloped through hell repeatedly and relished the challenge.

He shared with me the sorrow of having lost a brother in time of war, and while he'd never been imprisoned by the French, he was serving out a sentence similar to mine in nightmares and regrets. After years of exemplary service, St. Just had taken a bad turn in the wake of the fighting at Waterloo. Details were scarce, and one did not pry.

I'd sent for him before leaving Caldicott Hall, but I'd had no idea whether he would be free to join me, off shopping in Paris, or requisitioned by his ducal father for duty in the ballrooms of Mayfair.

"What the merry hell inspired you to come here?" he asked, extending a hand.

St. Just was travel-worn, suggesting a long ride despite the early hour. His hat, his cravat, and his jacket were all creased with fine dust, and his boots were coated with it. He was nevertheless a heart-warming sight.

We shook, his grip firm without being crushing. "Damned if I know," I replied, "but greet the earl, and..." The old fellow was no longer at his perch along the balustrade. The Welsh guard must have returned him to the garrison. The tray and its contents had already disappeared as well.

"Come for a stroll," I said, gesturing down the steps St. Just had just climbed. "Hyperia will be very glad to see you."

"And I will be glad to see Miss West, once I get some of the dirt of the road off my person. Her Grace tells me congratulations are in order."

The Duchess of Moreland was not St. Just's mother, but she was married to his ducal papa. These things truly did happen in the best of families. St. Just had a sister similarly situated, though any mention of their irregular circumstances was always quickly followed by an observation that His Grace had not yet been married or in line for the title when his wild oats had sprouted into by-blows.

The duchess had raised both children with her own brood of eight, and from everything I'd observed, the two oldest were as dear to the ducal couple as were the rest of the mob. St. Just was perhaps a little dearer, for having gone to war and come home the worse for his gallantry.

"Tenneby's cousin was a friend," St. Just said. "Major Cranston will long be remembered for his high spirits and low cunning. You asked me to drop by and…"

He sent a haunted look to the east.

"And any excuse to avoid Mayfair in spring deserves consideration," I said. "Moved, seconded, and passed. Tenneby is concerned about race-fixing."

St. Just's dark brows rose. "You're here in the capacity of steward? That's occasionally been my role. I would volunteer to fill it here, except that I'm only available for the first week."

Perhaps I could talk him into staying longer. "I am to engage in what has been called snoopery and I prefer to describe as preventive reconnaissance."

We ambled along a crushed-shell walk, the intersections and borders of the garden adorned with pots of red, yellow, and white tulips. Tenneby's racing colors were a cheerful combination.

"Are the stalls padlocked?" St. Just asked. "I disprove of the practice generally. It's a recipe for tragedy if there's a fire."

"Not padlocked, but the runners are housed on the inner side of the stable yard, the better to be kept under observation. Each groom is looking after his string to the best of his ability, but I might have already witnessed one attempt to swap out a pair of fillies."

I explained the imbroglio with Denton and the grays, while St.

Just and I strolled the perimeter path. I was still thirsty and getting thirstier, but this impromptu conference with an expert horseman was the answer to a prayer.

"Bad business," St. Just said, "when suspicions are aired so openly. Tenneby made a similar fuss at Epsom several years ago. Cranston was appalled, but he also said if Clary Tenneby claimed he'd been cheated, then Clary Tenneby honestly believed himself to be the victim of wrongdoing. Tenneby isn't known for needless drama."

"Horse racing generally is nothing but drama, or do I mistake the matter?"

St. Just and I rounded the sculpture most distant from the house, a winged Nike preparing to soar out over the park.

"Horse racing is supposed to be exciting," St. Just said. "Honestly exciting, a fair contest, with just the right mix of predictable and unpredictable factors. Have you walked the course?"

"Rode it just this morning. Puts me in mind of Epsom and Newmarket, but it's an oval rather than a horseshoe to allow for longer distances. Uphill out of the start, the first turn sweeps left, then downhill to the finish if the distance is less than a mile and a half, or around another circuit for the longer contests."

"We'll walk it," St. Just said. "We need rain, badly, but a muddy track is nobody's idea of ideal footing. The turf at Newmarket is as hard as weathered oak this year."

Meaning the horses' legs and feet would take a beating at speed. "How does one rig a horse race, St. Just?"

"Let's sit." He chose a bench in the shade, one that looked out over the park. "The simplest way to rig a race is to swap horses. Put a five-year-old in a contest for three-year-olds attempting an ambitious distance. The game works best if the original three-year-old was a mundane performer, and his mediocre talent is reflected in the betting odds."

"So... three-year-old Caldicott's Folly is given odds of ten to one.

If I bet one pound, I get ten back if he wins, but it's not Caldicott's Folly who is put under saddle."

"Right. It's his bigger, faster older brother—who looks just like him—Caldicott's Meteor. Put a hundred pounds on Meteor, and he is very likely to earn you a thousand. Be very careful to make sure any brands, hoof markings, and scars align on the two horses, and for at least one or two meetings, you have a near certain moneymaker. Never bet too much with any one party, but bet consistently, and you are likely to see a fabulous return."

If the substitution game had been done at Epsom previously, perhaps that was the least likely scheme to be attempted again.

"What else should I look out for?"

"The reverse strategy. Be the one generous, optimistic soul who will take bets on the favorite at odds the bettors will appreciate. Everybody else offers, say, a ten percent return, because he's the favorite and bound to win. You claim upsets happen frequently, which they do, but you also know the groom had the poor horse out galloping half the night away. The favorite loses, and you keep all the stakes from his loyal supporters."

"Diabolical. Why aren't the temperance leagues trying to have racing banned?"

St. Just smiled. "They will doubtless try, but who doesn't love a hard-fought match between noble champions?" Being Devlin St. Just, he referred to the horses, rather than their riders, of course. "Wellington spent two years with a cavalry regiment early in his career. I'm sure he saw plenty of horse races during that time, with all the mischief attendant thereto. You ask where he learned the knack for tactics, and I'll tell you—from a lot of Irish cavalrymen in the 12th Light Dragoons."

St. Just's mother had been Irish. He'd translated for Gaelic-speaking infantry more than once that I recalled.

"I will keep a close eye on the betting," I said, though I had no idea how to go about that. "What else should I be watching?"

"Fodder is always a question." He stretched out long legs and crossed dusty boots at the ankle. "You will recall that when cavalry mounts arrived from England, we had to ship English fodder with them, because turning them out in local pastures on the Peninsula or starting them on the local feed stores made so many of them sick. We had to blend rations, start them on grass gradually, if any grass was to be had."

Enlisted men had often complained that the army's equine stock had been better cared for than the average foot soldier. Cavalry regiments always had dedicated veterinary surgeons, farriers, and a plethora of serjeant specialists to look after feed, saddles, weapons, and recruits. The enlisted men, in other words, had sometimes had a point.

"Then I could switch up the feed so Caldicott's Folly got the wrong rations the night before the race?"

"Night before and morning of. Most horses will run better for having something in their bellies, though not a full meal. You could withhold feed altogether, though that's not necessarily enough to guarantee the desired outcome. Withhold supper, though, and offer moldy feed or drugged feed in the morning, and you are likely to achieve your goal."

God protect horses from human mischief. "Somnifera?"

"Somnifera is often used to deaden the pain of gelding a horse, but the farriers and veterinary surgeons have a whole herbal of concoctions for calming horses or agitating them."

"Could you kill a horse with such measures?"

"Possibly, though I wouldn't say probably. A fall can kill a horse too. Is there to be jump racing?"

A chilling thought landed in my mind: A fall could kill *a rider*, and somebody who'd steal twenty-eight thousand pounds and laugh at the victim wouldn't necessarily hesitate to put human lives at risk.

"Jump racing figures more prominently on the program for next week."

St. Just turned his face up to the sun. A handsome countenance in the black Irish tradition, with fine lines at the corners of his blue eyes and a smile that could be buccaneering or self-mocking. St. Just wasn't smiling nearly as much as he'd smiled before Waterloo.

"Pay particular attention to the last obstacle on the course," St. Just said. "The horses and riders are tired by the time they reach it, but the field has also been whittled down to those determined to win. In their haste to be first past the post, both jockeys and mounts can make poor decisions about whether to throw in an extra stride or take the long spot. Falls are almost expected at the last jump, and mistakes are easier to make."

More bad news. "Tenneby claims he's keeping fodder under lock and key. His head lad tells me the horses have been marked on the underside of the hoof with unique identifying designs. The grooms are on high alert, and if I have to sleep beside the final jump to avoid somebody tampering with it, I will. What else should I be watching?"

"You'll want to keep an eye on the no-hopers and unknown quantities. If the meet is crooked, at least one of those will pull off a spectacular upset."

"And in that case, anybody who backed the favorite will also lose." Was there no end to the ways a simple horse race could be turned into a confidence trick? "I am very sorry I agreed to attend this meet, St. Just, but appreciative of your tutorial."

"Pleased to oblige." He rose a bit stiffly. He'd probably ridden horseback all the way out from Town, if not from the Moreland estate in Kent.

"You're not too late for breakfast," I said, joining him on the path that took us back to the terrace. "You should also know the winter parlor is used as an all-day buffet to save the staff having to run around the shire all day with tea trays. The first match is this afternoon. A two-mile flat race for the fillies. The purse is modest, the aim to have a gallop around the course. Tenneby is meeting with his official stewards now."

"Ladies first, of course. Thank the benevolent powers I'm not a steward. The job is thankless at best. Let's see what's on offer in the winter parlor rather than subjecting the other guests to me in all my dirt."

As we made our way through the house, I wanted to ask St. Just how he was faring. Were the nightmares abating? Were the good days outnumbering the bad? But one didn't intrude.

"Go sparingly with the men's punchbowl," I said as we reached the sunny little parlor with its plethora of sporting art. "I suspect Tenneby's distinguished guests are taking turns emptying their flasks into the concoction, with the result that it will knock you arse over tea cups before you can pour a refill."

"My sisters perfected the art," St. Just said, ladling himself a generous serving from the smaller punchbowl. "If the brothers protested that the brew was too strong, we were unmanly. If we failed to protest, we allowed the ladies to think they'd scored victory over us in a sneak attack."

"What's a brother to do?"

"Only the potted palms know the answer to that conundrum, and they haven't survived to tell the tale. God, I'm hungry."

I filled my own glass at the smaller punchbowl, downed the contents at one go, and poured a second helping half full. I topped up the glass with water and drank most of the contents again.

"St. Just, could somebody tamper with a horse's water to ill effect?"

He paused in the creation of a third sandwich. "Horses are particular about their water. Unless they're moving from place to place regularly—as coach horses or cavalry mounts do—they often won't drink from an unfamiliar well."

I'd known that, but hadn't considered the consequences in a racing context. "Nobody shipped English water for English remounts to drink in Spain."

"Of course not. Before the remounts shipped, the grooms would start dosing the water with a bit of stout, just enough to give the water a hint of that beery, malty flavor. Send along cases of the same stout with the horses, and the different water sources were adequately disguised even from the discerning palate of the equine."

"Stout? Dark ale?"

"I'm told the idea originated in Ireland, but it makes sense. Enough stout to barely flavor the water won't hurt the horse, and we both knew artillery sergeants who shared their ale with the mules."

Indeed, we had. "Then I'm to watch the fodder, the fences, the water, the gear, the individual grooms, the betting, and each runner in every contest? What are the stewards doing?"

He considered his sandwich. "The same, I'm sure. But don't make the mistake of assuming the stewards are honest. Have you spies in the stable?"

I added *crooked stewards* to my list of responsibilities. "One pair of eyes—my tiger. He's good at not being noticed while noticing everything. I trust Tenneby's man Woglemuth."

"You can trust my groom, Piggott, but for the most part, trust only your instincts and the horses."

I knew exactly what St. Just meant. Horses were honest. They could not fake a bellyache, nervousness, or lethargy. They would not look over the odds and decide whether to win or lose based on their purses.

As for my instincts... They were telling me to develop a pressing need to quit the premises before the first race had been run. How I wish I had listened to those instincts much sooner than I did.

CHAPTER SIX

Walking the racecourse, as opposed to riding over the same ground, left me more morose than ever.

"Too many trees," I said as St. Just marched at my side down the declivity that led to the finish line. "All manner of mischief is possible thanks to the trees."

"I like trees," St. Just surveyed the venerable oaks, maples, beeches, and birches forming the boundaries of the race course. "What sort of mischief?"

"If you wait in a tree, you don't leave deep depressions on soft ground no matter how long you tarry. You don't cast a shadow. You elude a casual inspection of the hedgerow. Thirty feet up, with a spyglass, you can see much farther than anybody on the ground can see, and you can aim your guns accordingly."

St. Just stopped and gave me a steady stare. "The activity contemplated is *horse racing*. No guns necessary."

"Right." I came to a halt as well. "So, in the interests of securing the nominal sum of, say, ten thousand pounds—which no foot soldier ever earned in uniform—you pitch a rock at the head of the horse in the lead. A pebble will do, because all you need is for the beast to flinch, to go off stride, particularly as he's approaching a jump. A little swerve, a loss of focus. Have somebody else do it again in twenty yards."

St. Just studied the trees more closely. "A signal mirror might do the job. Angle the surface so it flashes into the eyes of the leader as he comes around the turn. Unless another horse is right beside him, nobody else will see what caused the spook. The jockey probably won't either."

"Because humans look ahead, while horses have a wide field of vision to the sides. St. Just, why does anybody, ever, for any reason assume a horse race will be honestly run?"

St. Just resumed walking, and I fell in step.

"For the simple reason, that most of them are. The Regent himself was cautioned by stewards for what appeared to be race-fixing, and his sole recourse was to leave the sport permanently. If the Regent can be taken to task, so can all the little lordlings and schemers on the periphery."

In a gesture of royal pique entirely in character for George, he had subsequently sold off his entire racing stable, from horses to hayracks. He'd abandoned the sport of kings without a backward glance. He'd also thus quit a tremendously expensive hobby while appearing to reel with injured dignity. The talk in the clubs had suggested that the race had likely been fixed, as had the prince's excusable retreat from a sport he could not afford.

We approached the bottom of the hill, and though the course was a mere mile and a half, I felt as if I'd hiked the length of the Sierra de Gredos. St. Just looked ready to cover the whole circuit again, double time, without breaking a sweat.

He was making progress, whether he'd admit as much or not. When I'd seen him the previous year, he'd not been in nearly such fine fettle.

"Why is your stay limited to only a week?" I asked.

"I'm heading north. Off to Yorkshire, of all places. One of His

Grace's little projects. I do like these downhill finishes. Makes for blazing fast runs to the post."

Whatever was afoot in Yorkshire, St. Just was reluctant to discuss it. "I dislike horse racing. I was neutral on the topic before—Harry seemed to think it was all great fun for a time—but I'm dead set against the sport now."

We crossed the finish line, and I turned to study the hill we'd just descended. "If you were going to toss these races, St. Just, what method would you prefer?"

"You know the answer to that." He stood beside me, his gaze on the rolling turf. "I'd have a list of options, from simplest to more complicated. I'd start on the simple end and, if that measure failed, graduate to the more complicated. I'd have already been contemplating my schemes for this meeting, running my slow-tops at Newmarket, where everybody could see how disappointing they were."

"But occasionally, say on a muddy day or an early morning match, you'd run your better horse, the twin, and lay a false trail. Caldicott's Folly has some potential—and he does well on a muddy course or in a match for morning glories—but not enough to redeem the horse's reputation."

"Precisely. Create credible doubt for the day when Caldicott's Meteor wins you a packet doing his impersonation of Caldicott's Folly. I made an early start this morning, and I could do with a nap. Let's call this maneuver complete, shall we?"

"How early?"

He shook his head.

"You left London around midnight, when the turnpikes were finally quiet, and rode through the night. Why?" The dust on his person when he'd arrived told me he'd been riding for miles, not merely hacking over from the nearest coaching inn at the start of the day.

"I made the night journey," St. Just said, "because I hate, with a passion known only to former dispatch riders, loitering about in a queue of carriages, pedestrians, drunks, and pickpockets when my horse could be at least trotting in the direction of my destination. Hate it."

Or he hated nights spent lying in bed, wide awake and remembering yet again all manner of purgatories.

"I'm glad to see you, regardless, and I wish you could stay the full two weeks."

He punched my arm, about as hard as Harry would have. Not a tap, but unlikely to leave a bruise. "You will manage. We're walking this course by daylight, stopping periodically and pointing and discussing, in part so that anybody running a filly this afternoon can see us taking stock."

"Parade inspection," I said, having figured out that much. "I assume we take a protracted tour of the stable yard next?"

"You always were a quick study. I want to meet your little tiger-cum-spy and introduce you to Piggott. We will peer into figurative cupboards, I will be taciturn and disapproving for form's sake, and you will be quietly observant while my smoldering Irish temper provides the distraction. I can be positively volcanic, you know. My legend precedes me."

He hadn't a temper... oh. "That business at Waterloo?"

"The last in a long line of half-mad incidents, to hear some tell it."

What fool had wanted to ask this poor man probing questions? "I've been mad. I don't recommend it."

"You allude to France?"

"Of course France. How is Westhaven? Hyperia speaks well of your brother."

St. Just allowed me the change of subject. He knew my past better than I knew his, perhaps because my disgraces were more spectacular than his had been. As we made our way to the stables, it occurred to me that if the race meet became the subject of scandal, that scandal would be associated with me rather than with St. Just.

He was on his way to Yorkshire, just passing through. I was the watchdog who still had very little grasp of how to identify or bring down my quarry. More fool I.

St. Just's man, Piggott, was a wiry, soft-spoken Berkshire native who regarded me levelly, though I was a good half a foot taller than he. Groom-cum-jockey-cum-spy was my assessment, though he was friendly enough to Atticus when I introduced the lad to him.

"Carrots or apples?" Piggott asked Atticus.

"Atlas loves them both, but in a dead heat, he'll go for whichever is fresher," Atticus replied, which was true enough. "I like apples better myself."

Piggott smiled, St. Just scowled, and Atticus—doubtless on the verge of a spate of juvenile loquaciousness—fell silent.

"Let's have a look at today's runners." St. Just strode off down the barn aisle.

I nodded at Piggott, winked at Atticus, and followed in the colonel's wake. He proceeded to make halfway disparaging remarks about this filly's quarters or that one's knees. When he came to Tenneby's entry, he offered grudging praise for Maybelle's well-set-on neck.

The grooms listened to all this gratuitous grumpiness without expression, but their very lack of reaction confirmed that St. Just was raising hackles. I, meanwhile, examined horses and stalls as closely as possible, even to the extent of lifting a few hooves and sniffing at feed buckets. So effective was St. Just's diversion that nobody gave me so much as a curious glance, save Paddy Denton, who kept his mouth shut.

"You're displeased," St. Just said as we concluded our impromptu inspection and trooped off toward the house. "That's a stable full of talented horses, if conformation has anything to say to it. They are all well cared for, and in good weight, for Thoroughbreds."

"Tenneby dragooned me into attending this meet in hopes I could deter crooked behavior. Other than the confusion between Maybelle and Cleopatra yesterday, I haven't seen anything to indicate there's a cheater in the herd."

"Because the proof will be in the race results. I see your dilemma, but happily for you, the racing will start in a very few hours. While I catch forty winks and a bath, you can get a feel for the betting. Starting with the fillies was a shrewd choice on Tenneby's part. The wildest gambling is always reserved for the colts. With the females, the wagers should start off with some restraint."

"Which means I am once again unlikely to see any patterns that would point me to guilty parties. Enjoy your damned bath, St. Just."

"Cheer up," he said. "The human fillies are likely to take an interest in this afternoon's contest as well, and their company makes any occasion sweeter."

Said a man with—I mentally counted—five sisters. "Valid point." And a reminder that I had yet to confer with my dear Hyperia, whose ability to gather intelligence among the distaff far exceeded my own on my best day.

I found my intended at the piano keyboard in the music room, rehearsing a trio with Miss Evelyn Tenneby on the violin and no less personage than Lord Wickley on the violoncello.

"I don't suppose you're musical?" Lord Wickley asked. "Mozart had a love affair with speed that my fingers do not share."

"Then dodge around the allegro assai and play the rondo," I suggested. "Ladies, good morning."

"You know this piece?" Wickley's tone suggested I'd somehow cheated.

"My sisters performed it regularly," I replied. "The B-flat major is his earliest trio." And it did begin with a ripping-fast allegro, which the ladies had treated as something of a horse race. "Miss West, I was hoping you'd come with me to select a spot from which to view this afternoon's races."

My ploy was meant to be obvious. If I'd cared to choose such a spot, Hyperia and I had viewed the entire racecourse on horseback only a few hours earlier.

"While I was hoping Lord Wickley would introduce me to his filly," Hyperia said. "Perhaps you might explore vantage points with Miss Tenneby?"

Ah. We were to divide and conquer. Neatly done. "Miss Tenneby, as a resident of the Acres, you will know all the best vantage points. Might you do me the honor?"

She curtsied with a flourish of her bow, as if concluding a performance. "Gladly. Herr Mozart and I were never the best of friends, and I agree with Lord Wickley. One wants fingers of flame to play the faster passages, and mine, alas, do not qualify. Meet me on the terrace in five minutes."

"We could all stroll to the stable together," Wickley suggested, setting his 'cello on its side atop the closed lid of the pianoforte. "A pleasant morning for such an outing."

Wickley no more sought to stroll in my company than I sought to play whist with his horse. "I've already admired your Cleopatra, and I'm sure Miss Tenneby has as well. Colonel St. Just pronounced your filly a bit over at the knee, but he found fault with just about every beast in the stable. He did have some praise for Maybelle. Liked how her neck was set on."

Wickley's diffident-gentleman act came to an abrupt conclusion. "St. Just is here? Colonel Devlin St. Just?"

"The very one, though I don't believe he has any runners, and he's not staying for the full two weeks."

Hyperia rose from the piano bench and closed the lid over the keys. "I will be so glad to renew my acquaintance with him. Such a droll wit, and the equine never had a more devoted champion. Come, Lord Wickley, let's repair to the stable with all possible haste."

Wickley looked like he was about to recall a pressing need to confer with his valet.

"St. Just has gone in search of a bath and a nap," I informed Wickley. "You won't find him in the stable yard at this hour."

"Very well, then we must make our obeisance before my fair Cleopatra. Miss West, shall I await you on the back terrace?"

"Please." She dismissed him with a smile, and he stalked off after treating me to a brooding perusal.

"I'll find you at luncheon," Hyperia said. "Please try to be good company for Evelyn. She's had to put up with Pierpont and Wickley's strutting and pawing, and the poor lady is quite out of patience."

"One sympathizes." I did not dare risk a kiss to Hyperia's cheek with the parlor door wide open. "Try to find out if Wickley owes St. Just money."

She stepped close enough to pat my lapel. "His lordship was less than pleased to hear of the colonel's arrival. Well done, Tenneby."

"Well done, me. I asked St. Just to attend, but I could not loiter at the Hall to await news of his availability. He rode through the night, Hyperia, and claimed he was avoiding the heaviest traffic."

"Hence the nap. Wise man. Is there anything else you want me to ask Wickley?"

"Is he genuinely fond of Miss Tenneby, or is he using her as a pawn in his ongoing competitions with Lord Pierpont? How are his finances generally, and why isn't he in Mayfair doing the pretty?"

"Hiding from creditors?" Hyperia asked, stepping back. "That would make sense."

"Creditors rank well ahead of matchmakers as blights on a bachelor's existence, and they would find it difficult to chase him down here at a private residence."

"Whereas at Newmarket, Wickley would be in plain view. If he's rolled up, he has a motive to cheat, Jules."

I mentally cursed the open door. "Try to get a sense of how he's betting, then, and let's plan on sharing a picnic blanket at lunch. A discussion of the particulars and possibilities with you is clearly in order. I suspect half of those who own racehorses are rolled up most of the time, and for the other half, simple greed might inspire them to cheat. The combination makes me uneasy."

Hyperia traced the graceful curve of the f-holes on Lord Wickley's 'cello. "You can spot the indications of poverty about a person's attire and habits, in the usual course. Greed and blind ambition aren't as easy to pick out, not in a crowd like this. The guests are all quite fashionable, and they can all legitimately claim a desire to win."

Good camouflage, to use the French term, and another daunting thought. "Until luncheon, my dearest. And, Hyperia?"

"Jules?"

"Be careful."

She nodded. "You too. Don't underestimate these people simply because they are turf mad. Madness of any stripe can be dangerous."

She did not need to remind me of that, but I was pleased that Hyperia was also taking the situation seriously.

Miss Evelyn Tenneby did not appear to take the race meeting or any of its attendees at all seriously. "Pierpont and Wickley are two among a herd of strutting nincompoops, my lord. Wickley expects me to be agog at his title, and Pierpont supposes that his brooding stare will set my heart aflutter."

"Most women would be agog to have a young, handsome earl in thrall," I replied, "and Pierpont's dark good looks, whatever his other failings, are all the current rage." May he and his curls rot in some poetical dungeon.

She grinned up at me, a russet-haired pixie poking fun at a gormless mortal. "Are you jealous?"

"You try having hair that makes you look like some sort of exotic badger. I used to have locks only a little darker than your own, Miss Tenneby, and I never appreciated how precious an unremarkable appearance was until I became something of a freak."

"Not a freak," she said, humor disappearing. "A casualty of war. You didn't die, but some of your innocence surely did. Never a pleasant experience. Let's admire the view from the folly, shall we?"

She took off up the hill that formed the center of the whole racecourse, an oblong swell of ground that rose a good forty feet at the center. Miss Tenneby negotiated the climb easily, suggesting a countrywoman's stamina and a sensible lady's approach to stays.

Atop the hill, some previous Tenneby earl had built a wooden structure larger than a gazebo and smaller than a cottage, most of it a terrace, though the center was under a high arching roof. The orientation gave excellent views of the start, finish, and long sloping straightaways, though portions of the sweeping curves were obscured by trees.

"Lovely prospect," I remarked when I arrived, puffing only slightly, at the top. "Somebody chose well."

"The present earl," she said. "Uncle pretends all his racing days are behind him, and he'll be least in sight at the formal suppers, but he was mad keen for the turf in his youth. If Clary had asked for an archery tournament or house party, the answer would have been no, but for the horses... his lordship is sentimental."

"What do you make of that business at Epsom several years ago?"

She took a seat on a bench facing away from the house and its outbuildings. The rolling Berkshire downs stretched green and glorious to the horizon, crisscrossed by lanes and wooded hedgerows. Unlike other parts of England, few sheep were to be seen here. The grazing livestock in this vista were mostly horses, including a liberal number of broodmares and gamboling foals.

"It's beautiful, isn't it?" Miss Tenneby said, untying her bonnet and putting it on the bench to her right. "Do have a seat. My brother and I are yet merely gentry, my lord, and impoverished gentry at that. No need for Mayfair manners. You ask about Epsom."

She was soon to be an earl's sister, and a simple writ would give her a lady's title for life. "All I know is that Tenneby's prodigy of a colt inexplicably ran out of puff when it counted, and neither Tenneby nor his jockey has any explanation. Many of the same cast are assembled here, and this course could be Epsom's twin. I'm concerned that a similar farce will play out again. Tenneby expects me to prevent that."

She patted my hand. "Clary sees the best in people, and if he's asked you to keep the weasels from getting into the henhouse, he'll put eggs on the menu every day, because he's that confident you will succeed. He was the same way when I made my come out, certain I'd bag a title, certain all of Mayfair would fall at my dainty feet."

She held up her feet, clad in boots for the occasion.

"Very diminutive." The lady herself stood no more than five feet and a couple inches, and while her contours were far from boyish, she was slender. "I gather Mayfair missed its cue?"

"I like horse races," Miss Tenneby replied. "You know who wins, unless it's a dead heat, and then you can do a rematch, and that will decide the matter. At Almack's, you think that quiet fellow lurking among the potted palms must be some dowager's penniless nephew dragged forth and kitted out on a hopeless quest for matrimony, and then you learn he's a hard-of-hearing duke and a confirmed bachelor."

His Grace of Devonshire was well liked, but he did find shouted public conversations tedious. Hence the lurking.

"You did not take?" My question was arguably rude.

"I received plenty of invitations—Auntie did her best—but as soon as it became known that my settlements were as diminutive as my feet, my dance card became populated by widowers and old soldiers. Many of them were quite dear."

"Were you tempted?"

She considered her feet again. "Sometimes I still am. I'm a burden. I know it, and yet, Clary is such a good brother, he claims he'd be lost without me. For a while, we hoped Pierpont might come up to scratch—he's bearable in small doses—but then he went to that race meet at Epsom rather than court me, and I realized that Clary was the attraction for Pierpont. I was just... a pair of pretty ankles."

Blessed Saint Eclipse. "Are you telling me that Pierpont paid you his addresses in order to learn more of your brother's racing ambitions?"

She twitched at her skirts. "Not his *addresses,* not in the manner your tone implies. He was friendly and flirtatious, and I was stupid."

And now she was sadder and wiser? "You doubtless chattered on and on about dear Clary's wonderful colt and his wicked-fast fillies, and all the while Pierpont encouraged you?"

She frowned at those small feet. "He did. He comes across as charming and dimwitted, but Lord Pierpont Chandler is accustomed to getting what he wants. Like anybody bitten by the racing bug, he wanted to best Clary at Epsom, and he succeeded."

"I'm sorry."

She tried for a smile. "Sorry Excalibur lost? So is Clary and so am I."

"Sorry Pierpont betrayed your trust and that you must extend the hospitality of the Acres to him now." How that must gall. "Shall I plant your brother a facer?"

"Why bother? Clary is right: I have to confront these people sooner or later, and another Season in Town—another expensive Season—is not how I'd prefer to do it. Then too, this group has money, and Clary needs them to bet that money against his stallion, or I truly will be a spinster for all the rest of my impoverished days."

He needed them to bet that money *and lose it—to him.*

"Speaking of the betting, what have you heard regarding this afternoon's inaugural match?"

"Put your money on Cleopatra."

"The opposition? Miss Tenneby, surely you blaspheme."

"Most of the fillies will run three times during this meet, and if I know my brother—and I do—he will give Maybelle an easy outing the first time 'round. Let the others try to impress with their initial performance, let them fall prey to vanity. Clary will instruct the jockey to make a good effort, but without exhausting the horse. The purse isn't worth the cost of an all-out effort."

"How much is the purse?"

"A thousand pounds."

Ye gods and little fishes. A small, thrifty family could live on that sum for twenty years, provided some interest accrued.

"That suggests," I said slowly, "that stakes will rise to celestial heights as the meet progresses. While the other fillies are recovering from a strenuous effort, Maybelle will still be fresh and ready to run her best. Why won't every owner instruct his jockey to take the same tack?"

Miss Tenneby rose and collected her bonnet. "They might, but one of the group will also reason that his filly will never win a race run at proper pace. She's too young, she's too slow, she's fast enough but lacks that winning drive. Her only chance for victory—which increases her value as a broodmare—is to take the opportunity presented today by all the watch-and-wait strategists."

Miss Tenneby shaded her eyes and regarded the course's starting line. "That mare, the mediocre talent, will be given her head, and the rest will want to catch her. Then any attempt to hold the other horses back becomes hard to disguise. The stewards would certainly question a jockey who *obviously* wasn't riding to win. It's a devious game, my lord, but I'm betting against Maybelle today."

I got to my feet as well. "Who took your bet?"

"Pierpont doesn't have a runner in this race, so he backed Maybelle, knowing she made no journey to reach the meet, and she has trained on this very turf. His reasoning makes sense, but he's also twitting Wickley."

My temples were beginning to throb from all the bright sunshine. Blue spectacles went only so far against Berkshire's golden sun, much less against all the intrigue possible around a seemingly straightforward horse race.

"I will suggest that Miss West back Cleopatra," I said, offering my arm. "I'm not betting myself."

"Very wise of you, my lord." She slipped her hand into the crook of my elbow. "Shall we return to the house?"

"You don't want to put your bonnet on first?" The same sunshine annoying my eyes would delight in causing the young lady the dreaded scourge of freckles across her cheeks.

"Why bother? I am not on offer here, the horses are. Clary has the best string of any of the owners. I know that, but this is not a sport where the best athlete reliably wins." She escorted me down the hill —or so it felt—a lady resigning herself to a dispiriting fate, though, in fact, she was much too fine for the likes of Lord Pierpont.

She should be comforted by that knowledge, but I suspected revenge for past insults would comfort her more.

CHAPTER SEVEN

"The wine is chilled," Hyperia said, on her knees before a wicker basket. "I could use a glass."

We shared a blanket spread along the ridge of the racecourse hill. The viewing folly was to our backs, as was the sun, and we had a good view of the start and finish as well as the lower curves of the oval.

At lunch, Hyperia had signaled that she'd remain in the company of Wickley and several others of his ilk—young men fiercely dedicated to the pursuit of handsome, witty idleness and the collective enrichment of their tailors and bootmakers. Their table had echoed with merriment and exchanges of knowing looks.

Not long ago, I might have been one of them, or longed to be. While the spectacle they made was on one level annoying—they were just loud enough to be un-ignorable—on another, I wished them the joy of their posturing. For many of them, posturing was what they did best.

"Allow me," I said, taking the bottle from Hyperia and making manly use of a corkscrew. I poured two glasses and took a cross-legged seat beside my darling. "To honest races."

She gestured with her glass toward the starting line. "To honest races and to the safety of the jockeys. The race card Tenneby put together lists only horses and owners, but it's the jockeys who are most likely to suffer a serious injury."

I realized I had seldom seen a race card that did name the jockeys. "And it's the jockeys, usually, who are serving as the grooms and thus doing the hard work of training gallops, mucking, feeding, poulticing, and so forth. I wish I could keep a closer eye on them, but for that, I'm relying on Atticus and St. Just's man, Piggott. What do you think of Wickley?"

Hyperia sipped her champagne and made a fetching picture on a fine spring day. The ground was hard, true, and that would affect the horses, but amid Berkshire's greenery, in this happy and handsome crowd, she was of a piece with the scene. She wore a wide-brimmed straw hat, a muslin dress printed all over with roses, and a bright red sash to match the red ribbons of her bonnet.

I wished we were merely spectators, indifferent to the races and the crowd, and intent on enjoying each other's company.

"Lord Wickley is new to his honors," she said, "and like Clary Tenneby, he never expected to inherit."

"Then he's making a hash of it, falling in with a bunch of wastrels in expensive plumage and trying to out-peacock them all. Understandable, I suppose." Younger sons and nephews were generally safe in assuming they would not inherit. Heirs, by contrast, were permitted to trade on their expectations, and thus life should go on.

Fate occasionally made other plans—witness, my own status as heir.

Hyperia glanced across the brow of the hill to where Wickley and chums, along with a smattering of adoring belles, were again indulging in audible merriment.

"I believe you are right, Jules. Wickley is trying to live up to somebody's ill-informed idea of how a young, bachelor earl behaves, and that path could lead to ridicule and foolishness."

If not bankruptcy. "What of duels?" I could mention such a

vulgar undertaking with Hyperia. Her brother had been known to engage in stupidities on the field of foolishness, but then, so had His Grace of Wellington.

"None yet, I gather. He's not exactly bright, but he has enough sense to grasp that nobody respects a peer trading openly on his consequence. He may trade subtly, he may wield political power directly, but he doesn't take seriously the deference shown him as a result of his inherited honors, especially among this crowd."

"Not your typical Mayfair drawing room, is it?"

Further along the hilltop, a pair of banker's sons lounged in the company of a pair of admiral's daughters. Wickley was one of two earls at the gathering, and beside St. Just—a duke's by-blow—sat a lady who was rumored to be the result of one of the Regent's youthful indiscretions. Wealthy gentry was represented in abundance, while the stewards were from among the many racing enthusiasts with whom the Acres shared property lines.

"I have enjoyed the meet thus far," Hyperia said. "If I can turn the conversation away from racing, the viewpoints are more varied than I'd find in Town and the humor just as clever but not as spiteful. What of you?"

The champagne was cool and lovely, fruity with just a touch of sweetness. Hyperia was lovely and sweet, too, but our discussion followed a narrower path than I preferred. Not quite small talk, not quite a substantive inquiry relevant to the job at hand.

"I am aware that Harry was a better fit for this gathering than I will ever be," I said, "but I can see why he enjoyed it."

"Do you ever forget Harry, Jules? Is he ever not on your mind, a source of comparison, guilt, and grief?" Her questions held a touch of exasperation.

"Sometimes, yes, I do, but his absence casts a long shadow, just as I'm sure both of your parents are frequently in your thoughts. Whatever else is true, Hyperia, I am glad to be here with you on this gorgeous day. I'm not in Spain, or France, or the shires while you bide in Town, and I am free to enjoy your company by the hour. My cup runneth over."

She blinked at her glass of champagne. "Jules, when you intend to turn up all heartfelt and romantic, you should give a lady some warning."

"Then you must dwell in a perpetual state of readiness, my dear, because we are courting, and I esteem you beyond words." I meant what I said, but a passing bit of sincere sentiment ought not to turn Hyperia up lachrymose. When I would have inquired as to the real inspiration for her tears, a trumpet fanfare heralded the arrival of the fillies.

"They're ever so pretty," Hyperia said, setting her glass down and taking up a pair of field glasses. "Wickley's colors are the purple and green. Pierpont is red and white."

"The fellow in red, white, and yellow is riding Tenneby's mare Maybelle. I was told not to bet on her by Tenneby's sister."

"I'm backing Cleopatra at Wickley's insistence."

"Who took your bet?" I was slightly shocked that the ladies were betting more or less openly, but that was another aspect of horse racing's egalitarian appeal. Most gambling in Merry Olde was technically illegal, but the ladies and lords, rich and poor, old and young were all equally welcome to risk their coin on the sport of kings. No expensive membership in a fancy club required, no invitation to some noted hostess's "charity" card party.

"St. Just took my bet, and he won't breathe a word, don't worry. I would tattle to his sisters if he so much as hinted that I'd been wagering with him, and his sisters would give him no peace. What else did Miss Tenneby have to say?"

The fillies—a field of seven—were reacting to the crowd on the hill and to one another's nervousness. As girths were checked and stewards inspected equipment, one entry began propping as if to rear, while another cantered in impossibly small circles.

"Miss Tenneby bears some resentment toward Lord Pierpont," I said. "He pretended to court her several years ago, when he was in truth just pumping her for information regarding Tenneby's runners. The stewards need to get this race started before somebody is hurt."

The spectators seemed to regard the confusion prior to the start as so much entertainment, but the horses—young, green, hot-blooded—were not enjoying themselves at all. By autumn, they might well be seasoned at the game, but on this spring afternoon, they were distressed and nervous.

"They're off!" Hyperia said, putting the field glasses to her eyes. "I've seen faster gallops."

So had I, suggesting that Miss Tenneby's strategy—watch and wait, hang back, live to gallop faster another day—was popular. The field ascended the first hill at a brisk but hardly punishing pace, though they did pick up some speed on the descent that completed the first circuit. The pace increased on the second circuit, with the field spreading out across several horse lengths the second time up the hill.

The curve to the left saw the gaps close up some, and the downhill rush to the post saw the third runner back making a good try to overtake the leaders, but leaving it a few yards too late.

"Cleopatra by half a length," I said, joining in the polite applause and occasional whoop. "Precisely as Miss Tenneby predicted."

I'd seen no odd flashes of light from the trees to suggest a spectator where one ought not to be. The horses had all run well and consistently, no sign they'd been tampered with. The jockeys had eschewed the dirtier tricks—using one's crop accidently on the face of an opponent or on the face of an opponent's mount, bumping one mount into another, shoving and kicking...

The sport was truly dangerous for the anonymous men in those featherlight saddles, and yet, this first outing had been conducted as if the *Code Duello for Horses* had been adhered to down to the last detail.

"That went well," Hyperia said, "particularly for Cleo's backers."

"Did you win a packet?"

She smirked. "Sixpence. Will you come with me to collect my winnings? The next race isn't for an hour."

"I will escort you to the loser and condole him on his ruin. Were you tempted to bet more?"

"No, not at all. Wickley hounded me to make what he called a truly sporting bet, but one harebrained fool in the family is enough. I do wonder when Healy will arrive."

I would have been quite content had Healy never joined the gathering. I happened to glance over at Pierpont, who hadn't had a runner in the field. He was looking distinctly unmerry, perhaps because his rival's horse had won.

"Jules, please can't you just enjoy the day?" Hyperia asked, following my gaze. "The race was honest, nobody's horse fell, no jockey had to be carried away on a litter. It might well be as Tenneby hoped—your presence is deterring bad behavior."

I mustered my best Venetian breakfast smile and assisted Hyperia to her feet, holding her hand a moment too long.

"I am relieved that all went well and hope you're right that my imposing presence is sufficient to keep order in the schoolroom. You must be gracious toward St. Just. He's probably not used to losing."

"Wickley seems very comfortable with winning," Hyperia said, studying the crowd around his lordship. The men were slapping his back, the women were patting his arm, and he was beaming like a schoolboy who'd taken top honors on Speech Day.

"He's off on a good foot and probably relieved."

"I feel sorry for him," Hyperia said. "He mentioned something about Pierpont making his life difficult when it became apparent that the earldom would befall him. Wickley insinuated that he'd been sweet on some young lady in her first Season, but Pierpont turned her head and soured her attitude toward all other suitors. I am not missing London, Jules, I can assure you of that."

"Did he name the young lady?"

Hyperia frowned at me. "You think it might have been Miss Tenneby? How awkward."

Awkward, yes, and enough to inspire a competition that could reach a very dangerous finish line for both of the strutting dunderheads.

"We can hope they've put that behind them, at least for the nonce," I said. "Let's find St. Just. You are entitled to do some gloating."

Hyperia was all pretty condescension, St. Just flirted shamelessly, and a fine time was had by all, except me.

I was certain that today's foot-perfect horse race was intended to create a false sense of calm, a false trust in proceedings that at some point would turn up dishonorable and dangerous. I simply did not yet know the when, how, or who of the matter.

Pierpont was unhappy with the result, and both Miss Tenneby and Lord Wickley had arrived to the meet already unhappy with Pierpont, so I'd make my next moves in the courtesy twit's direction.

"I placed a bet on Tootle Along," Pierpont said, waiting in line for the punchbowl with me. "Not much, but a tidy sum. She traveled only a short distance to get here and had plenty of time to rest. She has Herod on both the sire and the dam sides, and she was an early foal."

"Early?"

"May third, if you can believe it. According to Newmarket rules, all racing Thoroughbreds are born May first, though few actually are. Tootle's breeder tries very hard to see foals dropped on the happy side of that date, and in her case, he succeeded."

The line wasn't moving, in part because some young lady was trying to persuade the footman serving the libation to ladle the ladies' portion from the men's punchbowl, while her escort—an older brother, possibly—tried to jolly her past this hoydenish behavior.

"Who bred Tootle Along?" I asked, because racing people seemed to expect such questions.

"My brother-in-law, and she's damned fast, my lord. The jockey just waited too late to fire her up. I prefer to run mares because they are easier to keep focused on the job, and they have value in the breeding shed after their racing career is over. Colts can be fractious —I never buy them, I never run them—while the fillies grasp the essentials fairly quickly. Tootle's jockey didn't sort his job adequately in this case."

That had been my initial assessment as well, but given my suspicious turn of mind, I now wondered if Tootle's rider had been compensated to leave the final burst of speed a few strides too late.

"You expected her to win?"

"Why else would I have bet on her? Tenneby and Wickley should have both been saving their fillies for the races with bigger purses, and Toot's owner—Sir Albertus Reardon—hasn't schooled her much over the longer distances yet. She's a front-runner by nature, so this shorter distance was Tootle's chance to shine."

The line crawled forward.

"Who has your backing for the next race?" I asked.

"I'll keep my money in my pocket. I know my flat racing, especially the fillies, but over fences, on the longer distances, I am less certain of the runners. The jumpers will have a more difficult time with this hard footing. If I had to guess, I'd do whatever St. Just does. That man knows horses like the hostesses at Almack's know their bachelor peers."

Among whom Lord Pierpont did not number. "Do I detect a bit of envy directed at those peers, Pierpont?"

His air of genial bonhomie faded. "More than a bit, truth be told. My oldest brother is a prig and a fool. My own father despairs of the day when the title falls into Lord Vandyne's hands. We mustn't ever call him Freddie, you know. From the age of seven, he's had the heir's courtesy title. I can hardly stand the sight of him. Fortunately, he's afraid of horses, so if I must cross his path, I try to do so in the company of an equine."

Afraid of horses. Oh dear. "What of your other brothers? Are they denizens of the turf, or do their interests lie elsewhere?"

"They're busily getting their wives with child in hopes that Vandyne's nursery will remain empty. I'm the lone bachelor, though I have three nephews and two nieces, all of whom adore me. I'm quite fond of them too. I do envy my brothers their nurseries."

We came another two steps closer to the punchbowls.

"I was wondering if Miss Tenneby had caught your eye. I seem to recall some old gossip to that effect."

"Did *she* tell you that, or did Wickley?"

"Neither. I enjoy a full complement of sisters, Pierpont, all married, and my mother still keeps up with the Society pages. You are, after all, somewhat in the public eye by virtue of your family's consequence."

That bit of flattery should have earned me a rolled eye, but Pierpont merely looked annoyed. "I am a practiced flirt of necessity, but I entertain no plans at this point to take a wife. I'm sure Miss Tenneby is a lovely young lady, and we are acquainted—have been for some time—but merely acquainted. I know her brother through our racing connections far better than I know her. Ah, a serving of the good stuff for me."

The footman obliged and turned a questioning eye on me.

"A lady's serving, please."

Pierpont would have ambled away, drink in hand, except that I remained at his elbow. Because I socially outranked him—by a whisker—he apparently decided he could not ignore me.

"I'm sure Miss West will want her drink," he said. "The day isn't exactly hot, but my God, we need rain."

"We're doing better to the south," I said. "Berkshire is having a very dry spring."

Pierpont sipped his drink and surveyed the efforts of the grooms and groundsmen to situate a flight of brush jumps on the downhill portion of the course.

"Tenneby says the well in the stable yard is going dry," his lordship observed. "We're not to use it for the next week, to give it a chance to recharge. That will be tedious in the extreme. The stable lads are already grumbling about having to carry buckets from the kitchen garden well."

A well going dry was bad news indeed, the sort of thing old men recalled fifty years on and vicars mentioned in weekly prayers.

"Is Tenneby alarmed?"

Pierpont waved to a pretty young lady in a straw skimmer topped with pink silk roses. "He says that well has been unreliable for years, and they've been meaning to deepen it, but the opportunity to do so—this week, for example—never seems to arise when it's convenient. That's a lot of claptrap, if you ask me. Tenneby's in dun territory, his uncle has been for ages, and they cannot afford to keep the place up."

This bit of plain speaking was offered with a sidewise glance, suggesting a test of some sort. Would I fall in with bashing my host and his prospects or chide Pierpont for his rudeness? I was to choose a side, which struck me as puerile and a little sad.

I took a leaf from Harry's book: When in doubt, stick to platitudes. "Many old and respected families are dealing with a reversal of fortune now that the Corsican is buttoned up, and Britain herself is barely paying her debts in the ordinary course. That horse racing can thrive in such precarious times is a testament to the loyalty of its supporters. I see St. Just is in need of reinforcements. If you'll excuse me?"

I sauntered off, somewhat puzzled by the discussion. What had I learned? Pierpont had expected Tootle Along to win, and she hadn't. His lordship denied any previous friendship with Miss Tenneby, for want of a better word. He was a bitter young man and overly focused on finances—his, his family's, Tenneby's. He'd bet on a favorite, but he did not bet at all unless he knew the field well.

He was shrewd—the gambit about Tenneby's finances might well have been to distract me from Miss Tenneby's claims—and I neither liked nor trusted him. The discussion had been an exercise in confirming a first impression rather than gaining fresh insights.

Not that productive, in other words. I collected St. Just, and we took Hyperia her drink. For her part, she had attached herself to Clarence Tenneby and all but waved me on my way.

My intended was nearly avoiding me, and I did not care for that behavior at all.

"Tenneby's stable well is going dry," St. Just said, watching Hyperia wrap her hand around Tenneby's arm. "Bad timing and bad luck, that. He let the other owners know what their grooms doubtless noticed last night. Horses will be bathed at the river if it's necessary to bathe them at all. I understand the river is at an alarmingly low level too."

"You're worried," I said, though nothing in St. Just's expression conveyed anxiety. His gaze had gone watchful, though, and I could tell he was itching to assist the jump crews with the brute labor required to set the course.

"Drought is always worrisome," St. Just said, "but having to lug five-gallon buckets of water from the carriage house or the laundry or the kitchen gardens will be a sore imposition on tempers in the stable yard. Tenneby's little race meeting would run more smoothly with happy grooms and softer footing."

I strongly suspected that somebody wanted the race meeting to run anything but smoothly. "Should Cleopatra have won the first race, St. Just?"

He moved off a few paces from the sea of blankets and picnic baskets. "I don't know. Sir Albertus's filly was the grooms' favorite, and she had plenty left for the finish. I wouldn't think anything of it, but I saw Pierpont and Sir Albertus conferring at luncheon with the jockey."

"Isn't the owner supposed to confer with the jockey prior to the race?"

"Of course, but why include Pierpont in that conversation? The fillies don't race again until Saturday, and you might keep an eye on Pierpont between now and then."

In my ample spare time. "I'm also planning on having a gander at the stable yard by moonlight." If somebody wanted to ensure a horse lost, the dodgy well had handed them a perfect opportunity to ensure that outcome. A horse taken for an outing ostensibly to enjoy a late-night drink of cool, fresh river water could easily be taken instead for a clandestine gallop with nobody the wiser.

Several excursions of that nature, and even a fit Thoroughbred would lose his edge. "I foresee a lot of naps in my immediate future." And long nights on sentry duty in the stable yard.

"You always were a lazy sod." St. Just winked, passed me his drink, and strode off toward the crew wrestling another brush jump into place.

"Darling sister!" Healy West made a great show of taking Hyperia's hands, drawing her near, and kissing her on both cheeks. Never in my decades-long association with the West family had I seen such an effusive greeting for Hyperia from her brother, nor had I been so thoroughly ignored by him.

"Healy." Hyperia smiled graciously as she disentangled her hands from his. "Wonderful to see you. I trust the journey was uneventful?"

"Slow journeys usually are. Gives one time to review the competitions' form. Let's find me a drink, shall we? I seem to have missed the opening contest. Such a pity."

"The punchbowls are this way," I said, gesturing up the hill. "You can tell us all about your runner while we find a spot to watch the next race."

Healy was a handsome fellow with wavy brown hair, some height, and a muscular pair of shoulders. When he sneered, though, he looked about eleven years old and spoiled rotten.

"Imagine my surprise," he said as we scaled the hill, "to find not only my sister among the guests at the Acres, but you too, Lord Julian. Do I gather that your joint attendance is on my behalf?"

I waited for Hyperia to step in, but she remained silent.

"You do not. Tenneby invited me, and of course I asked that my intended be included. Hyperia and Miss Tenneby have a prior acquaintance. When I accepted the invitation, I had no idea you'd be among the competitors."

"Imagine my surprise," Hyperia said softly, "when I learned that my brother the playwright had gone not to some house party where he couldn't avoid the matchmakers, but to the Newmarket sales. Imagine my further consternation when I learned my brother is now competing in a sport in which our family has never taken an interest. Perhaps 'amazement' is a more accurate term."

"You haven't seen my colt run," Healy retorted a tad peevishly. "He's a wonder on four hooves."

We collected fresh servings of punch—Healy from the men's bowl, Hyperia and I from the ladies'—and located our blanket and basket.

"Tell us about your colt," Hyperia said, sinking onto the blanket. "I don't suppose you're interested in a sandwich or two?"

I was, but I said nothing while the last two sandwiches were surrendered into Healy's undeserving hands.

"George is bottomless," Healy said. "He'll run forever and jump anything. Dead sound, no vices. Will jump the moon. I'd trust you to ride him, Hyperia."

For present purposes, the horse was expected to be all of the above. More significantly, he had to be *fast*.

"You named your horse after the king?" Hyperia asked, arranging her skirts. "A bit naughty of you."

"He was named after St. George, and he'll slay the competition. These sandwiches are dry." Healy finished them nonetheless. "So why are you here, Julian? Harry liked the occasional race meet, but I can't recall you indulging in such frivolity."

"The better question," I said, "is why you are here. For St. George's first outing, why travel halfway across southern England for a private meet? The only races with stated purses for colts are next week, and your fellow could have joined in any number of informal meetings closer to Newmarket."

This question had apparently occurred to Hyperia, who took up her field glasses and studied the starting line. I knew that particular angle of her chin, and slight edge to the quiet economy of her movements. She'd wanted to interrogate her brother but hadn't dared.

Why not?

"Wickley put me onto this meeting," Healy said. "He claimed the field was a manageable size—no vast stampedes, as so many popular races are. Good company, comfortable accommodations, a well-kept course, some decent purses."

No penny press, no hostesses, and—Healy's priorities had become all too easy to discern—no worried sister and her nosy fiancé to muck up any dodgy schemes or intemperate wagers.

"With such a glowing recommendation," I said, stifling the urge to rummage in the hamper, "I'm surprised you didn't arrive in time to compete in today's races. Hurdles are becoming more popular, from what I understand—they are just the thing for young jumpers."

"The welfare of the horse comes first." Healy brushed crumbs from his fingers. "George needed the extra day lest he be taxed by the journey. St. Just is here." Said with more dismay than surprise. "I do hope his sisters haven't joined him."

Hyperia opened the hamper lid and produced a tin of petits fours. She took two before passing the tin to her brother, who helped himself to three and set the tin at his side on the blanket.

"You are a plain mister, Healy," Hyperia observed. "The daughter of a duke is unlikely to begin her search for a husband with a bachelor of your humble origins, as delightful as your company can be. That black horse is in want of manners."

Down at the starting line, a black horse was propping and dancing around, which upset the other runners trying to form up for the start. A chestnut began squealing and kicking out behind, nearly catching another competitor in the chest with a shod hoof.

Owners and grooms milled about despite the steward's waving them away, and Tenneby, smiling as ever, wandered amid the throng.

"Not my favorite part of a day at the races," Hyperia said, sliding the petits fours away from her brother's side and passing them to me.

"Nor mine." I ate two, a vanilla and a raspberry, and Hyperia replaced the sweets in the hamper without her brother apparently having noticed our maneuvers.

"Hyperia, lend me those field glasses, won't you?" Healy made an impatient beckoning gesture that would have cost him his finger had he tried it with my sisters.

Hyperia passed over the glasses as the stewards managed to line up the field. I counted fifteen runners, meaning some of the contestants were local talent joining the affray from their home stables. The course was narrow enough that they couldn't all run abreast over most of it, and by the first fence, the black was two lengths in the lead.

"That's not galloping," I muttered. "The blighter is bolting." The horse was in a flat panic, bucking, running, and kicking out at a blazing pace while his jockey tried in vain to pull him up. The difficulty—the danger—arose as the field approached the second fence.

"God help them," Hyperia murmured.

"That black should never have been allowed... Rubbishing hell."

The black had caught sight of the second fence in time to make an effort to clear the obstacle, but he only half finished the job. His front legs were over, his back legs... were not over. The rest of the field was obliged to swerve wide of the thrashing horse, which resulted in some swerving into others. Two simply chested the fence, and two others fell upon landing.

The black's jockey, still gamely aboard, extricated his horse from the hedge and then got tossed after a prolonged spate of bucking. The horse took off—still bucking—in the direction of the finish line, which set a herd of grooms chasing after it.

"Typical," Healy said, field glasses still glued to his nose. "The jump races are ever so much more exciting."

"The jockey is up," Hyperia said as that good fellow scurried to the side of the course.

I rose. "I feel a pressing need for more libation." Also a pressing need to avert my eyes from the mayhem on the course. "My dear, can I get you more to drink?"

"I'm parched," Healy said. "Damn, that little chestnut can jump."

Hyperia waved me away, and I took myself to the foot of the hill and into the brick building referred to as the rubbing-down house. Within five minutes, the black horse, head hanging, sides heaving, was led into view by a slender lad who seemed to be talking to the horse as a governess would scold a naughty child.

"Told ye to get hold of yerself. Told ye them others h'ain't got a patch on ye. Did ye listen? They'll be sending ye to the knacker's yard and yerself just a wee lad an' all."

The groom stopped at the doorway to the rubbing-down house. "If you bet on him, I'm sorry, mister, but he's not always so high-strung. Shouldn't have run him in such a big field."

"What's his name?"

"Blinken. Blink 'n' you miss him, like, because he's so fast. He's a good boy, but today he just..."

"Became overly excited. Let's walk him a bit."

I was not in St. Just's league as an equestrian, but I liked horses as a species. If I had to choose between guaranteeing Atlas's happy old age and my own, the horse would win the wager. Blinken looked to me, if anything, to be ashamed. He knew he'd not performed to standards, not done what was expected.

Horses had an ingenious gift for spotting patterns. If a lamp was lit in the carriage house window a quarter hour before the grooms mustered out in the morning, then every horse would be on high alert for breakfast before a single groom had put a boot upon a step. The grooms would call it uncanny, but the horses were simply aware of the pattern—a lamp is lit, breakfast to follow, day after day.

Blinken, green though he might be, knew that a starting line was no place for tantrums.

"Who saddled him up?" I asked.

"I did, same as I always do. I'm Corrie, by the way. Joe Corrie." The groom led his charge along the farm lane, two dusty tracks between an undulating line of brown grass. "Is Chalmers unhurt?"

"He was walking and probably cursing last I saw him. How old is Blinken?"

"Rising five. He likes to jump, especially the brush fences. Sir Albertus had high hopes for him too."

"You've loosened the girth?"

"Of course. Who might ye be, sir, if I might ask?"

"Lord Julian Caldicott. I'm a guest. I own no runners and hope to die in that blessed state. My personal mount is a dark gelding named Atlas, and his groom is a lad named Atticus."

"Seen 'em both. Handsome gelding. The lad dotes on him." The groom circled the horse so we wandered back toward the rubbing-down house. A whoop went up from the direction of the course, and if anything, Blinken's head hung lower.

"Let's take his saddle off here," I said. "The whole field will be invading the rubbing-down house."

"I'll never hear the end of this. Sir Albertus might sack me for it."

"Then he's an idiot. Were you at the starting line?"

"Nah. The stewards and their assistants do up the girths and such. Grooms and owners are to keep clear, though the owners seldom do." He halted the horse and stroked its sweaty neck. "You just got yerself into a temper, old lad."

I undid the overgirth and girth and slid the tiny racing saddle from the horse's back. The saddle cloth came next.

"Look at that," I said, pointing to brown spots on the dark blue cotton. The whole cloth was damp with sweat, but those two spots stood out to me like a full moon on a clear night.

"Wot?"

"Look closely." I turned the cloth over and revealed two small metal devices clinging to the fabric. They resembled miniature caltrops or tacks with four prongs. "Your boy was provoked."

"They wasn't there when I put his saddle on."

"I believe you. Blinken looked to be a perfect gentleman as you led him up from the stable. The mischief started when the girth was snugged up and the jockey leaped aboard."

Corrie looked ready to weep. "Sir Albertus will sack me for sure. I suppose that's what I deserve, lettin' me best boy get treated like that."

Ye gods, he was an innocent. "The sabotage might have occurred during that melee at the starting line. All it took was a hand slipped between the saddle cloth and the horse's withers before the girth was tightened. You could not have prevented that."

"Sir Albertus might still sack me. Damn. I like me job, and I like me horses. Blinken's a good 'un, and I know me jumpers. He'll get better as he grows up too."

Blinken's breathing had slowed, and he was looking less subdued.

"Take him down to the river, let him roll and play in the water, find him some grass to crop, and I'll have a word with Sir Albertus."

"Ye'll tell him about those spikes?"

"No, and don't you say a word either. Somebody is up to no good, and I intend to figure out who. I'll tell Sir Albertus that I fancy a horse with some gumption, and Blinken showed himself to be fast, nimble, and fit. Sir Albertus won't send anybody to the knacker's yard if he thinks I'm game to buy a half-mad jumper."

Groom and horse looked at me with equally bewildered gazes. "If you say so, milord. We're for the river."

I pocketed the little instruments of torture and handed over the saddle, girths, and cloth. "Say nothing, Corrie, but do keep a sharp eye out. I suspect more trouble is on the way."

Corrie saluted with two fingers. "Mum's the word, milord. C'mon, Blinkie. Time for yer bath."

CHAPTER EIGHT

"Would Sir Albertus do this to his own horse?" I asked, passing St. Just the tacks that had inspired Blinken's panic. Piggott stood with us behind the rubbing-down house, while grooms within yelled insults and encouragement to one another prior to the third and final race of the day.

"Piggott?" St. Just dumped the metal into Piggott's callused hand. "What say you?"

Piggott was small, as jockeys/grooms tended to be, his hands larger than one would expect for his frame. He looked to be in his late twenties—seasoned, fast approaching senior for his profession. His countenance was pleasant, as if smiles were more frequent than frowns. His hair was sandy, his eyes blue, and his gaze troubled.

"I've seen these put into a jumper's boots," he said. "Makes 'em bolt away from a fence because the points bite into the horse's flesh when he lands. He'll get around a course quick as lightning, though he might well wreck along the way."

Even when put to the low brush fences set up for the previous race, jumpers often wore boots to protect forelegs and pasterns.

"Both tacks were under the saddle cloth," I said. "Up near the withers. My guess is, they didn't bother the horse until the jockey's weight was in the saddle."

"That suggests Sir Albertus had a hand in matters." St. Just watched a tidy little chestnut colt walk past us across the lane. The groom holding the lead rope occasionally patted the horse's damp neck and kept up a soft, steady patter until the beast settled to lipping at a patch of dry grass.

"How do you implicate Sir Albertus?" I asked.

"Because," Piggott said, "at a meet like this, the owner tells the jockey whether to mount at the stable yard and then parade down to the course, or to mount just before the start. Chalmers didn't ride in the fillies' race. He coulda ridden down from the yard, but he didn't. He mounted up at the starting line."

"That doesn't necessarily implicate Sir Albertus." The baronet himself joined the chestnut and his groom, the conversation apparently genial. "Anybody in that throng at the starting line could have slipped these under the saddle before the girths were tightened."

St. Just swiveled his gaze to me. "If you were an owner, and you had paid one hundred pounds for a chance at fifteen hundred pounds, would you be watching the clouds and birds at the starting line, or would you be having a last word with your jockey, looking over the saddle and bridle, making sure the girth was snug but not too snug? Focusing intently on your horse?"

Clearly, St. Just would be doing those things. "If I wanted to signal great confidence in my runner, or that I had many hundreds of pounds to fritter away on his training, then I might offer cordial good wishes to the competition and eye them up carefully instead."

Piggott smiled. "Gotta point, milord. It's a damned farce on race day, half the time. Part fashionable parade, part melee. Sir Albertus is one of them bluff-and-hearty fellows, according to Chalmers. Beefsteak and porter for every meal, a hound snoring at every hearth."

"Blinken is a talented creature." St. Just watched the grazing chestnut. "Horses have memories that make elephants look absent-minded. Today's mistreatment will haunt that colt at every starting line."

"Every time somebody tightens his girth, more like," Piggott observed. "I don't see a hounds-and-horses man mistreating a talented youngster like that. Why would he do such a thing?"

Motive. It all came down to motive. So Blinken endured the worst five minutes of his life, which had probably been more frightening than truly painful, by human standards. Sir Albertus might have concluded that five minutes of misery for the horse was worth the cost of a month's oats.

"The chestnut won, didn't he?" I asked as across the way, Sir Albertus patted the chestnut's muscular neck and ambled away.

"Handily," St. Just said. "Damnation."

"Sir Albertus mighta been just congratulating the winning groom," Piggott said, though his tone was uncertain. "The better owners do. Makes 'em look sporting. They congratulate everybody—the jockey, the groom, the owner, his wife, the horse." Piggott handed me the nasty little tacks. "Will you say something to Sir Albertus?"

"Perhaps later. I would rather not make my first bow to Sir Albertus and then commence making accusations as well."

"You'll begin with some reconnoitering," St. Just said as Sir Albertus strolled back in the direction of the starting line. "Always a sound precaution. Piggott, our thanks for your perspective. Go do some reconnoitering of your own in the rubbing-down house, why don't you?"

"Always happy to lend a hand and reminisce about me days of glory," Piggott said, saluting with two fingers. "Milords, tread carefully."

"He can look after himself," St. Just said as Piggott marched off to gather intelligence. "I've met Sir Albertus. Would you like an introduction?"

"I would. Skullduggery at the starting line notwithstanding, protocol should be observed."

The runners for the third race were beginning to mill about

outside the rubbing-down house. A few horses yet had empty saddles, though not for long. The steward gave the signal to line up, and then another field of hurdlers took off.

"Whoever set out to take the race from Blinken chose well," I said as the initial cheers died down. "Between the first and third races, everybody would be busy, either collecting winnings from the first race or preparing a runner for the third. The timing speaks to a mind that can plan ahead."

"Or to blind luck." St. Just kept a keen eye on the thundering field. "Tenneby could have run the hurdles first."

"Then the flat racers would have had to navigate ground disturbed by the greater weight and thrust of jumpers. I don't know much about racing, St. Just, but I know the flat racers like smooth terrain."

He muttered something along the lines of, "Don't we all?" as we crossed the course. Sir Albertus made for the viewing structure at the top of the incline, and the old boy was spry, damn him.

I was tired, thirsty, and vexed.

The horses cleared the first set of jumps on the uphill side of the course without a mishap and continued on to the sweeping left-hand curve. The jumps on the downhill side rewarded boldness. A brave effort could pick up two strides on the competition, while a botched approach—taking off too close to the jump or too far away—could have the opposite result.

Sir Albertus joined a knot of spectators that included Pierpont and Wickley, as well as Evelyn Tenneby and several other ladies. Hyperia had apparently shaken free of her admirers for the nonce. Perhaps she was sorting Healy out, a thankless and overdue exercise.

The horses began the uphill climb for the second and final time, the smaller field able to navigate the jumps more easily. The pace picked up around the long curve, and the final dash—downhill, over jumps, then a short run-in to the finish—saw three horses pass the post simultaneously.

"A dead heat," St. Just said. "Don't have those very often. The stewards will confer. What's wrong?"

I was looking beyond the course to the tree line along the lane that led back to the stable yard. Hyperia faced her brother, though her back was to me.

"She's upset," I said. "You can tell she's upset from her posture."

"*You* can tell." St. Just spoke quietly. "West appears to be raising his voice to a lady in public. Shall you trounce him, or shall I?" St. Just started down the hill, while all around us the crowd speculated about who had won.

Rubicon by a nose seemed to be the consensus. A bit symbolic, that.

"St. Just, wait. Hyperia will not thank us for meddling."

I might as well have told the sea to quiet its surging tides. St. Just kept on marching, and thus I did as well.

"It's not meddling if the stupid git can still walk when I'm done with him." The rising blaze of a black Irish temper in full gallop illuminated his blue eyes.

"He is *her brother*," I retorted. "I don't like it, but he is the man in authority over her, and he controls her funds. Hyperia deals with him carefully."

We crossed the course again. The lane was deserted, but for Hyperia and Healy two dozen yards ahead. The whole crowd was waiting on the stewards' decision apparently.

When we were fifteen yards shy of the altercation, Hyperia backhanded Healy smartly across the cheek, then stalked off without benefit of an escort.

"She deals with him *carefully*," St. Just said, slowing to a halt and rubbing a hand across his chin. "I see what you mean. What in blazes is going on, Caldicott?"

"I don't know, and I intend to find out. The situation qualifies as a delicate predicament. Hyperia is protective of Healy. I am protective of Hyperia. I proceed cautiously."

"Who is protective of you?"

Hyperia had been, from time to time. I did not want her to have to choose between the dunderheaded males in her life, though.

"I look after myself. If you'd chat up West about his amazing colt, I'd appreciate it. I'm off to provide my intended my pleasant and doting escort."

"Dote from a safe distance, lest the lady deal with you carefully too."

Sound advice. I wasn't quite able to follow it.

"Don't ask." Hyperia stalked along the dusty lane, skirts swishing. "Don't ask, don't lecture, don't offer speculations meant to be interrogations. He is my brother, Julian, and I must deal with him myself."

"Far be it from me to meddle." I did not wing my arm or take the lady's hand either. "St. Just was threatening to thrash your brother simply for raising his voice to you. I dissuaded him."

"Good." Hyperia stomped onward, though her pace slowed slightly. "Would St. Just truly have used his fists?"

"He might have. He grew up with four brothers, and fisticuffs happen. He might instead have offered a tongue-lashing, which the colonel can do with telling accuracy. Had a bit of a reputation in the military."

"For?"

"He was jolly enough, at least before his brother was killed, but let him see an officer abusing his rank or anybody abusing a horse, and St. Just became the bright angel of justice, on the spot, no quarter given." Something along these lines had apparently landed St. Just in trouble at Waterloo.

"Nobody is to thrash Healy," Hyperia replied.

"Nobody save you, though you stopped after a single, symbolic blow. I'm not sure I could have."

She slowed further. "I should have ignored him, but he started going on about his horse. Healy rides well enough—I have the better seat—but he knows nothing about racing, much less racing over jumps. He says it's quite the latest rage, and he'll meet all the right fellows to back his plays at the race meets."

Equal portions of despair and bewilderment laced her tone.

"I am no expert," I said, "but as far as I know, the turf set prefer to waste their money wagering on horses rather than on playwrights. They do have money to waste, though, or they pretend to that happy status. Healy isn't entirely off the mark."

Hyperia laced her arm through mine. "You are being kind. I appreciate it. Please don't interfere with Healy, Jules. I will make him see reason eventually. I always do."

Well, no, she did not. On one or two memorable occasions, my assistance had been vital to preventing a Healy-induced calamity.

"Hyperia, will you let me help you?" I was tempted to remind her of all the times she'd scolded me for keeping my own counsel, for pondering my past in silence. "Just as you have access to venues a gentleman cannot frequent, I can keep a closer eye on Healy in some regards than you can. I will make regular reports and attempt no interventions without your guidance."

She had slowed to a stroll as we approached the stable yard. "I detest your penchant for logic."

"No, you do not. You find it a useful foil for intuition and theorizing, just as your own feats of logic often aid my hunches. Healy can be both scheming and impulsive, we know that. Two heads are better than one, and you will be at times kept busy foiling any attempts to fix the races. It's only fair that I should assist you by keeping an eye on Healy."

I would keep an eye on him, will she, nill she, but I'd rather do so with Hyperia's blessing.

"You won't act against him without my permission, Jules. No thrashings, no threats. He'll never grow up if he can't make mistakes and learn from them."

Healy West had already blundered so egregiously that learning from his mistakes ought by now to have imbued him with the wisdom of the biblical sages.

"No thrashings, no threats. I did ask St. Just to glean what information he could from Healy regarding this wondrous jumper. If St. Just can pursue one topic convincingly, it's horses."

"St. Just is unhappy," Hyperia said as we gained the shade of the trees nearest the stable yard. "He isn't quite as haunted, but his spirits are still diminished. Did you know him before the war?"

"I did, though he was more Harry's contemporary than mine."

"He was a joyous man, Jules. Much loved by his family, in some ways more dear to them than their late Lord Bart. St. Just can *dance*. He's grace itself in a ballroom, despite his size."

The agreement I had with Hyperia regarding her past was that I was to ask directly if a subject piqued my curiosity. She could either answer directly or guard her privacy. The decision was hers. At the time we'd reached this understanding, I had found the bargain reasonable and efficient.

I was no longer so fond of the terms, both because they were one-sided and because they denied me the right to conduct reconnaissance that touched on Hyperia's past. She'd had lovers, or at least one lover, but I knew not who he was or how involved she'd been with him.

"Why are you scowling, Julian?"

A groom led a pair of mares across the lane, taking them down the path that led to the river.

"St. Just was touched by some scandal either at or immediately after Waterloo. Nobody seems to know what happened, but he mustered out directly and went straight to the Windham family seat in Kent. Wasn't seen for months afterward."

"Neither were you seen for months after Waterloo."

"They were difficult months. I hope St. Just does make a full recovery, Perry."

"He seems in his element here. I take it you are not available to escort me to the house?"

Was that a request for my company? "I am absolutely available, but I'll be returning to the stable to chat up the grooms, and I hope to set up something like a roster of sentries for after dark."

The stable yard was deserted, many of its denizens still off at the racetrack. The red, yellow, and white tulips were particularly vivid splashes of color against dusty stone walls and dying grass, but the scene struck me as desolate rather than peaceful.

On the way to the house, I summarized the mischief done to poor Blinken, and Hyperia was appropriately appalled. We made straight for the winter parlor, where I downed two tankards of the ladies' punch in succession and made myself a large plate of ham-and-cheese sandwiches. Hyperia contented herself with half a sandwich and half a pint of punch.

If nothing else, I had focused her attention on the races rather than on her dunce of a brother. I would rather she confided in me regarding Healy's latest foolishness, but trust must be earned. I could not exactly comport myself like Healy—blustering and brooding in turn—and expect to garner any esteem in Hyperia's eyes.

Neither, though, would I sit on my hands and leave him a clear field for disrespecting his sister.

"We know one thing for a certainty," Hyperia said, putting her empty glass on the table designated for clearing away.

I knew many things for a certainty. I loved Hyperia, for example, and I would not let her brother come between us.

"What unassailable truth have we established?" I asked, refilling my tankard for a third time.

"Your august personage has been insufficient to deter mischief." Hyperia selected a tea cake from the epergne on the sideboard. "The first day on the racecourse, and somebody is already tampering with one of the horses. So much for your reputation for intimidating male-factors into submission."

She passed me the tea cake—raspberry icing, my favorite. "You are right, but I would rather the play begin, so to speak, than spend two weeks rattling around the Acres in a state of watchful anticipation. We have also established that Tenneby was right to be concerned about foul play. We have a place to start. That's an odd sort of relief."

She brushed her hand through my hair. "Only you, Jules. Only you. I'll see you at supper."

My darling swanned off and left me to effect further depredations on the buffet. I also took a full tankard of punch to the veranda and sat in the shade, pondering the various ways Healy West could have provoked the dearest woman in the world to violence upon his person.

"I knew your brother." Sir Albertus extended a hand to me in a blatant breach of etiquette. "Fine fellow, was Lord Harry."

I shook, choosing to appreciate his forthright manner rather than quibble over protocol.

"Your brother had a wonderful sense of the absurd," Sir Albertus went on. "Had a keen eye for the jumpers too. Not quite as reliable when it came to the flat racing."

"What would Lord Harry say about Blinken's performance this afternoon?"

We were enjoying the relative cool of early evening in the shade of the stable yard maples. Sir Albertus had come to look in on his string, a common later-afternoon practice among those who owned racing stock.

While we watched, some horses were led out for a night at grass. Others were given a final grooming for the day. Still others—the mares, predominantly—were taken down to the river.

"My lord, you must believe me when I tell you that Blinken has never behaved in that manner before. He's a good, steady lad, is Blinken, with plenty of bottom and heart. I was so very disappointed I nearly sat down and wept. Another outing like that, and I won't be able to sell him to the knacker."

"If he's never behaved like that previously, and he's competing barely a mile from home, what do you suppose got into him?"

"Chalmers is at a loss, and he knows Blinken as well as anybody could. Claims our Blinkie has the makings of a champion, and I did have hopes. One must nevertheless develop a certain stoicism in the racing business, my lord. The horse that runs like blazes on the dawn gallops cannot muster a decent canter for a midafternoon match. The filly who passes her female competition like a Congreve rocket can't be bothered to settle if there's a colt in the field. One learns these things the hard way, of course."

Sir Albertus fell silent as the victorious chestnut colt, Rubicon, clip-clopped past, the sole charge of the groom holding his lead rope.

"Handsome little devil, isn't he?" Sir Albertus muttered. "The leggy Thoroughbred is all the rage, but that fellow will stay sound until Judgment Day. Perfect conformation for a jumper, or what we called perfect in my day. Now, if a horse isn't half starved and walking on stilts, the young gents won't look at him."

The chestnut was compact compared to those he'd beaten. "He's nimble, isn't he?" I asked. "Puts me in mind of the Iberian breeds. They can lengthen and shorten their strides on the spot and hop a jump as tidily as a cat. Tremendous stamina too."

Sir Albertus looked at me as if I'd just recited Eclipse's pedigree for eight generations on the sire side.

"You are correct, sir, and though we don't bruit it about in polite company, many a mare has that heritage buried in her past. One forgets those details at his peril. Old Temerity used to bang on about Iberian stamina and such. He always rode the Andalusian stock, if he could get it. The build is a bit cobby for me, but he hasn't my height, you know."

"I've only seen the earl occupying a Bath chair, and our conversation was brief. I don't suppose Blinken's groom has any insights to offer?"

Rheumy blue eyes gave me a slow perusal. "Why the curiosity, my lord?"

I thought back to Blinken's panicked rush from the starting line. "My life depended on my horse in Spain, and many an officer would say the same thing. I'll introduce you to my gelding, if you like."

"You brought him here?"

"I am seldom parted from him for long." Only as I spoke did I realize the truth of my words. I was more willing to leave Atticus behind than I was to part with my mount.

We threaded steps past horses, muck carts, grooms, and other owners as we made our way to Atlas's stall. My boy was alert, probably anticipating a night under the stars munching what grass he could find, given the dry weather.

"Now that is a handsome horse," Sir Albertus said. "Seventeen hands? The Iberian types don't usually come so big."

"Draft on the dam side, Spanish on the sire. He's up to my weight, reliably sound,"—I rapped on the nearest wooden board— "and steady as Gibraltar. Gaits as smooth as the Serpentine on a May morning and the manners of a duke."

Sir Albertus extended a hand toward Atlas. "You might not be smitten with racing, my lord, but you are smitten with this horse. Understandably so."

"We served together." I said the words softly, another truth hitting me from a fresh angle. "He knows my secrets."

Atlas politely sniffed at Sir Albertus's hand, then turned a questioning eye on me.

"He's wondering where his groom is," Sir Albertus said, which was doubtless correct. "Time to romp around the pasture and have a chat over the fence with the lads in the next paddock. Or maybe he's eager for a turn at the river. Don't you have a water bucket hung in his stall, my lord?"

"Speak of the devil..."

Atticus came up the barn aisle, using two hands to hold up a bucket. "Guv. Brung himself his water. Had to go to the smithy for it."

"Don't let us keep you," I said, stepping aside so Atticus could open Atlas's stall door. "You'll turn him out soon?"

"Aye, when it's quieter. Never seen such a busy stable, and all for horses ridden for less than thirty minutes of an afternoon."

Sir Albertus found that sally amusing, though I perceived agendas resting on those short, fast rides that extended to family pride, sibling rivalry, dynastic fortunes, and probably even courtship.

"Let's leave the boy to his labors," Sir Albertus said, ambling down the barn aisle. "People accuse the racehorse of flightiness, but nothing could be further from the truth. Of all horses, the bloodstock must become accustomed to bustle and hum, to hard work, to regular handling, and to farriery from a young age. They simply like their routines, and I cannot fault them for it, being of much the same mentality myself."

"Blinken knows the starting line routine, doesn't he?" I'd waited until we were once again out in the fresh air to pose my question.

"You suspect foul play." Sir Albertus sighed in a manner that conveyed a bowing to the inevitable rather than irritation. "The horse's groom is a young Yorkshireman, and if ever such a one was sentimental about anything, it's that young man about his charges. Joe Corrie would not harm a horse in his care for all the gold in Aladdin's cave. As we speak, he's probably praying I don't sell the colt to a passing tinker."

"Would you sell him to me?"

Sir Albertus studied me more closely, probably trying to determine if I was making a brilliant offer or proving myself to be a fool.

"Not at the present time, and not for the pittance you are likely thinking of offering." His tone was civil, just. "That's a good horse, my lord. A very good horse who had a very off day. Nothing more."

"Have you had other offers?"

"Pity offers by the side of the course. Gestures of consolation. Those are not meant to be taken seriously. I've made a few myself. Blinken is not for sale, and he will be back in good form before his next outing."

"He will be." I fished the metal tacks out of my pocket. "These were found under his saddle cloth when his gear was removed. Both were bloody, as was the cloth. Do you recognize them?"

Sir Albertus glowered at the tacks and then at me. "They are considered by some to be a training device, not by me. The usual method is to put them in a jumper's boots so he moves off smartly after landing, as if stung, or so the theory goes. As far as I'm concerned, that's a quick route to ensuring an otherwise capable horse embarks on the dangerous habit of refusing jumps and ends up with needless infections. I hate the damned things."

"I believe you. Do you believe me when I tell you that Blinken was set up to fail? Your groom put the saddle on in the stable yard and led Blinken to the starting line. I suspect that while the other jockeys were mounting and owners were tightening girths, somebody slipped these under Blinken's cloth. As soon as Chalmers was aboard, the colt started acting up."

"Damnation, my lord," Sir Albertus swore with quiet vehemence. "That is a serious accusation, and I cannot be heard to entertain such suspicions. Men have been called out for less."

"Men have been called out for reciting poetry beneath the wrong moonlit window. Do you believe me?"

He stole another glance at the evidence in my hand. "I'm getting too old for this game," he muttered. "The young fellows think it jolly great fun to break the rules. They are all cordial good sportsmen to look at them, but they don't know the difference between a prank and cheating."

"Joe Corrie knows what I found." I put the offending articles back into my pocket. "I will keep this development under my hat, but if I were you, I would not sell that colt any time soon, and I would keep a close eye on him for the duration of the meeting. I will explain to my groom that a watch is to be kept over Blinken, just as the boy keeps watch over my Atlas."

Sir Albertus looked torn, but common sense prevailed. The evidence I'd presented fit with what he knew of Blinken and what he'd observed of Blinken's behavior. Brushing the incident off as a prank—a prank that could have seen Chalmers or any number of jockeys or equines dead or maimed—was beyond him.

"Your discretion is appreciated." He strode off several paces, then stopped. "Mind your step with this bunch, my lord. They are not a troupe of harmless overgrown boys, though the press likes to depict them that way. They play to win, and I am apparently no longer up to their weight."

"I take the opposite view. Blinken is sufficiently talented that somebody had to eliminate him as competition for their runner. Your horse's ability has been noticed, and you had the training and breeding of him."

He frowned, shook his head, and strode back into the barn.

Atticus chose that moment to emerge with Atlas in tow. I wished, not for the first or last time, that we were all back at Caldicott Hall, enjoying the advance of mild spring weather.

CHAPTER NINE

"You take the early shift," I said, "when I'll be expected at supper and cards. I will arrange for Joe Corrie to take the hours following your stint, then I will relieve him. St. Just will take the last watch."

"Corrie's a good sort," Atticus replied as he led Atlas to a paddock bordered by stately oaks. "Sings Welsh lullabies to his horses."

"I thought he was from Yorkshire."

"He's Welsh on the dam side. Says Atlas is a handsome specimen. Denton agrees but says Atlas has too much bone to be fashionable."

My tiger had gone horse mad with a vengeance. "I have too much bone to be fashionable. Ergo, my mount must be sturdy. What else did Denton say?"

"That Blinken coulda beat Rubicon by two lengths. Says Rubicon has speed, but he overjumps, like he's afraid to let the brush touch him. That means he's spending more time in the air than he needs to, and a horse with a tidier style and equal speed can gain on him at every fence. Denton said some other things."

We reached the designated paddock, which didn't offer much in the way of grass. Near the oaks, which would provide morning shade, some viable grazing remained. The rest of the patch was brown for want of rain.

"He'll eat this down in two nights," I said. "What else did Denton say?"

Atticus turned Atlas out, and the horse, being a sensible fellow, rolled thoroughly upon gaining his liberty. He was fit enough to roll from side to side, which he did several times, then got up and shook, sending a cloud of dust wafting on the early evening breeze.

"Berkshire needs rain," Atticus said as the dust dissipated. "Woglemuth said he's never seen it this dry so early in the year."

A verse from the book of Matthew popped into my head: *He maketh his sun to rise on the evil and on the good, and sendeth rain on the just and on the unjust.* Who had unjustly benefited today from Blinken's torment?

"Tell me what else Denton said."

"That the hard ground will see more than one horse lamed and more than one jockey brought low. It's good for taking off in front of the jumps—solid, like—but murder on the landings. A half ton of horse needs the ground to give some when he comes down, or that's what Denton says. He don't race over fences if he can help it. Says that's a foolishness reserved for younger men."

And Atticus, who had only rudimentary experience riding over the lowest, safest of obstacles and mostly at a trot, considered himself one of those younger men. Heaven defend the boy.

"Atticus, I realize you are learning a great deal of horsemanship from the jockeys and grooms, and that is all to the good, but somebody tampered with a horse today. Our primary focus must be on determining who and why."

Across the paddock, Atlas made unerringly for the remaining green grass.

"None of the jockeys expected Rubicon to win," Atticus said, "but Woglemuth won a packet on him. Said he's seen the horse at the gallops, and today's race—three miles, low jumps—was perfect for him. He's no good over longer distances or higher jumps. Perfect for Blinken, too, or was supposed to be."

This was news. "When did Woglemuth place his bet?"

"Before the parade down to the start. He was watching Rubicon being saddled and said the horse had fire in his eyes today. Put a fiver on him and won twenty-five pounds. That's a fortune, guv. A bloody fortune."

"Language, young man." Though Atticus was right—a footman new to his livery could expect annual wages on the order of five pounds, along with an allowance for beer, candles, and livery.

"Who took the bet?"

"Sir Albertus. They know each other because they're neighbors."

The bet went some way toward exonerating Sir Albertus of interfering with his own horse, if my earlier interview with him had not.

"Who else lost money on Blinken?"

"Lots of people. Blinkie's a good 'un, according to Woglemuth. Sir Albie's pride and joy—one of 'em—and a local favorite. Pierpont took some bets that backed Blinkie, so he's ahead. Wickley took some, too, because Pierpont did. They favored Rubicon because he's out of... I forget who. Some mare who's horse royalty. They liked Rubicon's breeding better'n Blinkie's, though they don't care for Rubicon's build. Too stocky."

Atticus started back down the path to the stable, chattering away about shoulder angles (very important for a jumper), pasterns, quarters, and other equine anatomical features. While I was happy to see him expanding his knowledge in a useful direction, I was also preoccupied with his report.

The *stable master* had made twenty-five pounds on a single bet with the local squire. I expected the lordlings and popinjays to throw money around with studied carelessness, but I hadn't realized how far the wagering side of the game could extend.

For twenty-five pounds, Woglemuth, Denton, Corrie, or even Atticus might be tempted to toss a race. To toss several races, and they were each in a position to do exactly that.

"Atticus, I know you will take utmost care with Atlas, but I'd also like you to keep a close eye on Rubicon."

"Why?"

"I don't know. A hunch. He was an unlikely winner today, or a less-than-certain winner, and Pierpont and Wickley both made money on his performance. The odds of him winning go up every time he's victorious."

Atticus stopped on the path and stared at the hard-packed ground. "So not the next time out, but three races on, he'll be the favorite who's put out of commission?"

"Possibly. You'd best take a nap if you're to remain up past your bedtime. The day has been long, and you'll go short of sleep tonight."

We resumed walking. I was intent on returning to the manor house and making myself presentable for the supper gathering. I had no idea what thoughts filled Atticus's young head.

"May I take Atlas out for the gallops tomorrow?"

Well, of course, complete with polite diction. "You may hack him up to the gallops. Walk, trot, a little canter. You are not to race him, Atticus, or you will lose your saddle privileges for a very long time."

"I can ride out with the jockeys?"

"Yes, provided you keep to a sedate pace and go as an observer." My own words filled me with foreboding. "Look for who is pushing his horse too hard for a mere practice run, who is having trouble getting a decent pace from his horse. Eyes open, Atticus. Ears open. Trouble is afoot, and we're supposed to sort it out."

I was supposed to sort it out, but Atticus had a valuable contribution to make as well.

"Right. I'll see everything and hear everything and report everything, guv, and keep my mouth shut. Promise." He sped off, doubtless to polish a spotless saddle and spread the news of his good fortune.

All through supper—I was paired with Sir Albertus's spinster sister, Miss Cornelia Reardon—I worried that I should have denied Atticus tomorrow's outing. I distracted myself by watching Healy

West flirt with Miss Tenneby and Hyperia flirt with Wickley, while Pierpont tossed his curls and smiled knowingly at his wineglass.

"When were you going to tell me about Blinken's bad luck?" Tenneby asked as we returned from escorting the ladies to the parlor for their postprandial tea.

"I take it Sir Albertus has already alerted you?" We spoke quietly, while Wickley called for toasts in honor of a fine day of racing.

"Sir Albertus was furious," Tenneby replied, "and I'm none too pleased myself. A simple tactic, and one that should have been simple to prevent had the stewards been doing their jobs."

"One steward to oversee fifteen horses and jockeys isn't enough. I'll want to have a look at the card for the day after tomorrow. At all the cards, in fact. What do you know of Rubicon's owner?"

Footmen opened the French doors, which was the signal for those who preferred to smoke to enjoy their cigars under the night sky. Tenneby motioned me onto the terrace.

"I hardly know Rubicon's owner to greet her in the churchyard. She's a widow. Inherited the horse from her spouse and said the old boy would want the colt to have his outings. The deceased, one Mortimer Tucker, has a property about five miles to the east. Cut from the same cloth as Sir Albertus. Family made a fortune in cooperage, I believe, and Tucker always had a runner or two in his stable. Tucker Junior is here. The blond fellow with the ruddy cheeks. Goes by his middle name, Quillon. Seems a pleasant sort."

I made a note to chat with Tucker Junior when he was less flushed with victory, so to speak, and we had some privacy.

"If you'll make my excuses, Tenneby, I'll find my bed. This has been a long day."

"One understands, but, my lord..." Tenneby's usually cheerful countenance looked for once serious. "I did not appreciate hearing from Sir Albertus of the sort of mischief you are here to prevent."

I was tired, I wanted a full soaking bath, and I was uneasy about Atticus joining the morning gallops. I was not about to put up with a birching from the man who'd invited all and sundry to his race meeting and recruited me only as an afterthought to see to security.

"Shall I leave, Tenneby? If it weren't for me, neither you nor Sir Albertus would have any idea what went amiss with Blinken. Sir Albertus was willing to assume Blinken had simply had a bad day. The next bad day might see a jockey injured or killed."

"You mistake my point. I'm very pleased that you found the reason behind Blinken's poor performance—I have already alerted Woglemuth to the method used—but I hope in future you will bring your findings directly to me."

Now that I'd aired the offer, part of me did want to leave. These men and their motives were too numerous and devious for one former reconnaissance officer to best in the time allotted. I would fail, the next jockey would not be so lucky as Chalmers had been, and I'd have an injury or a death on my already overburdened conscience.

But if I blew retreat on the first day of the meet, I'd be abandoning Hyperia to her dimwitted brother and disappointing Atticus, who was keenly enjoying the gathering.

No retreat. Not yet. Not when, as Hyperia had pointed out, we'd established that foul play was most definitely afoot.

"Let us agree," I said, "that I will drop by your apartment each day prior to supper. If you have need of me at some other point in the day, send word through your first footman, assuming he is loyal. We can meet in the earl's suite, if that suits, and I'm sure his lordship won't mind the intrusion."

"That will do."

"When can I have the race cards?"

"They're in the desk in the library. I was planning to ask the ladies to copy them out tomorrow morning. Do you know if Blinken will scratch? I forgot to ask Sir Albertus."

"I have no idea. I'm off to bed, though in future, Tenneby, before you relay word of my activities or findings to your staff, I wish you'd first confer with me."

Tenneby stared past my shoulder into the night. "Are you saying I cannot trust Woglemuth? You might as well insult my sister, Caldicott. Insult the earl, if you must, but don't impugn my stable master."

Such a straightforward soul, bothersomely so. "Your stable master made twenty-five pounds off Rubicon's win. He knew both horses, knew their prospects and abilities, and he still bet five pounds on Rubicon. I don't question where he came by such a sum, but I do wonder how he had the confidence to risk it. Whether he was involved in today's scheme or not, he'll mention the tacks to your grooms, and they will mutter into their beer when other grooms can overhear them, and thus my job has become harder."

"Because nobody will dare try to use the tacks again? How can that make your job harder?"

Cupid in his clouds wasn't this devoid of guile. "Because the malefactors will use *other means*, Tenneby. Means harder to discover. Moreover, now that they know we're on to them, I've lost the advantage of surprise. If I stay out here with you much longer, I will lose the advantage of relative anonymity too. You'll have my reports, but I'll have your silence in return. Are we agreed?"

He nodded at me, though his expression suggested I wasn't a very nice fellow and whoever had invited me should think again before adding me to another guest list.

I was halfway across the terrace before it occurred to me that Tenneby might like to know I planned to do sentry duty in the stable yard, but then, he hadn't asked for my plans. He'd asked me to report results.

I went up to my room, and when I rang for a bath, I was told the gentlemen guests had been asked to limit their bathing to the river for the nonce in light of the shortage of water.

To the river I did go, and by the light of a half-moon, I did bathe at length. The water was too low to admit of swimming any distance, but by the time I was finished, I was considerably cleaner and cooler. I sat on the ground, my back resting against a handy birch sapling, and prepared to snatch a much-needed forty winks.

I was floating on the outermost reaches of slumber when I felt the ground reverberate with the regular rhythm of a horse moving at the walk.

I am afflicted with a peculiar defect of memory. At intervals having no discernible pattern, I forget nearly every fact and experience ever to befall me. I say *nearly*, because faculties such as speech, how to ride a horse or brew a cup of tea—faculties having a strong physical component—yet remain. A much larger catalog is obliterated: My name, my familial connections, my course of studies at Oxford, my entire Peninsular misadventure, and my country of origin elude me. I know neither the day of the week nor the identities of my nearest and dearest.

The familiar becomes alien, and I am a stranger to myself.

Thus far, the lapses have been temporary, lasting from a quarter hour to the better part of a day. I dwell in fear of the moment when my memories abandon me permanently, though I have yet to see a progression in that direction.

Upon first rising from the drifting slumber I'd enjoyed beside the river, I felt the same disorientation that occurs when my memory fails. For the space of a half-dozen heartbeats, I knew not where I was, why I'd come to be there, or why the sound of hoofbeats should hold my interest. The moon and stars told me night was not well advanced, and yet, beneath the trees, all was dark.

As the horse walked by not six feet from where I sat, my mind righted itself. I was at the Acres, grabbing a catnap prior to taking a shift on sentry duty. A groom might be taking a horse to the river for watering, but... no.

Human footfalls had not accompanied the hoofbeats. Either the horse was at liberty, or somebody was on its back.

"No drink for you, me lad," said a soft voice. "You're for the Downs and a hearty gallop."

The rider spoke too softly for me to discern an accent, and the hoofbeats faded into the night. I let myself resume dozing, confident that Atticus would have noted the identity of any groom or jockey taking a horse out for solitary exercise.

The horse came back some thirty minutes later and was followed shortly thereafter by another mount bound for the Downs. One groom was apparently working without assistance. When a third horse had been ridden out to the Downs, I made my way to the stable.

"Pleasant night, isn't it?" I remarked, the signal prearranged to let Atticus know who approached. He'd chosen to secret himself outside Maybelle's stall, where his perch would be in shadows, but he'd have a view of the whole stable yard.

No prescribed reply met my ears. Fearing the worst, I advanced on Maybelle's stall and found my loyal tiger sitting on the ground, back against the stall door, side anchored to a half barrel of drooping tulips. A nudge to the sole of his boot confirmed that the lad was far gone in the arms of Morpheus.

Too much excitement and too much responsibility loaded onto his small shoulders, when I should have known better. He was a growing boy, and however much he might demand to be part of my investigations, he needed his rest.

I retreated across the stable yard, found a pebble of appropriate size, and pitched it against the stone wall beside Maybelle's door.

Atticus stirred, stretched, and snuggled closer to the potted flowers. I approached, making certain that my boots scraped the hard earth. When I offered the greeting a second time, I was rewarded with a sleepy answer.

"Bit warm," Atticus said, yawning and rising. "The stars are glorious, though."

"That, they are. Off to bed with you, unless you have anything to report?"

We spoke softly. The sounds of horses munching hay and stirring in their stalls counterpointed our speech. A precocious nightingale began his courting arias, and I was taken back to nights on Spain's north coast. Battles had been won and lost, war waged for miles in every direction, and yet, the little bird graced the air day and night with his song.

"Nothing to report, guv. Cobbles make a miserable bed."

"To the manor with you, then. If you're of a mind to take a bath, stop by the river. Male guests are asked to make that substitution in light of the dry weather. I can't imagine staff is permitted the freedom of the laundry if guests are being restricted."

"Getting on to parched weather. Denton says the heat will start to build tomorrow, and storms should follow."

"We will trust in Denton's prognostications, for the sake of the horses, crops, and humanity. Get thee to bed, Atticus."

The longer we stood chatting, the more likely we were to deter the late-night galloper from returning his horse to its assigned stall. I was reluctant to let Atticus know he'd failed to uphold a sentry's role and very much did want to learn who was taking horses for moonlit rides.

"I'm done in," Atticus said, yawning again. "I mighta dozed off a bit."

He'd been dead to the world. "We're not in the army. A bit of dozing is to be expected. I'm sure you would have awoken if anybody had been stirring."

"Aye. I woulda. Can't have any more tampering with the horses. Night, guv."

"Sweet dreams."

He toddled off. I found a handy patch of shadows on the colt's side of the stable yard, because the rider had referred to his first mount as a lad.

I used the time to think through potential suspects and found the exercise daunting. As competitive as the owners were, as varied as their stories and as manifold as the means of throwing a race were... my villain could be anybody, several anybodies, or Tenneby himself. He was a bit too dense when it suited him and too shrewd otherwise.

Then too, the notion that my presence would ward off mischief had originated with him and was a measure any self-respecting race-fixer would take if he wanted to build a case for his own innocence.

He'd been at the starting line when Blinken had panicked. Most of the owners had been.

I'd been parsing conundrums such as that for a good half hour before the rider returned. As luck would have it, the sole cloud in the entire firmament chose then to obscure the light of the moon, and not a single lantern or torch was lit in the whole stable yard.

My ears still functioned quite well, though, and on the cobblestones forming an apron before the stall doors, I could make out the sound of hooves purposely muffled with cloth. The rider confirmed my suspicions when, after dismounting, he knelt by the horse's front legs.

I could make out movement but could not discern exact forms, and in no time, the horse had been returned to his stall. The groom mounted the steps above the carriage house, and silence reigned over the stable yard.

I moved cautiously, counting doors, until I came to the stall of the horse who'd just been returned. Dasher, owned by Sir Albertus. A cursory inspection determined that the coats of Sovereign Remedy, owned by Wickley, and Excalibur, Tenneby's pride and joy, were also slightly damp.

In about five hours, the sun would rise, the stable would stir back to life, and these three horses would be again galloped on the Downs. If tomorrow night's routine followed the same pattern, by the time colts were again raced the day after tomorrow, these three would be tired young fellows.

"Pleasant night, isn't it?"

St. Just's voice startled me so badly I nearly jumped out of my boots. "Bit warm," I replied softly. "The stars are glorious, though."

"No rain tomorrow," he said. "We need damned rain, Caldicott. Tenneby has overscheduled this meet, and the horses won't hold up for long on this hard ground." The patch of darkness that was St. Just moved under the overhang, becoming indiscernible from the Stygian shadows. "I had a chat with Healy West about his prodigy of a jumper."

"I take it the news is discouraging?" Hyperia would scold her brother all the way to Coventry if he'd bought a sorry specimen.

"If St. George is who I think he is, then he's an infamous morning glory. Has all the speed and will to win in the world if the dew is yet on the grass. Run him after midday, and he's happy to lollop around a course in excellent form. He'll clear every jump in perfect style, but he'll never win, place, or show."

"And Tenneby has scheduled every race for midafternoon or later. Have you persuaded West of his error?"

"I suggested the horse bore a close resemblance to a colt renowned for fading in the later heats, but quite capable of speed at daybreak. West dismissed the very notion. Bought the horse from a close albeit recent acquaintance. West would never attribute foul motives to such an upright member of the sporting brotherhood."

"That's more bad news?"

"The upright member of the sporting brotherhood sells St. George, whose previous *nom de scène* was Zeus, with a guarantee to buy him back for half the price if he doesn't perform up to standards. He argues that if Zeus leaves his control, then all manner of bad training or vices might result, so half the price is enough to show good faith."

Good faith, my blooming aspidistra. "Then this paragon of sporting integrity doubtless demonstrates the horse's speed in the cool of the next morning, and the bargain is struck."

"The bargain, as near as Piggott could recall, has been struck four times in two years. Twice for the spring meets, twice for the autumn meets. The purveyor of the equine goods is always careful to subtly alter the horse's appearance before each sale—roaching the mane, banging the tail, dabbing charcoal on the pasterns—so that only a very thorough examination reveals the ruse."

"How did Piggott figure it out?"

"St. George's coat forms double whorls above his eyebrows. You don't see that very often, particularly not when coupled with spur whorls that point downward."

Little swirls of hair that remained fixed during a horse's life were often used to identify an individual specimen if branding was to be avoided. Brands could, in fact, be altered, but the whorls were reliably consistent.

"Are such whorls rare?"

"In that combination, yes. The Byerley Turk was said to have spur whorls, and I do believe West's horse, whatever its name, has Highflyer in his pedigree."

"He's related to Eclipse?" Weren't they all?

"How can you not know this? Both Eclipse and Highflyer of course trace their lineages back to the foundation sires, but Highflyer is the great-great-grandsire rivaling Eclipse. Highflyer was born two years before Eclipse, and old Richard Tattersall made a fortune breeding Eclipse mares to Highflyer, hence the name of his country manor, Highflyer Hall. Highflyer's progeny regularly win the Derby when Eclipse's descendants don't grab it for themselves. Perhaps you've heard of the noted stud Sir Peter Teazle?"

"Somebody names his horse after a knight?"

"I despair of you, Caldicott." Real consternation came through in those few words. Truly, St. Just, like most cavalry officers I'd served with, was horse mad.

"I despair of Healy West. He's been taken for a fool, and he's pinning his fortunes on a no-hoper."

"Or a late bloomer. Some horses just take time to become competitive, especially over fences. That is not a game for tender youth."

"Somebody is playing games." I recounted the evening's earlier developments. "Somebody is quite possibly over-conditioning those three colts. They're strong contenders, so they should inspire a lot of wagering."

"Can you thus eliminate Wickley, Tenneby, and Sir Albertus from among your suspects?"

Good question. Why would an owner tire his own runner? "Doesn't that depend on how the horses are exercised in the morning? The real conditioning might be intended to happen at night, so an outing in the morning—a mere hack—won't yield an accurate notion of the horse's abilities, and neither would it tire him."

"Devious, but I can tell you it's been done before. The bookmakers are notorious for watching morning gallops through field glasses and telescopes. They base their odds in part on what they or their spies have seen."

Logic suggested that Sir Albertus, Tenneby, and Wickley would not have all used the same jockey for a bit of clandestine exercise. Each man would have used his own rider and kept his nocturnal stratagems from the other owners—or tried to.

"Tenneby disclosed the whole business with tacks and Blinken's tantrum to Woglemuth," I said. "He doubtless told his lads, and they put a friendly word in many an ear among the competitors. My hunch is, somebody is still intent on fixing races, but they've switched tactics."

St. Just was quiet for a moment. An owl hooted over by the river, a death knell to any mouse daring to come forth for a nocturnal drink.

"You are facing a determined opponent, my lord, and you can be damned sure he or she knows Highflyer from Herod. He'll have more tricks up his sleeve before you catch him. If you catch him."

"I know watching and waiting, St. Just. I know evidence forms patterns, and patterns point to answers."

"Seeing any patterns yet?"

"Not a blessed one."

I left him chuckling in the darkness, found my bed, and fell into a slumber far more troubled than the respite I'd enjoyed beneath the stars.

CHAPTER TEN

Denton's predictions proved accurate. Morning brought a precursor to the heavy, cloying heat usually associated with high summer. The day qualified as pleasant, though the air was still, and the ladies were keeping fans close by. The horses, as they came in from their morning gallops, were drenched in sweat.

One by one, their grooms led them to the river, where the beasts were thoroughly rubbed down and permitted to drink when cool.

"How did Excalibur, Sovereign Remedy, and Dasher go?" I asked as a beaming Atticus led Atlas up the barn aisle. While Atticus and I had shared a morning tray in the predawn gloom, I'd mentioned that those three had been taken out for nighttime gallops.

Though the tray, strictly speaking, had not been shared. It never was. Atticus hovered under the guise of tidying up the bedroom while I ate enough to take the edge off my hunger. As I finished dressing, Atticus returned the tray to the kitchen, always mysteriously devoid of leftovers by the time it arrived belowstairs.

Atticus had his notions of class distinctions and defended them ceaselessly.

"Them three ran like the wind," he said, unfastening Atlas's girth and then replacing the horse's bridle with a halter. "They all run like the wind, and the jockeys have to hold them back, and the owners yell at 'em to let them sprint to the finish, or not, and they all run like mad, and if they won't, then the Congress of Vienna convenes to figure out why. The dewfall was heavy this morning. Denton said galloping like that on wet grass was folly. Said Excalibur, being older, knew better than to go flat out over wet grass."

Or Excalibur, having galloped like mad six hours ago, had been overtaxed. "What of Dasher and Sovereign Remedy?" I lifted saddle and pad from Atlas's sweaty back.

"They ran against each other. Tenneby left room for match races at the end of next week, so some of the gallops are being done in twos. Piggott says the betting on match races is worse than the auction for two year old's at Tatts."

"Then listen to Piggott and keep your coin close."

"You got that blowin'-up-castles-in-Spain look about you, guv." Atticus took the saddle and pad from me and set them over an open half door, then draped the bridle over the saddle. "What you thinkin'?"

The stable yard was oddly deserted for the morning hour. The first string had come back from its exertions, and the second had gone out. No grooms were at leisure in the morning sun, and what horses weren't at grass or exercise were content to doze in their stalls.

Like Denton, they could sense the building heat.

"I'm thinking," I said, "that Tenneby makes up the gallop rosters, so he would have known Dasher and Remedy were to pace each other. If both horses are tired, that's less evident when they run against each other."

Atticus shook his head. "The rosters have been posted for the week, in pencil, at the bottom of the carriage house steps. Every groom knows the schedule, and so do the owners. They like their whole string to run together, if they have more than one runner, but sometimes if they own both colts and fillies, that don't work."

He was picking up his own version of an Oxford education without cracking a book.

"Then everybody knew that Dasher and Remedy would be paired this morning, and Denton had an excuse for Excalibur being tentative."

"Excalibur's getting on, according to Piggott. He's rising seven, and that's old for a runner."

"Excalibur's racing over fences these days, and seven is not old for that undertaking. Seven is arguably young. Like you."

Atticus stuck out his tongue at me and took the horse's gear into the saddle room.

I considered my mount, who was considering me. "We are not old. We are in our prime, and that child knows nothing about anything."

Atlas swished his tail at a fly, which I took for agreement among the senior ranks. When Atticus returned, he took up Atlas's lead rope and they sauntered away in search of green grass, to be followed by a doubtless mutual roll in the river.

My boyhood summers had been filled with such pleasures, mostly shared with my brother Harry, or with a canine or equine companion. I dearly hoped that Atticus had many more years to savor innocent joys and that his enthusiasm for all things equestrian would not end in grief.

My own agenda was to find Tenneby and report the previous night's developments. I stopped by his apartment, to no avail. I looked in on the breakfast parlor, half hoping to find Hyperia and coming instead across her brother.

A brief conference with Healy was also on my agenda, so I put together a plate at the sideboard and suggested to Healy that we enjoy the morning sunshine on the terrace. He heaped his plate full of second helpings and obliged me.

"Did you go along for morning gallops?" he asked, taking a bench that looked out over the park. The balustrade made a handy table, and I was famished.

Healy looked entirely too rested and relaxed for my liking, when I was again in want of a bath and short of sleep.

"Atticus, my groom, tiger, and general factotum, took my horse out for me by way of a hack. He's enthralled with the whole race meeting. I trust St. George will be joining the excursions as soon as he's rested from his travels?"

"He well might, but if you think to lecture me on the care and training of my jumper, spare your breath. You sat on a horse for a few years in Spain, I grant you, but I have known the magic of Newmarket. Nowhere will you find a greater abundance of wisdom relating to all matters equine than in Newmarket."

Sat on a horse for a few years in Spain. Not altogether wrong, but still. I pushed aside the urge to smack Healy's toast from his hand.

"Newmarket is certainly the capital of Thoroughbred racing," I said, "but you'd be hard put to learn the deepest mysteries of the pony or the plow horse there. I found Newmarket a bit like a rummage sale. Unless you are looking to buy trinkets, it's all so much gossip and money changing hands."

Healy took a bite of toast soaked with butter. "Philistine. You have allowed Hyperia too much influence over your masculine sensibilities, and you a former soldier."

I tore off a bit of hot cross bun and mentally counted to five. "Tell me about St. George. Where does he shine?"

"Over fences, and not those puny hurdles gaining favor with owners whose runners are too slow on the flat. Fences, Caldicott. Fences are where the excitement and the true athleticism lie. Any dog can run fast on the flat, but fences require strategy."

"I had no idea you were so keen on jump racing."

"Getting keener by the day. You know old Richard Tattersall made his fortune off one stud. A fortune from a single horse. That's why it's called the sport of kings, you know, because the right horse can make any man a king of sorts."

And here, I'd thought royalty had had something to do with that epithet, or perhaps needing a royal fortune to be able to afford to participate.

"And St. George is that horse?"

Healy paused in the demolition of his omelet. "He's fast, Caldicott. He's blazingly fast and brave as the devil. If he doesn't make me a fortune, he'll die trying. He's that kind of horse."

He was that kind of horse, apparently, until midmorning or so. "What does Hyperia think of this venture?"

"Oh, she's against it, of course. She's against all of my ventures. She expects me to sit around a second-rate club reading newspapers and hoping for some modestly dowered viscount's daughter to smile upon me. Hyperia hasn't any sense of adventure, but then, we don't expect that of *ladies*, do we?"

Thrashing was too good for this dimwit. "She's engaged to marry me. That took some courage, I'm sure you'll admit. When shall we get around to discussing settlements, by the by?"

Healy took a sip of his tea. He pushed his eggs around on his plate. He shot me a sidelong glance and took another sip of tea.

"Is there any *reason* those discussions need to take place immediately?" The question was frosty with fraternal authority, and I took no offense. A brother was entitled to know if scandal was afoot, even this brother.

"None that I know of, but if the lady should take a notion to set a date, the preliminaries had best be dealt with sooner rather than later."

"I thought you weren't to set a date until Waltham returns, and he's off somewhere in the Peloponnese, last I heard."

"My brother left Greece some time ago and should soon be touring southern France." The very notion of France, any particle of its accursed terrain, made me shudder.

"Then he won't be home for quite some time, will he?" Asked with far too much good cheer.

"I am prepared to be very generous regarding the Caldicott contribution to Hyperia's settlements. I have property of my own, considerable means, and every intention of seeing the lady honored in the particulars of her dower estate. The discussions should not take long, West."

"Good to know, but I'll be having those discussions with Waltham. He's the head of your family, and that's how these things are done."

That Healy West, gentry, should dictate to me, a ducal heir, how *these things* were done was so far beyond ill-mannered as to be proof positive of imbecility.

"His Grace might decide to settle in France, West. Your solicitors will negotiate with the Caldicott family solicitors under my direction —I have His Grace's written delegation of authority. Unless you'd rather risk an elopement? If Hyperia attempted to kidnap me, I'd capitulate to her scheme willingly."

I would not consent to an elopement all that happily, in truth. The whole business usually had a hole-and-corner aroma and hinted of unsteady motives and anticipated vows.

Healy should have exploded with indignation. Instead, he shoved the last bite of eggs into his mouth, chewed, and patted his lips with his table napkin.

"You'd elope? Truly?"

"I'd rather not, but the manner and timing of the wedding lie within the lady's marital purlieus." Would he *like* to see us elope? Whyever...?

Ah, because a bride who eloped forfeited any claim on her family's obligation to contribute to her settlements. If she eloped, she came to her husband as a pauper—shame upon Healy for ignoring that fact —but the family wealth would be undiminished by her marrying.

"I try to avoid marital purlieus myself," Healy said, finishing his tea. "Though, to be honest, Hyperia is not the most tolerant of sisters. She's all up in the boughs about St. George, for example. You'd think I'd taken to printing seditious pamphlets."

He'd probably consider that scheme, too, if it made money. "She worries about you." I did, too, in my more patient and forgiving moments.

"She needn't. St. George will slay all my dragons, and Hyperia should for once have some faith in me. I'll bid you good day. Let me know when Waltham is expected back on Albion's shores, there's a good fellow."

He rose and strolled across the terrace, quite the young man in charity with the world.

I was out of charity with him, and not only because of the casual slights he'd tossed at Hyperia's character and judgment. She wasn't merely up in the boughs about Healy's acquisition of St. George, she was livid.

Healy's refusal to negotiate settlements with me and his sanguine consideration of an elopement all but howled that Hyperia's rage was justified.

I finished my eggs—cold now—and my toast and bun. Finished my tea and was less hungry but still unsatisfied. Hyperia was angry with Healy, justifiably so.

But I could not resolve her difficulties with her brother without also provoking her ire at myself, and that, I was loath to do.

"Wickley's not a bad sort," Hyperia said. "If he were a horse, I'd say he's overfaced. Scrambling to get over jumps he lacks the strength or coordination to manage, but galloping gamely on."

We were finishing a round of cribbage in the early afternoon shade beneath an octagonal stone folly by the river. A picnic basket had been duly raided. The river at low water sang over shallows, and a slight breeze stirred the branches of the oaks above us.

The moment should have been pleasant, but I was burdened with the knowledge that I owed Hyperia a report, and the news regarding St. George was not good.

"You are doubtless trying to gently steer Lord Wickley onto a steadier course," I said, collecting the cards.

Hyperia was as softhearted as she was fierce, and I loved that about her. Mostly. I also haunted myself with the notion that our engagement was the result of pity on her part rather than true esteem. She would one day soon admit the error of her decision to marry me, and I'd be bereft of her company for all the rest of my days.

"'Gently' being the operative word," she said, rising from the bench and shaking out her skirts. "To little avail. He seems to think that if nobody is laughing or gossiping, the conversation is a failure. Shall we walk awhile? The path is shady, and I've played enough cribbage."

As had I. "What of Wickley's credentials as an owner of race-horses?" I asked as I got to my feet. "Does he know what he's about?"

Because we had taken a meal and played cards, our hands were bare. When I offered Hyperia my hand to assist her down the steps, she took it and laced her fingers through mine. I ought to have stolen a kiss, but St. George's poor prospects dulled romantic inclinations considerably.

Drat Healy West and his deuced horse, anyway.

Hyperia set us on a trail that meandered by the river. "I cannot tell if Wickley is truly turf mad, or if he's simply doing what he thinks is expected of him, Julian. He's also mentioned that he wanted to get back a bit of the family's own by besting Lord Temmington's heir."

"What could that allude to?" My friend the nightingale was in good form, though he was singing at an unusual hour. Perhaps the dry spring was upending his courtship schedule.

"Pierpont whispered something about the earl and Wickley's father having a parting of the ways years ago. They'd been great friends, but something went amiss—a wager was involved or possibly a lady's honor—and they stopped speaking to each other."

"Was there a duel?" Dueling was falling out of fashion, but in Temmington's day, it would have been nothing remarkable between hotheaded young men.

"If there was, Pierpont didn't say, but then, he wouldn't, would he?"

Because Hyperia was a lady. "You are uncovering motives, Perry dearest. If Wickley's family came out badly in the elders' day, Wickley has the basis for a grudge, and that grudge might be behind last night's unscheduled gallops."

We strolled hand in hand, and my resentment for the investigation grew with each step. I wanted to *marry* Hyperia, to devote myself to her happiness, and here we were, discussing cheaters and schemers on a pretty spring day.

Best get it over with. "St. Just had a discussion with Healy about St. George. The report is mixed."

"Tell me."

"The horse has speed and ability—a great deal of speed and ability, apparently."

"But?"

Let's go wading. Let's find some fishing poles. Let's shed our clothes and feel the cool water on our bare skin.

"St. George is what's called a morning glory. He'll run like the devil on a dawn gallop, all the speed in the world. Put him in an afternoon match, and he's a different and much less motivated horse."

Hyperia walked half a dozen yards in silence. "I suppose it could be worse," she said. "He could be a mudder. Not much chance of a muddy track at this meet."

I could feel the stoicism in her words, the self-discipline that set disappointment at a remove from speech and action.

"There's more. St. George is a serial joke among those in the know at Newmarket. He's sold for a hefty sum based on his obvious talents, then bought back for half the price after somebody has paid his shot for a few months of inexplicably slow going."

"Healy has been taken for a fool?" She might have been inquiring about the offerings on the sweets table at tonight's buffet.

"By experts, but yes. The probability of St. George doing well at this meet is small."

Hyperia stopped walking and dropped my hand. "Wickley put Healy onto this little gathering. I don't know if Wickley obtained an invitation for Healy, or if Healy wrangled that for himself. Perhaps my brother has deduced that St. George would not do well against serious competition at Newmarket."

"Healy is not without brains, Hyperia. We know that." He could write clever satire and do basic sums. He'd have to take notice of a series of lost wagers, one after the other after the other.

"But my darling brother can also be exceedingly lacking in sense." She blinked at the river, though I doubted it was the afternoon sunshine putting a sheen on her eyes. "Damn him, Jules. Damn him for a selfish, shortsighted, ungrateful, impulsive... I wish I had slapped him harder."

I took Hyperia in my arms, though she did not reciprocate the embrace. She leaned against me, her forehead against my shoulder, her posture conveying a bewildered weariness of spirit.

"Tell me," I said, rubbing her shoulders slowly. "You often say to me, 'What are you thinking, Jules?' Or, 'What has put that look on your face?' and I want to put the same questions to you. I love you. I want to spend the rest of my life with you, and I am willing to move mountains to bring that happy occasion about."

"Unfair, Jules, to use my own tactics against me." She pushed away and scooped up a handful of pebbles.

"Unfair, but effective, I hope. I know he's in over his head, Hyperia. I can bail him out, if you like, but I don't see any point in supporting the myth that he'll recover his fortunes at this race meet."

One by one, she tossed the pebbles into the water. We'd come to one of the few places where the river still had some depth, and each stone created concentric ripples on the quiet surface.

"He has the rest of his life to recover his fortunes. The fate of my fortune concerns me more. Until I've taken care of that detail, I cannot marry you."

If she had kicked me in the jewel box, I could not have been more shocked. "*Cannot* marry me?"

She nodded, her gaze so impassive that I would not have given tuppence for Healy's old age in that moment. Insight befell me like another blow to sensitive regions.

"*He spent your settlements.* He abused his authority over your funds and squandered them." A modest fortune, but that wasn't the point, at least not to Hyperia. I could replace the funds. We could manage splendidly without them.

Though the pragmatic half of my brain begged to make that very point, the suitor in me knew better. Healy had robbed Hyperia of dignity as well as coin. Setting matters to rights would take more than bank drafts or economies.

"You must not call him out, Jules. I forbid it. I've forbidden him to call you out as well, not that he'll listen to me. You will respect my wishes, of all the ironies, while I can't trust my only brother as far as I could throw him."

The enormity of Healy's transgression subsided under the weight of my concern for Hyperia. "How have you not murdered him? He has stolen the sum designated by your parents to guarantee your security in this life. The only means you have for ensuring a roof over your head should matrimony not appeal to you. He has pillaged your contented old age, forced you to consider marriage on terms abhorrent to you, and disrespected you as the sole female for which he has any responsibility. This is... God in heaven, he needs a thrashing, Hyperia. At least allow me that."

She was, of all the inexplicable things, smiling. "You understand."

"Of course I understand." Reluctantly, but I did. "This is why horse thieves are hanged, for pity's sake. You take a man's horse, you steal his livelihood, his safety on the road, his greatest asset, his companion on the battlefield, or his sole legacy from the only uncle who had any blunt. It's *not done*, to steal a horse. What possible excuse could Healy put forth for this heinous behavior?"

My rage, for that's what it was, seemed to comfort Hyperia. "He went to Newmarket. That's all it took, Jules. All the best fellows have a runner or two, and that crowd has informal match races by the dozen. I gather wagering is like drinking tea for them, and Healy was very, very thirsty."

"He was dodging the Season in Mayfair, just like most of those other *best fellows.* Hyperia, I commend your restraint. You are doubtless Healy's heir. If sending him to his Maker hasn't occurred to you yet, it surely should."

She threw the last of the pebbles into the water. "I suspect, Julian, I would inherit a pile of debts, some heavily mortgaged properties, and one boring little scandal. Another spinster who should have married when she had the chance. Such a pity. I will bring Healy day-old bread when he's rotting away in the Marshalsea debtors' prison. I don't mind the thought of poverty for myself, up to a point, but I mind very much that I am not in the situation you thought me to be when you offered to marry me."

And without settlements, Miss Hyperia West would not marry anybody. Her sense of honor, which I also loved her for, precluded a marriage on those terms.

I wasn't so keen on her sense of honor at the moment. "This is why Healy refused to embark on settlement negotiations with me. He said only Waltham has the authority to handle those discussions, but I have Arthur's written delegation to deal with all matters personal, ducal, or familial."

Hyperia nodded once. "Healy has nothing to bring to the negotiation table, except that blasted horse and a fine wardrobe. He hasn't even tried to sell his play, Julian. That was just a passing distraction, according to Healy, though it's a good work, and writing for the stage is work a gentleman can do."

The question burning in my soul was too fraught to ask: *Are we still engaged?*

"I do love you," Hyperia went on. "Madly, even when I'm vexed with you. I hoped I could sort Healy out this time, as I have on several previous occasions, but he's not a boy with an essay to write before morning. His messes have grown messier and more serious, and this one... He never means to cause me any difficulties, but he never stops to think about the consequences of his actions."

"It's not the money, is it? That's not why you feel you cannot marry me now."

"Oh, the money matters, Julian. For the sake of my pride, if nothing else. I cannot so much as hire a scullery maid without my brother's permission, though he's never set a booted foot in the scullery himself. This is money my parents meant for me to control, though perhaps not until great old age. If nothing else, I could direct that the sums be shared among my daughters, but Healy has taken all that away. I have nothing of my own, and that is not how any lady seeks to begin a marriage."

"The worse problem, though," I said, "is Healy himself. You are ashamed of him and loath to burden any husband with Healy for a brother-in-law. You are concerned that he will be a plague on the marriage."

I'd surprised her, and her impersonation of the serene lady faltered. "Jules, he's been a blight on *our courtship*. Deny that if you can."

Having only the one sibling, Hyperia apparently did not know, as I knew, that family was in part meant to blight our existence, to challenge our capacity for compassion, to force us to develop some self-respect. Harry had done that much for me, both by leading me into trouble and helping get me out of it. Family—good family as well as the other kind—was a crucible for building character.

"Healy has been a challenge, Hyperia, but I have hope for him yet. His road has not been easy, though I make no excuses for this latest stunt. At the rate he's going, I won't have to call him out. Half of polite society will beat me to it."

Hyperia put her arms around my waist. "No duels, Julian. Not with Healy, not with anybody. You didn't survive the worst-imaginable horrors of war to lose your life over stupid male pride."

What about intelligent male pride? Where would Society be if honor was lightly held by the gender wielding most of the money and power?

I kept those arguments to myself and hugged Hyperia gently. "We are still engaged, Miss West. You will not jilt me before all these peacocks and popinjays. Such behavior is firmly under the heading of Not Done. Worse than stealing a horse, in fact. A man's pride matters, even his stupid pride, and I see no reason for hasty measures in any case. Promise me we will remain engaged for the nonce."

She gave me a squeeze and stepped back. Letting her go cost me more gentlemanly restraint than the Bank of England had coin.

"I won't jilt you, Jules, I promise. We might quietly decide we don't suit, but not yet. Certainly not here in the middle of an investigation. You must promise me not to get up to any duels."

She was truly concerned for her brother, despite the grief Healy had caused her. "I give you that assurance easily, and if he's to be thrashed, I will leave you to finish the job you so ably started yesterday."

"I did wallop him soundly, didn't I?"

"St. Just was impressed, and he has five sisters."

Hyperia slipped her hand into mine, kissed me soundly on the lips, and returned with me in silence to the gazebo.

We were still engaged, and she had confided in me the worst of her situation. That much was encouraging.

That Healy West had stolen her entire fortune, and behaved like a ninnyhammer, jackanapes, highwayman, and fool all under one top hat, was more than a bit daunting.

"Why wait until the day is almost gone to tell me this?" Tenneby whipped his cravat into a simple mathematical and surveyed his reflection in the cheval mirror. "Didn't you agree to report to me after breakfast, my lord?"

"You were not in your apartment after breakfast, and a meeting before supper also figured in our agreements."

Earlier in the day, Tenneby might have been napping in this tidy little dressing closet. Unlike many chambers of its kind, this one had a window that overlooked the back terrace. The other appointments were predictable: two sizable wardrobes, a vanity with dressing stool, a cheval mirror, and a clothespress. Shelves boasting hatboxes, boots, and slippers rose above the clothespress, and a wicker hamper sat by the door.

The space was tidy, predictable, and unremarkable, much like Tenneby appeared to be.

"After breakfast? I was out and about, you're right. You might have found me sooner, though. This is a bad business, somebody larking about by moonlight on my best horse." He dragged a brush through his hair, though no amount of styling would turn his red locks into a fashionable coiffure.

"Somebody was larking about on *three* promising colts, Tenneby, not only yours." Though Excalibur was no longer a colt in racing parlance. "For all I know, more runners were galloped last night, but I could not take up surveillance until nearly midnight." I thought it prudent to keep any mention of Atticus, St. Just, or Joe Corrie to myself.

"You could not stay up all night, could you? I suppose I'll have to post guards. Every owner on the premises will be insulted."

My befuddlement with the racing crowd grew by the hour. "They should be grateful that you take the integrity of the races seriously, though if you put a stop to the extra gallops, then the next tactic might be to tamper with the feed or something even worse. I propose that you allow me to continue keeping a quiet watch instead."

He spritzed the air above his head with the scent of bergamot. "My lord, at the risk of pointing out the obvious, it's dark at night. You, with all your experience under Wellington, could not tell who was riding those horses. Last night was *dark*. Tonight will also be *dark.* This falls under the heading of eternal verities. Nighttime is *dark,* and you have poor eyesight, unless I miss the mark. You are not the ideal fellow for the job."

"Which *makes* me the ideal fellow for the job. I have no horse in the race, literally, and I am not betting on any horse. My night vision is actually quite good. You asked me to keep the races honest, and I cannot do that if you dictate means and details, Tenneby."

"Well, you haven't managed the one job you're assigned, have you? Blinken was tampered with. Three horses were run ragged by moonlight. At least three. This is not how I foresaw matters unfolding."

I wanted to kick him, because this was exactly how I'd seen matters unfolding. Mischief on every hand, suspects lining up twelve deep before the punchbowls. Tenneby had had more than an inkling such mayhem might ensue—to wit, he'd dragooned me into attending.

"Tenneby, did you honestly think you could parade me around and your race meet would magically escape all the tricks that are apparently perennial ploys when the turf set gather around a course?"

He set the brush down and turned his profile to the mirror. "I had hoped so, yes, and the earl agreed with me. He's sensible, for all his faults. Do you expect me to say nothing about what amounted to temporary horse thievery last night? Somebody takes out my stallion, runs him over badger holes and heavens know what else out on the Downs, tires him thoroughly, and may be preparing to do the same again and again. I'm supposed to say nothing?"

"You are supposed to say nothing. You may, however, post torches in the stable yard as a courtesy to all the grooms who, unlike your own staff, can't be expected to find their way to the river and back after dark. That water is their only bathing option, and bathing must take place at night if we aren't to risk scandalizing the ladies."

I paced the length of the room. "You may swap around where you stable each of your horses on any pretext you please, assuming anybody notices—a rathole that needs plugging, a horse who prefers afternoon light. You may make late-night calls upon your colts and fillies, as a sentimental owner will. Wind straw around the latches on the stall doors so you'll know if they were taken out, and let those same horses miss the morning gallop, again on any pretext you please. You can take all the evasive maneuvers in the world, but do not—pray heaven, *do not*—inform your enemies that they need to employ yet another race-fixing tactic."

Tenneby pocketed a gold watch and threaded the chain through a buttonhole on his waistcoat. "I can't think like you do, in pretexts and evasions. I haven't a devious mind, and I do not want to develop one. I hate that my race meet is disgraced by these goings-on."

"But you anticipated that it might be. Could somebody have been galloping Excalibur to exhaustion at Epsom three years ago?"

He patted his watch pocket. "Yes, blast the notion. Yes, they could, though the facts don't exactly conform to that theory. I did not post any guards on my string. Why should I? The grooms slept above the stalls, for the most part, and the lads are devoted to their charges."

The lads, like soldiers on campaign, like my own Atticus, were also doubtless exhausted at the end of their days and in need of every moment of slumber they could snatch.

"Was Excalibur's defeat consistent with a horse who'd been over-trained?"

"Possibly." Tenneby took a yellow iris from a bouquet on the windowsill and extracted from his jewelry box a minute vase resembling a pewter lapel pin. The vase he filled with water from the washstand, and the iris he inserted into the tiny opening of the vase.

"Would you mind?" He gestured with the iris assembly. "One can't get the angle just so if one's hands are raised. Spoils the lines of the jacket."

I affixed the pin on his lapel, though I would have chosen a purple iris rather than yellow for a man of his coloring.

"You know," he said, surveying his reflection, "Excalibur might have been overtrained at Epsom, meaning galloped hard when my back was turned, but he came out at the start like he'd been shot from a cannon. Full of fire, exactly as I'd hoped he would. He went around most of the course in fine style, but then, when he should have been giving his all into the finish, he simply... ran out of puff. I have never seen anything quite like it. If a horse is tired, he's tired all the way around, you know?"

Well... yes. Nervous energy could make for a lively start to any ride, but it didn't last for a flat-out three-mile-long gallop. Terror could inspire a horse to heroic feats of speed, but equine high spirits alone couldn't overcome fatigue indefinitely.

"We can't undo the past," I said, "but you can prevent any more clandestine training outings, or allow them to go on, but then give the horse back his morning rest. That's up to you. Please do not put a word in Woglemuth's ear, either way."

If I'd taken away a toddler's puppy, I could not have earned a more intense scowl of dismay. "Not tell Woglemuth? My lord, you *blaspheme*. He is my *stable master*. He is responsible for the *stable* and all the horses in it. I might conceal a delicate matter from my sister or the earl, but not from my *stable master*."

The world was not meant for hearts as pure as Tenneby's. "Precisely because he is the stable master, the grooms keep a close eye on him. He holds their livelihoods in his hands. If he's seen conferring with you, the grooms and jockeys will all know it. They will watch the whole exchange, while pretending to curry horses or clean bridles. If Woglemuth is summoned to the house, they'll take note of his mood when he returns. He is their commanding officer, more or less. They will ply him subtly for information. He already spread the word about the metal tacks, and that has made him a greater object of scrutiny going forward."

"I don't like this." Tenneby picked up a pair of gloves from the vanity. "I do not like this *at all*, my lord. I will explain to Woglemuth that I've heard some rumors over the cards, and a few torches in the stable yard will quiet gossip. Is that oblique enough for you?"

"Have him move Excalibur to a stall that catches a better night breeze, but ask that he see to it personally and deliver the request with a wink or two."

"Winking is for pantomime charlatans."

"If you say so, Tenneby. I'll see you at supper." I had yet to change for dinner myself, and my interview had accomplished its purpose. Tenneby was warned, countermeasures had been agreed to. That was progress for the nonce.

"Caldicott!" he called as I was halfway across his bedroom. "A moment." Tenneby emerged from the dressing closet looking exactly as an earl's heir ought—except for the color of the iris at his lapel. "If I do have the torches lit, and move Excalibur to a different stall, and wander around the yard myself at midnight, then you won't have to keep watch yourself, will you?"

My first thought was, *He knows who took the three horses for gallops and doesn't want the guilty party caught.* But no, Tenneby lacked the guile for such measures, and he'd been genuinely surprised and horrified that Excalibur had been among the runners taken for an outing.

He was concerned with *appearances.* Spying was bad form all around. On that score, polite society had ever been in agreement. Just as Wickley was trying to live up to some Drury Lane impersonation of a bachelor peer, Tenneby had his own standards to uphold.

"As you've noted, Tenneby, I cannot remain vigilant all night every night. I am in the habit of looking in on my own mount at the end of the evening, though. I have also been known to hack out at dawn, particularly if the weather is warm."

"One expects that much. Very well. No more skulking about, then. I'll see you at supper."

I nodded and decamped without agreeing to anything. I was damned good at skulking about, and that skill had already yielded valuable information that might well see Excalibur best his rivals in a lucrative fashion.

I'd skulk about however I pleased to, and Tenneby's delicate sensibilities would just have to deal with the results.

CHAPTER ELEVEN

Dawn brought a sultry, unpleasant heat. The horses came back from their early morning gallops, heads low, coats matted with sweat. I waited in the shade of the stable's overhang, more than a little anxious on Atticus's behalf.

I spotted him on Atlas near the end of a returning string. Atlas's coat was damp as well, but not wringing wet. The boy was chattering and gesturing, despite the reins held loosely in his hands, while Piggott, mounted on a cob beside him, listened with seeming patience.

Several yards behind them, Wickley rode the elegant dapple-gray Cleopatra while Denton walked at his side. They, too, were engaged in conversation, or Wickley was holding forth while Denton periodically nodded.

"Guv! We watched the gallops. Piggott says Atlas could whup half of 'em if the distance was more than two miles." That announcement, bellowed for all of creation to hear, inspired smiles from the sweaty jockeys and a scowl from Wickley.

"Mind your manners, boy," Wickley snapped, "and stop bleating your ignorance about for half the countryside to hear. Your nag hasn't the breeding for proper racing."

"He ain't got no breedin' a'tall," Atticus retorted. "Like me. But he can run like the wind for miles, and he'll jump anything. My Atlas *served under Wellington*, and if there's bad manners on display, they ain't comin' from me or my *horse*, who is a perfect gentleman."

Pierpont, atop a chestnut gelding, was grinning outright.

I strode forth from the cool of the shadows. "Hush, lad. We all know you love that horse. Down you go and get him to the river once you've walked him out."

"Aye, guv." Atticus slid to the ground as gracefully as an otter and patted Atlas's shoulder audibly. "Good boy, Atlas. Very good boy." With a chin raised to royal heights, he led the horse into the stable yard and to another patch of shade.

Wickley swung down by virtue of lifting his leg over the mare's crest. "A lad that cheeky would make a good jockey, once somebody beat some respect into him. I don't suppose you'd give him up?"

Denton loosened the mare's girth and led her away, though the remark had to have offended him.

"I would not part with that child for all the colts at Newmarket, Wickley, though where he earns his coin is his decision. Aren't you a bit tall for that mare?" Cleopatra, rising four, still had growing to do, and Wickley was no sylph.

"Builds strength for her to carry the occasional full-sized rider. Pierpont is appalled that I'd ride any sort of mare, and Denton disapproves because a female mount for one of my standing is *infra dig*. Annoys the hell out of them both. Doubly satisfying for me."

Infra dignitatem. Beneath his dignity. I wanted to spank his rubbishing dignity. A horse's back, especially the back of a young horse, was easily injured and slow to heal.

"Do you mind if I have a word with Denton, Wickley?"

"As long as you don't interfere with his duties, have all the words you please. I'm famished and looking forward to Miss West's lovely presence at the breakfast table."

He strode off, swinging his crop at a patch of lavender growing along the barn wall, and I went in search of Denton. I found my quarry walking the mare along the lane that led to the racecourse.

"How is she going?" I asked, falling in step beside him.

"She'd go better if his lout-ship kept out of her saddle. Says he's building up her strength. He's keeping his fancy boots dry. Doesn't want the morning dew spoiling the leather."

That reasoning sounded credible where Wickley was concerned. "And he won't ride a hack up to the Downs because he likes forcing you to walk? Why put up with that? Woglemuth would lend you a mount."

Denton strode along with the sweaty mare. "It's the besetting sin of the Irish that we will insist on eating from time to time. We're happy to sleep in the hedges, as is known to all, and we're not too fancy about our dress, nor do we set great store by footwear or hygiene. We do, however, relish the occasional crust of bread to go with our insatiable appetite for ale. If I have to walk while the great man rides, I'll walk to earn my pay packet."

The Irish and Welsh, with their lilting intonations, could deliver a scold more bitter than any conveyed by the most articulate Oxford don. The majority of Denton's pay packet was doubtless sent home to aging parents or younger siblings.

Perhaps even to a wife.

While Wickley worried about keeping his boots dry.

"Somebody took Excalibur out for an unscheduled gallop last night. Tenneby did not authorize the extra exercise and is taking measures to ensure it doesn't happen again."

Denton eyed the mare, whose respiration was gradually slowing. "You expect me to peach on a mate?"

"I hope to see anybody who thinks to throw a race held account-able, though I doubt last night's jockey is the responsible party. Had he been caught on the Downs riding a horse he'd no business riding, he could have been charged with stealing that horse."

"Aye. Same thought occurred to me. Sir Albertus's brother-in-law is the magistrate, according to Woglemuth. Cut from the same cloth as Sir Albie. He'd go spare with any mischief involving horses."

"Then you knew somebody was absent without leave from the dormitory?"

Denton led the mare to a patch of shade along the hedgerow, where she proceeded to crop at the spindly green grass at her feet.

"Somebody is always leavin' the dormitory, milord. Out to take a piss, to canoodle with the cook's assistant, to smoke, to check on his horses. The younger lads will leave under darkness to sit under the stars and weep for home. We're all going down to the river after dark of late, too, and not just to water the horses. This weather is gettin' oppressive, and as thee and me learned in Spain, heat takes a toll on a body."

Heat could be deadly. A single day was bearable, but day after day, marching under a blazing sun in wool uniforms, many a man had succumbed.

"Whoever went abroad on horseback last night took out Excalibur, Sovereign Remedy, and Dasher."

Denton rubbed a hand across his chin. "Are you asking me if I'm the culprit? If I'm so put out with Lord Witless that I'd tire his own colt on purpose and go for a romp on a couple others because I'm that keen to hang? Don't you know the Irish are almost as fond of lying as they are of their drink?"

Denton's bitterness was excusable. England had been alternately oppressing, exploiting, and slaughtering the Irish for centuries. The Glorious Revolution of 1688 that had seen William and Mary put on the throne to replace the papist James VII was taught to schoolchildren as a peaceful transition, politely arranged by Parliament for the good of the realm.

Peaceful in Ireland had meant thirty thousand deaths and the decimation of the Catholic portion of the Irish peerage.

Then too, like the Scots, the Irish had paid a high price in the fight to defeat the Corsican, only to find no jobs, no places to dwell, and no appreciation from the crown upon returning home. The wounded veteran begging on a London street corner was a common sight.

"I don't know about Irish people generally," I said. "I know you served loyally and marched at all times with honor. I know your family had reason to mourn, as did mine."

Denton's smile was wry. "Now you trot out the fife and drums. My lord is ruthless. I knew your brother. Very democratic fellow and played merry hell with the ladies. Democratic in that regard too. Lord Harry hadn't your seat, but he could give a good account of himself in the saddle."

Denton played Long-Lost Lord Harry to my fife and drums. He'd have made a very competent officer.

"Who went out last night, Denton? A second sortie like that could see them hanged or transported."

If Denton was my culprit, I was duly warning him, one soldier to another, of the consequences to be paid. Wickley would not protect him, and Pierpont would call for Denton's blood out of sheer spite. If Denton was not my culprit, he'd likely keep his mouth shut—the denizens of the dormitory were his mates anywhere but on the race-course, apparently—as long as Wickley's horses won.

"Somebody went out," Denton said, moving a few steps to keep pace with the grazing mare. "The door opens and closes all night, for reasons stated, and sometimes we prop it open for the sake of a breeze. Gets a bit close up there on a warm night. I woke up maybe halfway through the middle watch. Moon was setting but not down. I don't know who it was, don't want to know, but he smelled of sweaty horse and the wind on the Downs when he came in. I noticed mud on Remedy's left hind fetlock this morning. The only place you'll find mud these days is along the riverbank, and I hadn't taken him there since his last grooming."

"You're hauling buckets to his stall?"

"Most of us are, for the runners kept in at night anyway. Your lad makes sure that big gelding of yours always has a full bucket too."

Effort expended simply out of respect for the horses. "Whoever took out three horses apparently rode them hard. He's a jockey or a very competent groom."

The mare raised her head and gave Denton an impatient look. The grass was doubtless not up to her standards, for all it was as good a patch as she'd find anywhere outside the garden walls.

"Come along, then," Denton said, leading her back to the lane. "I can ask Hercules Smith if he knows anything. He's Lord Pierpont's head lad and a decent sort, despite his lamentable taste in employers. We get on as best we can, and he's a notoriously light sleeper. I don't know who your midnight rider was, my lord, but I suspect he knows you."

I fell in step on the opposite side of the mare. "What makes you think that?" I was certainly in evidence in the stable yard, and Atticus would make no secret of my identity.

"'Cause there was talk yesterday at the river suggestin' your lordship were slouching about in the stable yard by moonlight. The tone was not flatterin' to one o' your consequence."

A warning for a warning. Whoever was attempting to fix the races was taking countermeasures of his own, maintaining surveillance and guarding his flank.

For even a portion of twenty-eight thousand pounds, such measures were warranted.

"Do you ever think about giving it all up, the race riding and meets?" I asked as we approached the stable yard.

"Every day, but a jockey makes a bit extra if he wins, and I'm a good jockey. One of the best, still. Soon enough, I'll take a fall or get knocked off, and then the bit extra will be beyond my reach."

"Make hay while the sun shines?"

"If you try it on the wet days, you can kill your whole stable with the moldy results. I'll bid your lordship good morning." He led the filly to the ladies' side of the stable, her hoof falls echoing on the cobbles.

"Same to you, Denton, and thanks."

He waved a hand without turning.

"He's an excellent jockey," Sir Albertus said, coming up on my elbow. "I'd hire him away from Wickley, except that Wickley would make my life hell if I were successful. Pierpont has doubtless offered him the moon, despite having a very competent man of his own. If your lordship has a moment, I'd appreciate a word."

Sir Albertus's brother-in-law was the magistrate, and his colt had been among those taken for a hard gallop without permission. What could it hurt to hear him out?

"Tenneby took me aside this morning," Sir Albertus began, "and informed me that owing to the building heat, Excalibur would be given a very light ride this morning, and he suggested I take the same measure with Dasher. He apparently had a similar conversation with Wickley, who said he'd been given the same advice by Denton."

"Let's find some shade, shall we?" I strolled off without waiting for the baronet's reply. He came along readily enough and marched for the path to the river.

"Not that way," I said. "Let's have a look at the racecourse, shall we?"

"I have seen that damned racecourse in my nightmares, young man." And yet, he changed tack and accompanied me along the lane. "I wish I'd never agreed to bring my horses to this meeting. Even the weather is conspiring against me."

"Then the weather is conspiring against every competitor equally, no?"

His pace slowed. "No, no, it is not. Just as a mudder loves the sloppy going, or a morning glory shines in an early match, some horses thrive in the heat. Larger horses have a harder time with it, and I tend to breed mine for some size. If they go on to race over fences or into the hands of the hunt crowd, size is an asset."

"Dasher isn't particularly big."

"Give him time, my lord. His line tends to mature slowly, which is a disadvantage if they're over-raced. They can break down if too much is asked too soon, and hard ground is particularly difficult for them." Now that Sir Albertus was holding forth about his runners, his demeanor was almost chatty.

"You are careful not to overtax them, I take it?"

"I am obsessively careful. You've doubtless had to put down a mount or two, and it is a horrible business when you can blame the necessity on an accident. When your own avarice is responsible, when you think only of the purse and not of the horse, firing that bullet is intolerable."

He loved his horses, and I respected him for that. "Is somebody trying to overtax your horses?"

He came to a halt. Such was the heat that when he took off his top hat and swiped a sleeve across his brow, his white hair bore a damp ring of sweat.

"You tell me, my lord. You were in the stable yard last night, according to sources I trust. Your military reputation is dubious, for want of a more delicate term, and left you well-versed in the art of sneaking about. I apologize for the insult implied, but the appearances want an explanation."

We were about halfway to the racecourse, still in full view of the stable yard and also visible from the eastern façade of the manor house.

Eyes everywhere, in other words. "I could not sleep. Many a former soldier will tell you he's similarly afflicted. I came to the stables to visit my horse, whose company is a comfort. While I was paying my call, I heard somebody taking a horse out, and because of my military experience, I easily recognized the sound of hooves muffled with cloth boots. I remained to observe what I could, which turned out to be precious little."

Sir Albertus considered his hat, then considered me. "Plausible. Just. I'd rather pressing business demanded your immediate departure, my lord."

Fair enough. "Would you rather Blinken's poor performance had gone unexplained?"

He shook his head. "But that's the trouble, you see? If you wanted to ensure that I trusted you, that I placed you above every suspicion, that's exactly the sort of device you'd employ. Sabotage my horse, then reveal the sabotage."

Also plausible, dammit. "I wasn't at the starting line when the mischief was done."

"You could have delegated the deed."

"To whom? I brought only the boy, and he wasn't near the starting line either."

Sir Albertus whacked his hat against his thigh. "I don't know who might be desperate enough to accept coin for such a deed. Racing attracts all sorts, and the stakes are high. It didn't used to be like this, so, so... fraught. We raced for the pleasure of good sport, toasted the winners, consoled the losers, and called it a fine day. Now..."

"Now, Tenneby recruits the likes of my dubious, lurking self to keep the races honest, and I'm having a devil of a time accomplishing my stated mission. Tell me about Dasher, Sovereign Remedy, and Excalibur."

Sir Albertus put his hat back on his head and turned for the stable yard. "Dasher is coming into his own, my lord, and I say that not as the man who bred and raised him, but as a good judge of horse-flesh. That colt will sire winners before it's all over, and he will be a winner. He's the best colt to grace my stables, ever, and that is saying a great deal. I hope to breed him to my Juliet, who is his equivalent among the fillies."

"Speed and stamina, both?"

"Dasher and Juliet have much more than just speed and stamina. You can breed for speed and train for stamina, but Dash in particular is also a sensible lad. Knows the job on race day and loves his work. The jockeys adore riding him because he works with them, not against them. We've put him to a few fences over the winter, just for variety, and by God, he's as nimble as a deer and as brave as a lion. I'll not see his like again."

This was not mere paternal fondness for a bright child. This was the doting devotion of a new grandpapa for his first grandson. All things bright and beautiful lay before that child, and the wonders of the universe shone from his eyes.

"How does Dasher stack up against, say, Sovereign Remedy?"

"Give Wickley credit—he has an eye for horseflesh. Sovereign Remedy *looks* like a champion, while my Dasher wouldn't appear much out of place at the local hunt meet. Wickley's animal has perfect conformation, my lord, perfect. I've heard it said Remedy could have hired out as a model to the late George Stubbs, had their seasons overlapped. Remedy is fast, he has heart, and he looks the part. A bit short of stamina, but that's Wickley's problem to solve. The horse is more than capable."

"And Excalibur?"

Sir Albertus paused again. "Excalibur is... He doesn't simply look the part of a champion, he knows himself to be one. If he isn't the best horse here, if not the best horse over fences in my lifetime, I will eat this dusty hat."

"But he's not raced in several years, from what I understood."

"Exactly what that horse needed to develop his full potential. Was the same with Eclipse, more or less."

Not this again. "In what way?"

"Good heavens, everybody knows the story. The colt was fractious and difficult. Should have been gelded, but his owner at the time, Wildman, decided on a different tack. He turned the horse over to a fellow who tried to ride the temper out of the beast, but Eclipse loved the hard work. He'd spend hours under saddle and be happier for the exertion. Another horse would have broken down. Eclipse *settled* down. His jockeys always let him decide the pace of the race, and the result was an undefeated record followed by very lucrative years at stud. That's what can come from rejecting the received wisdom of the experts, you see."

"Tenneby rejected received wisdom regarding Excalibur?"

"Not exactly." Sir Albertus resumed walking. "Good Lord, this heat is miserable. One expects this in July. One is accustomed to it by then."

Accustomed or not, I'd never grown comfortable with the heat in Spain, and that had been dry heat, for the most part.

"Excalibur has benefited from his years at home. Is that what you're saying?"

"That is exactly what I'm saying. I'm a neighbor. I frequently run into Tenneby's string on the Downs. We all mill about up there, watching each other's runners go, sometimes pacing them against each other in a spirit of good sportsmanship."

"Excalibur is good?"

"He's fast, he's nimble, he can go forever, and he'll jump anything. The Eclipse of racing over fences, mark me on that, but Tenneby has acquired some shrewdness. He wants and deserves decent odds on the horse after what happened at Epsom. He's being very casual about Excalibur's chances, though I know better. I'll be backing Dasher on the flat, of course, but over fences, my money will be on Excalibur."

"Good to know, though I am not making any wagers."

The old fellow gave me a sidewise perusal. "Best you don't, my lord. I still wish you'd leave the gathering, and not just because your nosing about implies an insult to every honest owner with runners on the cards. If you did not take those horses out last night, then somebody else did, and they are busily casting suspicion in your direction."

"Suspicion and I are long acquainted. I don't care for the company, but neither does it intimidate me."

"Then you're as much a young fool as the rest of 'em, sir. They get to drinking and declaring and vowing and swearing... Pierpont and Wickley are both said to bring their dueling pistols with them everywhere, and a rumor like that doesn't get started without some basis in fact. As if the Creator, with the entire universe to oversee, can be bothered sorting out strutting dunces who think playing with loaded guns can settle a matter of honor. Since when has honor ever been confused with sheer, lethal inanity?"

He stomped off, his gait slightly uneven but quite brisk.

If I was very lucky, and that same Creator was kind, I might grow up to be just like Sir Albertus. Fierce, honest, nobody's fool, and very fond of his horses.

Before that happy fate could befall me, I'd have to expose the party, or parties, trying to ruin Tenneby's race meet. Three promising prospects all interfered with—four, counting Blinken—and the only suspicious activity anybody had noticed in the stable yard last night was my humble self, who'd kept expressly to the shadows.

Very curious indeed.

CHAPTER TWELVE

"The three colts taken out last night aren't on the card for today," Hyperia said, waving her fan gently beneath her chin. "We're to have a flat race and a hurdle for the fillies, then a steeplechase for all comers. I'm told the steeplechase is mostly local lads showing off for one another."

"I looked over the card,"—I'd memorized it—"but Tenneby uses so many abbreviations that other than names of horses and owners and the basic race description, I'm not sure what other information it conveys."

"Age limits," Hyperia said, nodding at Evelyn Tenneby some yards across the crowd. "Five and up, three-year-olds only, that sort of thing, and weight requirements, if any. The card should also state the purse of record. Pierpont gave me a lengthy tutorial. The big races next week will be run with each horse carrying the same weight. These earlier matches are more of a come-as-you-are."

"This week is the artillery barrage."

Hyperia linked her arm through mine and led me along the crest of the viewing hill, until we were in the shade of the trees at the first sweeping, left-hand turn.

"Artillery barrage, Jules? I hear no guns."

"In the military, the first phase of battle was often an artillery barrage, intended more to unnerve the enemy than to decimate his numbers. A skilled gunnery sergeant could listen to such a barrage, correct for wind and terrain, and know exactly what sort of guns the enemy used, how many were firing, and where they were placed."

"A display of power, but at a strategic cost?"

The shade was a relief, though nothing could dull the brightness of the midafternoon sunshine. This outing would have a strategic cost to me, in throbbing eyes and possibly a megrim.

"That strategic cost—revealing the strength, number, and position of the guns—could be turned to a strategic advantage."

Hyperia's fan paused, then resumed its languid motion. "I see. You keep half your guns silent during the initial barrage, or fire them once or twice, then move them about. That's what horse artillery was for, wasn't it? Get off some telling shots, then change positions and land a few more cannonballs from a better vantage point."

"Exactly, and those artillery teams made the hostlers in the best coaching inns look like sluggards by comparison. There's art to war, Perry, but it's art with deadly purpose." We moved to the near edge of the curve, against the white rail that kept horses on the course and spectators off the course. "The horses are more settled today."

Down at the starting line, fillies, jockeys, owners, and stewards were nearly decorous compared with the situation at the previous races. The heat was perhaps to thank for some of the apparent calm. Horses waited patiently for jockeys to be tossed aboard, then ambled placidly to the designated starting area.

When a dozen fillies were positioned more or less evenly across the grass, the starter dropped his flag.

"They're off." Hyperia handed me her fan and produced a pair of field glasses from her reticule. "What sensible animal wants to go at top speed in this weather?"

The fillies galloped along the short straightaway at the bottom of the course in a tight bunch, then turned up the hill. The combined impact of tons of horseflesh moving at top speed created a thunderous tattoo against the dry ground, and abruptly, I was nauseated, dizzy, and filled with terror.

A cavalry charge was a fearsome experience to survive, and I'd survived several. Standing in formation, shoulder to shoulder with other riflemen, I'd waited while the mounted enemy first trotted, then cantered, then galloped at our infantry square.

The test of nerves on both sides was excruciating. The oncoming riders faced a wall of bayonets, bullets, and gun barrels, sixty men on a side at the start of battle, four lethal ranks deep. The horses with any sense swerved the human obstacle as best they could, and a man with any sense would never have taken the king's shilling in the first place.

And we stood there, sighting on the enemy as we waited for the order to fire, and tried to think only of hitting our targets. I suspected most of us aimed at the horses despite being told to aim at the riders, but the whole point of a formed square was to launch a barrage of ammunition into a barrage of cavalry. The point of the exercise was damage rather than accuracy.

And damage invariably resulted.

"Jules?" Over the pounding of hooves, Hyperia's voice sounded as if from far away, and I had the vague thought that I might be fainting. One often did in the midst of battle.

"Julian?" Hyperia was nearly shouting as the horses swept past us, leaving a choking cloud of dust in their wake. "Julian, can you hear me?"

"I can hear you." I could also feel her hand wrapped around my elbow, and on that steadying sensation, I focused all my awareness. My head swam, but I resisted the temptation to gulp and pant for air.

Steady breaths. The image of the lime alley at Caldicott Hall. Shade, repose, quiet. Hyperia's hand on my arm. *Breathe. It's only dust and horses, no scent of blood. No screams.*

Hyperia took the fan from my hand and used it gently near my face. "You're very pale. The heat must be getting to you. My old governess claimed that once a lady had fainted from the heat, be it in a ballroom or at a Venetian breakfast, she was more susceptible to the same mortification. I'm babbling."

"You are wonderful."

Her expression went puzzled then scowling. "Are you delirious, Julian? Must I call for assistance?"

"I am in love, which is a form of delirium. You can cease waving your fan at me. I had a bad moment, is all, and the bright sunshine doesn't help." I hesitated, but this was my beloved, who insisted on rummaging through my worst memories when they came calling. "A cavalry charge came to mind, or rather, awaiting the arrival of a cavalry charge."

Her scowl became thoughtful. "The horses? The horses coming at us right up the hill? They gave you a bad turn?"

"The whole business—the sounds, the concussion of dozens of hoofs on the ground, the speed of the approach, the bright sun, the heat... Bad moments in Spain came to mind, very like when the cavalry gallop full tilt at an infantry square. You stand there on the ground, praying to kill rather than be killed, and to not disgrace yourself, and knowing such prayers are in themselves disgraceful. I will avoid watching other races from this same location."

Many a man lost control of his bladder while waiting for the order to fire. It wasn't spoken of and, in the mess and gore of battle, didn't matter. Thank heavens I'd not fallen prey to that humiliation, though I was not as calm as I'd sounded.

My heart still thudded against my ribs, and my head was light, but I could form words and manage the business of basic respiration.

"Miss West! Lord Julian!" Lord Pierpont joined us along the rail. "What did you think of my Minerva? She'll be leading the pack next time around, see if she isn't."

A roar from the crowd went up, suggesting some sort of near disaster or fall on the far side of the course.

"She's the darling bay with the four white socks, isn't she?" Hyperia said. "Beautiful eyes and a nose as soft as velvet."

Pierpont beamed. "The very one, though her markings and her sweet nose aren't why I run her. Caldicott, are you well? You look as pale as a winding sheet."

I'd been studying his boots, for want of something else to focus on. Dusty, a bit worn down at the heels. The broguing across the toe of the left boot—the decorative pinhole pattern—didn't quite match the broguing on the right.

"The heat disagrees with me," I said. "Had rather too much of it in Spain and Portugal." The South of France had also been overly warm, once I'd won free of the mountains.

"We're in for worse, I'm afraid." Pierpont took out a plain handkerchief and mopped his brow. We both wore top hats, which was beyond foolish, given the weather. "If the result is rain, I'm all for it, but the grooms say rain is at least a few days off. Here they come again."

I stepped back from the rail and made myself scan the oncoming horses.

Pierpont's Minerva appeared to be leading the pack. She moved with the steady determination of a horse who liked to run in front and was being allowed to indulge her preferences. A chestnut filly with a crooked blaze was coming up on her right, but either the jockey was holding his contender back, or the chestnut was saving her best effort for the run in to the finish.

Hyperia surreptitiously squeezed my fingers and kept hold of my hand until the horses had passed. I breathed. I counted backward in Latin from twenty. I considered Pierpont's slightly frayed shirt cuff and the plain pewter sleeve button holding it closed.

"Don't you want to be at the finish, Lord Pierpont?" Hyperia asked. "Minerva was in quite good form."

"I will take myself there now, though I don't like to watch the final run in. One is supposed to appear at his ease, graciously aloof, and so forth, but I do love my fillies. I'd end up cheering for them like an ill-mannered schoolboy, and I will leave that loss of composure to such as Lord Wickley."

He touched a finger to his hat brim and sauntered off.

"He was doing so well," Hyperia said, "until he had to bring up Wickley's enthusiasm. Are you withstanding more cavalry charges in Spain, Jules?"

"Not at the moment, thank you. Let's see who won and get us both some punch." I offered my arm, and we followed in Pierpont's wake toward the viewing structure. "I was ready for the second onslaught, fortified by the affection of my loyal intended."

"I might not be your intended much longer."

"Never say it, never think it. In any case, I was preoccupied with Pierpont's boots, Perry. They don't match. His handkerchief is plain and worn. His cuff is going frayed. Those are the signs of a man who might be avoiding creditors."

"Or the signs of a man far gone into bachelorhood."

Possibly. "Motive, though, Perry. A fellow in want of coin has a reason to fix a race."

She sighed gustily, a governess marshaling her patience. "One doesn't enter a horse in a race with the intention of losing, Julian. Every owner here has a pecuniary motive for cheating his way to victory."

Or to defeat. Wagers could be profitable if one knew which horse was to lose.

We took our places in line before the punchbowls, while all around us, people chattered about Minerva's victory. The initial betting had put her second favorite behind the chestnut apparently, but she'd romped away with the victory by five lengths.

"It was the oddest thing," Miss Evelyn Tenneby said. "Sir Albertus's chestnut was gaining handily when they started down the hill, and I thought we'd have at least a close finish. Halfway down the incline, the chestnut just… gave up. The jockey tried a whack or two with the crop, and the filly dropped from the canter to the trot, sides heaving, head down. Poor thing broke my heart. Simply lost her wind, apparently, though Juliet is noted to excel over longer distances."

The recitation had a familiar ring, though it took me until I was sipping cool cider and envying Hyperia her fan for the recollection to settle in place.

Excalibur had been positioned to win at Epsom, coming on for the final push well ahead of the pack, and then he'd simply *run out of puff*.

I would have pointed out the coincidence to Hyperia, but Healy chose then to join us, and from the expression on his face, he'd bet on the chestnut to win.

Of course he had.

"Nobody will dun you for debts of honor," I said as Healy trudged at my side back to the manor house. The second race had been run at a nearly sedate pace, until the dash for the finish, when the favorite filly had pulled out a victory by a nose.

The steeplechase had finished without injury to horse or jockey— the definition of a successful race, according to Piggott and St. Just— and Hyperia had been swept into Wickley's coterie. She'd left her fan with me, which would make a handy pretext for me to seek her out prior to supper.

Clever lady. Dear, clever lady, who might be lost to me because of Healy West's gormless schemes.

"Debts of honor are to be paid the most swiftly of all," Healy retorted. "A gentleman is as a gentleman does."

A gentleman did not steal his sister's security. "We have plenty more races yet to go, and you might yet win back what you've lost. When does St. George have his first outing?"

"Not till next week."

When the big races were run, the ones with substantial purses. *Idiot, idiot, idiot.* "You didn't want to give him a canter over the course in a hurdle race for practice?"

Healy tugged at his limp cravat. "He practices running up on the Downs, Caldicott, like all the other runners."

St. George was a jumper, not merely a runner. "Have you walked the course?"

"I just got here! One needs to recover from his travels, for pity's sake. I'll walk the course this evening, when the sun has eased off and all the lads and grooms are busy in the yard. Honestly, Caldicott, I wasn't born yesterday."

I wanted to plant him a facer, because having stolen Hyperia's last groat, her pride, and her future, Healy still managed to muster a thorough pout.

"West, I have seen your finances. Where did you locate the blunt for the stakes involved in next week's contests?"

"Backers, Caldicott. St. George's abilities have inspired backers, and you are not my nanny. I vow, I do not know what Hyperia sees in you."

"Neither do I, but one doesn't argue with a lady. Just know that if you get into a spot of bother, I am the next thing you have to family, and you may call upon me for assistance in any regard. I'll bid you good evening."

I quickened my pace, still wanting to plant him a facer, also to trip him, wash his face with dust, and think up a nasty nickname for him in the best schoolboy tradition. West rhymed with pest, distressed, infest, inquest—that one had possibilities—undressed, detest...

"You saw the first race." Tenneby caught up with me on my march back to the manor, though I had set a good pace. "My lord, tell me you saw the finish to the first race."

"I did. The chestnut wasn't up to the distance in this heat, apparently."

"That chestnut, Juliet, can go for miles at a blazing pace. She's local and hacked over after a gallop last week. She's rested. She's, if anything, better suited to the longer distances, and she should have won that race."

"You bet on her too? I believe West is in the same leaky boat. My condolences. Is Minerva really so lacking in talent?"

"Minerva is a steady performer, but she's a front-runner. Gets to the head of the pack and tries to stay there. Juliet has more than enough bottom to best her over three hilly miles. That's why Juliet was the favorite."

The day had been long and not all that enjoyable, but for time spent with Hyperia. For her sake, I summoned more patience. "Favorites often lose."

I set myself to play devil's advocate, though the exercise would doubtless be unpleasant. The last thing the race meeting needed was Tenneby reeling with conviction that wrong had been done, and not a shred of evidence to support his accusations.

If nothing else, I might argue him into keeping his conclusions to himself for a time.

"Favorites lose about twice as often as they win," he said, "but Juliet was more than a favorite—she was a certain winner. Everybody knew it except Pierpont, apparently. At least he was humble in victory, as well he should have been."

"You just said that naming a horse as a favorite tilts the odds *away* from that horse winning, Tenneby. Perhaps Minerva deals more effectively with the heat, or was better rested, or better ridden. I realize the finish put you in mind of Epsom. A good, fast horse poised to win is nearly becalmed at the moment when she should have been pushing for the post. A sad spectacle."

"Not sad, Caldicott. Crooked."

I spied St. Just and Piggott walking ahead of us, and though I was weary, I resumed my faster pace. "Do you accuse Pierpont?"

"Of course not. He was simply lucky. Somebody set out to make Juliet lose, though, and they succeeded. I want you to find out how, lest the same thing happen again next week."

"I'm to find out how, but not to frequent the stable after dark, when the mischief is likely perpetrated. When every guest you've invited as well as their grooms, jockeys, sisters, wives, and valets have a motive for tossing the races. When the whole meeting will be over in ten days. It's not like you're asking me to find fifteen thousand French soldiers on the Spanish plain, Tenneby."

"Even I could do that."

That little outing had taken me weeks and seen me facing death twice. "Without getting killed on the way back to report what you'd seen? Right. Child's play. A lark, a mere frolic. A gentleman's eccentric though harmless pastime." I was graduating from testy to angry, and St. Just glanced over his shoulder at me, then dropped back to my side.

"This heat makes one irritable," he said. "The change has come on too fast and too soon. The horses don't like it either."

"The heat," Tenneby said with the air of one ready to repeat an entire sermon at volume, "did not throw the first race."

"Nothing threw the first race," St. Just said, quite calmly. "Juliet wasn't sufficiently accustomed to a downhill finish. Downhill finishes can be blazingly fast, and she exceeded her own limits pushing a habitual front-runner that hard. She's a fine animal, with many victories ahead of her, but her owner failed to train her for this particular course. A common oversight."

I could never in a thousand race meets have come up with that reasoning. I doubted another horseman in all of England could have.

Tenneby regarded St. Just owlishly. "The downhill finish did Juliet in?"

"That is my considered opinion. You watch the gallops on the Downs every morning, Tenneby. How often are the horses asked for their maximum effort on a downhill slope? Almost never, because we want to strengthen their hindquarters and test their wind by galloping them *uphill*. The well-rounded horse must be asked for both sorts of efforts, just as they must be run on both left- and right-handed courses. Jockeys understand that much, but they don't care for a downhill rush—takes more skill—especially for an early morning training gallop when the grass is wet, and we cannot blame them for that."

Entire vistas of training possibilities were opening before Tenne-by's wondering eyes. "A downhill finish. Quite fast. I see what you mean. Very interesting, St. Just. A cavalryman's seasoned perspective, doubtless. I don't suppose you've shared these notions with the other owners?"

"They haven't asked for my opinion, Tenneby, and I doubt they will. Besides, I'm leaving the day after tomorrow, and the issue is unlikely to arise before I depart. Everybody thinks Wellington always sought the high ground for the sake of his artillery, but his choice of ground also forced the enemy's cavalry to charge uphill, if they survived long enough to mount such an attack. Ask the French cuirassiers how well that went for them at Waterloo."

At Waterloo, the exhausted French cavalry, galloping uphill time after time and having to navigate ground turned to muck by heavy rains, had been mowed down like summer wheat. The memory put yet another blight on a challenging day.

"Very interesting, St. Just," Tenneby said. "Fascinating what you military chaps know. Perhaps we can chat more about this before supper? In fact, I insist upon it. I must have a word with my grooms at the moment, but please do plan on joining me for a drink before the meal." He touched the brim of his hat with one finger and jaunted off toward the stable yard.

"Thank you," I said as we took the lane that led to the manor house. "From one military chap to another. He was ringing a peel over my head for the finish to the first race. Do I conclude that some-body tampered with the horse?"

"What do you think?" St. Just put the question neutrally, so I did the only thing I knew to do and reviewed what evidence I had.

"The race was fixed. The objective was not necessarily for Minerva to win—though she was the second favorite—but to make Juliet lose, which she did."

"And you base this conclusion upon what facts?"

St. Just had doubtless been present when many a reconnaissance officer had reported to his superiors what had been observed in the field. After the facts had been summarized, the speculation began. What did it mean that the French were buying up horses? What was the significance of this or that general nipping into Madrid for a week?

"The heat should be affecting all the horses more or less the same. They are in good health, pampered by equine standards, and kept in top condition. Juliet has excellent conformation, the will to win, and a reputation for stamina."

"And?"

I thought back to the chestnut mare, faltering from canter to trot, head low, as the rest of the field had rushed past her.

"She was *bewildered*, St. Just. The horse herself didn't know why she could not continue running, but she simply could not. She had no more fuel to throw on the fire."

"That was my sense. Doped, would be my guess, but earlier in the race, I saw no evidence that she'd been drugged. She was ready to run, eager for her chance, very much on her mettle. I've seen horses dosed with a touch of somnifera, and the listlessness is evident shortly after the drug is administered. The symptoms increase thereafter, as inebriation becomes more evident with a sot. Juliet wasn't showing any signs of drugging at the start."

"She wasn't showing any signs of drugging for the whole first circuit of the course and right up to the last push."

St. Just cast a look back toward the racecourse. Stragglers, some none too steady on their pins, toddled along the lane, as did grooms slowly leading spent runners back to the stable yard.

"The race was fixed," I said. "Whoever is tossing these races knows exactly what they're doing. As I uncover one scheme, they hatch another. Tacks under the saddle, midnight gallops, now some sort of drugging. Tenneby's worst fears are coming to pass, and I have been powerless to intervene."

"Not powerless, just one step behind."

"Horse races can be won or lost by a nose, St. Just, and I am losing this one."

"You have some time to gain ground. The significant purses don't start until next week, and the colts' races the day after tomorrow should mostly be sightseeing tours of the course."

"Today was supposed to be a friendly outing for the mares who didn't run earlier in the week." Another thought occurred to me. "Is it true that Wickley and Pierpont both travel with their dueling pistols?"

St. Just cursed in his native tongue. Something about testicles and playthings for Saint Brigid's cats. "If one of those nincompoops hauls his Mantons about, so does the other."

"Hyperia frowns on dueling."

"Good. So do I. I frown on horse racing, come to that. Let's find the punchbowls tucked away in that corner parlor. I'm parched."

So was I, now that St. Just mentioned thirst. "You are bound for Yorkshire?"

"I am. Not a frolic, a duty, and one I am all too tempted to shirk." So he'd make himself see to the situation dealt with, whatever it was. "I wish I hadn't mentioned Waterloo to Tenneby."

For St. Just, that was a heartfelt confession. "I had a bad moment when the fillies thundered past. Expected to hear the order to fire at any moment."

He nodded as we gained the house. "Your guts clench, you can hear your heart beat in your petrified ears, and you wish to God... Well, none of that. We're at peace, by heaven. My own ducal father insists that it's so."

"As does my ducal brother." We both had two servings of cider, and still I felt worn out and frustrated by the day's events. My head throbbed from all the bright sunshine, Hyperia was threatening to jilt me once the meet was over, and Healy was heaping foolishness atop desperation.

"You could come to Yorkshire with me," St. Just said when he'd drained his second tankard. "Just a thought."

"I cannot abandon the mission, St. Just, much less abandon Miss West, or her clodpated brother, but thank you for the offer."

"The whole sport is clodpated," St. Just said, going to the windows that looked out over grass turning brown in the park. "I understand cavalry officers indulging in a steeplechase or two to keep their mounts fit or to alleviate boredom. But all this wagering…"

"I know. And Tenneby is in some ways the worst among them, hoping that this venture will bring his finances right, when the whole business can be rigged six different ways."

"Oh, at least." On that cheering observation, St. Just decamped.

I poured myself a third serving, took it to the terrace, and considered what avenues of inquiry remained to me that wouldn't earn me a thrashing, or worse.

CHAPTER THIRTEEN

"I saw that race," the farrier said, gesturing with a pipe on the dusty square of ground outside his smithy. "Damnedest thing. I like Juliet. She's not simply a fast horse, she's a lady. Good temperament, and to the man who's responsible for putting on and pulling off her dancing slippers, that matters."

Caleb Bean, like many in his profession, was a sizable specimen. In addition to height, he had massively developed musculature over the arms, shoulders, and chest. He was clean-shaven, flaxen-haired and possessed of Nordic blue eyes.

"I'd rather chat in the smithy, if you don't mind." I was squeezing in this conversation when most of the other guests were either changing for supper or loitering in the stable yard. St. Just's theory regarding training that ignored the need to practice downhill finishes was likely changing the future of racing, at least in this corner of Berkshire.

Bless him for his quick thinking. Curse the duty that drew him to Yorkshire. My own mental processes had slowed to a plod, and the only next step that had occurred to me was a chat with what passed for the local horse doctor.

"Perhaps your lordship doesn't want to be seen poking around yet again?" Bean wiggled pale eyebrows. "The grooms were grumbling about you, but then, that lot lives to grumble." He ambled with me back into the dim confines of his workplace. The space was ventilated by a couple of open windows—one low, one near the ceiling, doubtless the better to create a draft.

The only light source other than the windows was the forge and its glowing bed of coals. Smithies were kept dim by design, because the precise color—and therefore temperature—of a metal heating or cooling was easier to discern in low light. The walls were a tool box writ large, with every manner of hammer, tongs, rasp, testers, hoofpicks, and more arrayed on tidy rows of nails.

"I am happy to be seen talking to you, Mr. Bean," I replied, "but bright sunshine bothers my eyes, and we've had nothing but sunshine for days and days."

"Hence your blue specs." He took out a square nail from a pocket of his leather apron and scraped at the bowl of his pipe. "Juliet deserved to win that race, to shine before her home folks. I've not seen a horse falter as she did, at least not in a race."

"I asked St. Just for his opinion, and he was stumped. He said drugs would not have taken effect like that, after two and a half miles of good effort. I've wondered about the feedstuffs, but haven't dared to inquire too closely."

"The owners generally bring their own fodder and keep it under lock and key. Your lordship had best not temp fate by poking into oak sacks or sniffing the fodder."

Bean tapped the dottle from his pipe onto his coals, where it crackled and turned to smoke. "Juliet didn't look drugged. Anybody with sense will drug a colt prior to gelding him. A touch of the poppy and the poor lad doesn't feel the cut, nor object to the operation. If a horse is particularly high-strung, we might do the same for his first few outings to the forge, though a drugged horse can also be a horse easily spooked."

I propped a hip against a stone water trough. "You're saying Juliet's gaze was focused. She was alert to sounds and movement around her." I'd observed that much.

"Aye, and she wasn't getting snorty and proppy. She wasn't going all hot and cranky like some noxious weed was disagreeing with her, though as to that, most noxious weeds are slow poisons."

"You know your business."

The grin was in evidence again, this time a bit wistful. "Horses have been my world since I was a wee lad. I wanted to be a jockey. Alas for dear little me. Papa was a stable master, my uncle was a farrier, so I took to the forge. My missus is as good a blacksmith as I'll ever be—she comes from a long line of smiths up near Oxford—and we're bringing our children up in the trade. I dearly hope they don't end up working for the racing set, though."

"Why is that?"

Bean produced a pouch, thumbed some tobacco into his pipe, and used the square end of the nail to tamp it down.

"Woglemuth says you served under Wellington. Denton says you were nearly drummed out of the corps, but he seems to respect you for it."

"I did serve under Wellington. I was nearly drummed out of the corps. You would have to apply to Denton directly to gain his opinion of me."

Bean used a taper to light his pipe, puffed gently, and cradled the bowl in his massive palm. "You don't fit in with them, with Tenneby and his supposed racing friends."

Bean didn't fit in as a typical blacksmith either, or the usual caricature of one. He was neither dark, nor obnoxiously merry, nor unkempt. His speech was educated, and he chose his words with care.

"Tenneby asked me to attend," I said, "because I have a talent for sorting out mischief, albeit usually after the fact, while his situation calls for preventing mischief. In this regard, I have been a singular failure."

"This lot,"—Bean gestured with his chin toward the manor house

—"wouldn't be caught dead admitting failure. They wager fortunes as if money grows in every hedge just for the picking. You think the racehorses are pampered, and for the present, that might be true. But where will these youngsters be in two years?"

"Some of them will be racing over fences?"

"Aye, until they wreck at some bullfinch or hedge on a sloppy day. The mares, if they're fast and lucky, will have a few babies, but the best that most of the colts can look forward to is gelding and a few years in the hunt field. The rest will end up in the knacker's yard because they are too fine-boned and hotblooded for anything but the racecourse. It's a waste of a good animal, to breed only for speed, my lord. If you think about it for two seconds, you'll reach the same conclusion."

He was angry, harboring the slow rage of one impotent to right a wrong.

"That's why Juliet's defeat bothers you so? Because she has speed, stamina, *and* a calm temperament?"

"Aye. She should be bred to champion studs. More to the point, she should be retired from racing before she's ruined. She's proved her abilities already, but her owner will send her off to Newmarket, where she'll be expected to win a fortune or die trying. Only if she survives that ordeal will she be allowed to join the broodmares."

"I thought Sir Albertus owned her. He seems a decent sort." A decent sort who'd all but asked me to leave the gathering.

"Juliet is owned by Mrs. Trelawny, the old vicar's widow. She's put the horse in Sir Albertus's keeping, and he's not the worst of the lot by any means, but neither is he in Tenneby's league. If I might pay my employer a sideways compliment, he puts the horses first, and that rare integrity will mean his downfall among the racing brethren. Too many of them are far more concerned with purses, wagers, and victory, than with the lowly beast who does the hardest work."

Another philosophical puff of the pipe.

The conversation had ruled out noxious weeds or poisoning and confirmed my hunch that Juliet's defeat had been by design. Not much progress, but some.

As if we'd summoned him, Sir Albertus loomed in the doorway to the smithy, a dark shadow against the late afternoon sun.

"Exactly what is my lord doing here?"

Bean set his pipe on the edge of the stone trough. "His lordship's gelding will need new shoes before the journey home. The more notice I have for such extra tasks, the more likely I am to get the job done timely. What can I do for you, Sir Albertus?"

Atlas did not need new shoes.

"I want you to look at Juliet's shoes. They seem sound enough to me, and she's trotting up sound, but her performance today was disappointing. Pierpont is quietly rubbing it in, offering to buy her for a quarter of her value. I am ensuring that next week Juliet will be first past the post."

Pity offers. I'd bought Atlas out of pity for his previous owner, an officer down on his luck who hadn't the coin for passage home. What a fortunate day for me that had been.

"Juliet's shoes are fine," Bean said, using the bellows on the coals. "I check the next day's runners the night before they race. Unless she found a way to loosen a shoe while dozing in her stall, you can't blame her defeat on me."

Bean nonetheless took a pair of hoof testers, a file, and a mallet down from the wall and eased past Sir Albertus, who would insist on remaining in the doorway.

"You'd best not be seen here alone, my lord. The lads are already wondering why you were lurking in the stable at night, and now they'll be wondering why you'd privately consult Bean after an inexplicable upset."

I rose from the stone trough, dusted off my backside, and took my time going to the door. "Is that not the nature of an upset, Sir Albertus? They are inexplicable by definition, though I'm told Minerva was the second favorite. And who exactly will pass along to the lads that I'm asking Bean to reset Altas's shoes? You're the only person to see me here, besides Bean himself."

We joined the blacksmith who busied himself studying the ground, though I suspected he was enjoying the exchange.

"They watch, those lads." Sir Albertus tramped away from the smithy. "They see everything, and they will know you came here. I won't have to tell them anything."

"I agree they are observant, so why aren't you asking *them* what they think of Juliet's disappointing performance? I'm sure they all have theories, and their opinions will be better informed than mine could ever be. Bean, my thanks. You'll find Atlas to be *a perfect gentleman*."

Sir Albertus inhaled through his nose. "Of all the cheek. Bean, I'll see you in the stable yard." Off he went, exuding the air of one who had been denied an opportunity to kick the hapless dog.

"Is he sweet on the widow?" I asked.

Bean considered the baronet's retreating figure. "My lord speculates in a direction familiar to all the local ladies, including my wife. Supposedly, Sir Albertus has added Juliet to his string to honor the late vicar's wishes. Nobody expected her to shine as brightly as she does— as she did. But horses are expensive on a good day, and racehorses are extremely expensive. Why take on that bother when the mare could have been put in work as a hack or bred to produce saddle horses?"

"And now, Sir Albertus will look foolish before the woman he was trying to impress. Splendid. Why can't horse racing just be a matter of horse racing?"

Bean sighted down the length of his rasp. "It can. Today's steeplechase was all in good fun, but that's not what gets the brotherhood of the turf to Newmarket. Tenneby is too decent for them, really, but he's too stubborn to cut his losses."

"If the earldom goes bankrupt, what will you do?"

Bean stuffed the rasp into a pocket that looked designed to hold that particular tool. "Emigrate. I can make a living anywhere that life involves horses, as long as I have my tools. Since the war ended, the government has turned mean. Lord Liverpool's tariffs on foreign grain will see the peasantry starved for the sake of the gentry—and when English peasants starve, we tend to riot and revolt, usually to no avail.

"Even Tenneby," he went on, starting for the stable yard, "a basically decent man, can't admit the truth. He says the Corn Laws will safeguard English merchants from unfair competition. Bollocks to that. I have children to consider. A government that allows my children to starve while Wickley and his ilk bet a thousand pounds for an afternoon's diversion... My wife would scold me for getting above myself."

"I am not your wife."

"I don't want to leave England, but neither will I tie my fate to that of a man gone turf mad. When the old earl goes to his reward, I will likely gather up my tools and my family and seek a foreign shore."

Hence his slightly disrespectful attitude. He would soon muster out, so to speak, and his regard for the established order of his present situation was eroding apace.

"Best of luck to you," I said, holding out a hand. "If a character from a courtesy lord will aid your cause, don't hesitate to let me know."

I'd surprised him. I'd surprised myself, too, but Bean had given me covering fire with Sir Albertus's attempts to interrogate me.

Then too, Arthur took a dim view of the Corn Laws and thought Britain ought to make up in shipping revenue what it was losing in agricultural revenue. The population in England was growing quickly while our arable land was, if anything, shrinking. In Arthur's mind, that put the country on a collision course with starvation, which was a short step away from revolution.

None of which told me why Juliet had so spectacularly lost her race.

"One more question, Bean. You said you'd never seen a foot-sound racehorse precipitously fade like that on a course before. Have you seen it happen to other horses?"

"I have. Saw it once myself. Heard of the same thing happening to another horse, both coach horses. They were trotting along with the team one moment, then stumbling, then able to move at only a walk. No lameness, no swelling, no inability to flex joints. It's as if the wind dropped from their sails, and all they had left was inertia to get them into port."

"Did the condition progress?"

"No. Both were fine the next day and right back in the traces."

We parted, though I was more puzzled than when I'd left the racecourse earlier in the afternoon. If a horse could somehow be made to falter halfway around a racecourse, then somebody stood to make a deal great of money and others to lose just as much.

But how in blazes was the horse tampered with, and by whom?

"I miss Lady Ophelia," I said, passing Hyperia her glass of punch. "Godmama would be right at home among this crowd."

I missed St. Just, too, though I'd seen him off only that morning. He'd promised to write and let me know of developments in York-shire. He'd quit the race meeting with the sort of reluctance officers tried to hide when they were posted to a new and less appealing billet.

The last set of first-week races had drawn a larger group of spectators than either of the previous outings. Distant neighbors, a few owners at loose ends from the vicinity of Windsor and the royal race-course at Ascot, perhaps even a bored lordling or two escaping the London Season. The local inns would enjoy the additional custom, but Tenneby did not look to be enjoying his own gathering.

Mine host paced about behind the starting line, doubtless trying to be everywhere at once and failing miserably. Denton was there as well, exchanging good-natured shoves with Pierpont's man, Hercules.

Sir Albertus towered over Chalmers and gestured to various points on the course.

"Her ladyship would know everybody's pedigree," Hyperia replied, "also the scandals throughout those pedigrees. What do you think she'd say about Lord Pierpont?"

"He needs to make an appointment with his barber before all that curl-tossing dislocates his neck." I accepted my glass of punch from the smirking footman wielding the ladle. "Let's find some shade, shall we?"

We made our way among the throng, some of whom were on shooting stools, some of whom were on blankets. Others were milling about the viewing structure, while many more stood in line before the punchbowls.

"Tenneby is running Excalibur later today," Hyperia said. "Expect that's half the draw for this crowd. I wish it wasn't so hot. The horses aren't used to these temperatures so early in the year."

Some of the horses would still be sporting the last of their winter coats, though Thoroughbreds tended not to grow as shaggy as their plow horse cousins.

"I wish I could spend this afternoon napping." I'd continued intermittent nighttime patrols of the stables, though I'd heard no more muffled hoofbeats and seen no more midnight riders. Atticus had reported no suspicious activity, and yet, Juliet's defeat lingered on everybody's mind.

"Julian, shouldn't you be among the owners and runners behind the starting line? If somebody is up to no good, that's their last opportunity to interfere with a horse."

The first race was for three-year-old colts only, the young fellows who'd learned the ropes and were ready to show the world how to run a race. They were fit, eager, and fast, also dangerous when upset or riled in confined circumstances.

"We can see the starting line quite well from here."

Wickley appeared at Hyperia's side. "Care for a small wager, Miss West? Ten pounds says Golden Sovereign leaves them all in the dust, which applies literally, thanks to our present weather. Golden is Remedy's half-brother, and every bit as impressive."

Hyperia patted his sleeve. "I'll keep my money, though I'm sure your colt will do splendidly. Ten pounds is rather more than I'm comfortable risking on a horse race."

He leaned nearer to her. "Pierpont has wagered a thousand against my Cleopatra in Monday's opening contest. Considers himself the reigning expert on the equine distaff, you know, and says Cleo has already peaked, but then, he would say that."

Hyperia did not oblige his lordship with a polite riposte. "*A thousand pounds? On a single race?*"

"Ten thousand is nothing on a hotly contested match, Miss West. The denizens of the turf know how to take a risk. Win today, lose tomorrow, and keep your head either way. By week's end, the wagers will boggle your mind. What of you, Lord Julian? Are you inclined to chance a few quid on a runner?"

"No, thank you. I comprehend the need to take a risk from time to time, but it's the why of it at a race meet that puzzles me. Risk your life to defeat Boney? That makes sense. He was choking England's commerce with his Continental System and pillaging his way from Cairo to Copenhagen. Risk your fortune and the livelihoods of all who depend on you for the sake of...? What, exactly, Wickley? What drives a man to such a reckless flirtation with ruin over a mere horse race?"

Wickley regarded me evenly. "Perhaps you refer to Tenneby? He's the only fellow here peering into the depths of the River Tick. We must afford him some understanding, my lord. He believes himself to have been wronged at Epsom, and he has some grounds for that belief."

Wickley had dropped the insouciant air and was regarding the growing chaos behind the starting line. "Tenneby is making a last desperate charge, my lord, and surely even you can understand that. We respect him for it, even as we try our best to defeat him. That's the nature of the sport."

Behind the starting line, Wickley's chestnut was propping and dancing, wheeling willy-nilly into other competitors despite Denton's attempts to settle the horse.

"Good Lord," Hyperia said. "Jules, please get down there before somebody is mortally injured."

I had no idea what she expected me to do, but I passed Wickley my drink and sallied forth. When nobody else seemed willing to take on the task, I grasped Golden Sovereign's reins near the bit and shook my finger in his face.

"You are setting a poor example for the enlisted men, young sir. Settle your feathers, or the starter will disqualify you for conduct unbecoming."

"Been tellin' him that," Denton said as the horse followed me to the starting line, his steps gingerly and his ears pricked. "He'll leave all his fire in the saddling enclosure, rate he's going. Foolishness I expect out of a two-year-old."

I produced a bit of carrot left over from my morning call on Atlas. "Is he too wound up, Denton? Worse than usual?"

"Naw. Bigger crowd. All the ladies waving their fans. He likes you."

The chestnut was a handsome young devil of about sixteen-two hands. Elegant, glossy, muscular, and lean, he was another epitome of the George Stubbs ideal. I patted his neck as he crunched the little bit of carrot into oblivion.

Dasher came up on Golden Sovereign's right, and I pretended to fish in my pocket for another treat.

"Best hop it, my lord," Denton muttered. "Starter might actually give the signal before the wash dries."

I patted both horses and ducked under the railing that separated the course from the spectators. Why hadn't Wickley bothered to see to his own horse, and was Golden Sovereign merely excited, or had he been somehow interfered with, such that he'd end up plodding across the finish line?

I made my way up the hill to where I'd left Hyperia and Wickley and instead found Healy West, swilling punch and smiling fatuously at Miss Evelyn Tenneby.

"This lady knows her horses," Healy said. "She says my George has perfect conformation for a jumper."

"He does," Miss Tenneby said, "but one needs speed, agility, timing, luck, and stamina for that conformation to mean anything on a racecourse. A brave and competent jockey figures prominently into the equation as well. My lord, has Wickley promoted you to head groom? I saw you calming Golden Sovereign. He's more hot-tempered than Sovereign Remedy, though Wickley says he's also faster."

If Wickley had bet a thousand pounds on Monday's race for the fillies, how much was riding on today's performance by his skittish colt?

"I was merely being helpful at Miss West's insistence, though I seem to have lost track of her. The heat makes the owners and jockeys fractious, and that communicates itself to the horses."

"Precisely," Miss Tenneby said, slapping her closed fan against her gloved palm. "The horses would be perfectly calm if the humans would be perfectly calm. But there's my brother, along with half the owners, grooms, passing vagabonds, sightseers, and—"

"They're off!" Healy shouted, rather unnecessarily.

Miss Tenneby produced a pair of field glasses and fell silent.

I was more prepared for the spectacle of a dozen horses, each weighing better than half a ton, galloping up the hill at more than thirty miles an hour. They thundered into the first turn all in a bunch, and that spacing held for the whole first circuit of the course.

Golden Sovereign was among the front-runners, trading the lead off with a bay and a lean gray. The pace was quick to my eye, but then, what did I know of racing paces?

"The second uphill will sort them out," Miss Tenneby muttered. "They can't keep this up in this heat."

The leaders pulled away, or the back of the field fell behind, on the second ascent. Denton had maneuvered Golden Sovereign to the rail, which meant a shorter circuit than horses to the outside had to travel. Golden Sovereign, running second, pulled even with the gray, then ahead by a nose.

The crowd was on its feet, yelling madly as the two horses approached the final declivity before the run in to the finish. The third-place bay was holding on gamely, perhaps saving something for the final push, and then... the bay was running second.

The smooth, pounding rhythm of Golden Sovereign's gallop slowed to the three-beat tattoo of the canter and then faltered further, until the horse was approximating the gait of a rocking horse, despite Denton applying the crop smartly twice. The pack thundered past Golden Sovereign, and when he was once again visible, he stood, head down, sides heaving.

Denton took his feet out of the stirrups, gave the horse a kick in the ribs, and the miserable creature shuffled forward.

"Poor lad ran out of puff," Healy said. "Glad I didn't bet on him. Wickley will be out a packet, and he'd hoped to send Golden to stud, you know. Lots of money to be made, standing a stud." He rattled on, about Eclipse's stud fees, and then old Tattersall making a mint off of Herod, and how Pierpont must be gloating.

Miss Tenneby was apparently so absorbed with the spectacle before us that she didn't bother correcting him. Tattersall had made his fortune standing *Highflyer* at stud, not Herod, who had the honor to be Highflyer's sire.

"This wasn't supposed to happen," Miss Tenneby said, jamming her field glasses into her reticule. "Friday was supposed to be a fluke. The heat, the challenge of the terrain, Juliet having an off day. That mare has never had an off day in her life. Golden Sovereign might not have been the favorite, but he shouldn't have been hobbled like this."

She spoke figuratively, of course, but the same tone of disbelief and dismay ran through the conversations all around us.

"Damned strange, if you ask me."

"Wickley will cry foul, mark me on this."

"Reminds me of Tenneby's bad luck at Epsom two years ago. No, three years ago. Made quite a fuss about it."

"Who won?" Healy asked.

"The gray. Moonglow." Miss Tenneby was confident, though we hadn't been able to see the finish from our vantage point. "The bay hasn't the bottom to overtake a steady performer like that. Moonglow gets stronger as he runs, at least over three miles. He settles into a rhythm, and his jockey can rate him to an inch. The bay is a young three, and in a race like this, that shows. We should never have started racing Thoroughbreds younger than five. My brother will be beside himself."

"Let's find him," I said. "Healy, if you locate your sister, please give her my regards and a promise to see her at supper."

As Miss Tenneby and I moved through the crowd, I heard more muttering and speculation. The mood was sour and suspicious, as well it should have been.

"Lord Julian." Sir Albertus inserted himself onto my path, causing Miss Tenneby to halt beside me. "I want a word with you."

I did not want a word with him. "Ladies present, Sir Albertus."

He blinked, then nodded at Miss Tenneby. "Miss Tenneby will excuse us."

"No," the lady said, "she will not. Lord Julian is my escort, and I am not giving him up for your convenience, Sir Albertus. Whatever you have to say, you can say it before me or save it for a more private situation."

She was small but formidable and the nominal hostess of the gathering. Sir Albertus tried glowering and got nowhere with it.

"I know what you're about to say." I kept my voice down, because Sir Albertus was doubtless determined to make a spectacle of the discussion. "You saw me among the runners, chatting with Denton and leading Golden Sovereign to the starting line."

"I most certainly did, and I saw you slip something into that horse's mouth, and then we have this abject farce coming into the finish. You were present on Friday when my Juliet ended up in the same condition, and I wasn't about to let you move among the runners without keeping a very close eye on you."

Juliet, in the strictest sense, wasn't *his*. Now did not seem the time to quibble over details.

"You saw his lordship feed Golden a bite of carrot," Miss Tenneby said. "I had my field glasses trained on the start, and I know a carrot when I see one."

"A drugged carrot, then," Sir Albertus said. "A carrot hollowed out to hide some foul weed or tincture of mischief. If nobody else here will hold this meddler accountable, I will see to it."

He would have slapped me, but I jerked my head back out of range. One didn't outgrow schoolyard reflexes.

"No blow has been landed," I said, "and no challenge will be accepted, because I have no need to face death for lending a hand behind the starting line. Miss West urged me to it, and Wickley was standing beside her at the time. It's his colt who suffered a defeat, and if there's a complaint to be made, I will hear it from him."

A circle of gawkers was forming around us, and that circle included both gentlemen and ladies.

"I demand satisfaction," Sir Albertus roared. "Twice now, the best horse hasn't won, and both times, you have been implicated. Your dishonorable reputation precedes you, and if Tenneby won't—"

I took a step forward. "Enough. I am an expert, Sir Albertus, with small arms and long guns. I have shot to kill my fellow man more often than you've brought down grouse, and I've hit my target more often than not. I fed the horse *a carrot* from the supply in the stable yard. Denton was in the saddle and saw everything. Speak to him and speak to Miss West and Wickley. Gather your facts before you make accusations you'll regret."

Hyperia had forbidden me to duel, but the temptation to brawl, to drop this posturing dolt with a hard right... but no. Ladies were present. I also wanted to inspect Golden Sovereign, to have Bean inspect him, and to talk to Denton somewhere private.

"Listen to his lordship, Sir Albertus," Miss Tenneby said. "Consider St. Just's theory, that we don't train our horses on downhill finishes. Consider the heat and leave it to Lord Wickley to raise difficult questions. Excuse us."

I bowed before offering Miss Tenneby my arm. The crowd grew quiet and parted for us, and through the stillness, I heard raised voices from the direction of the rubbing-down house.

"You will excuse me, Miss Tenneby. I'll see you at supper, and thank you."

She looked as if she wanted to follow me, but I made my about-face and departed quick time. Another day, another accusation of dishonor. I was so angry by the time I reached the rubbing-down house that the least provocation would have inspired me to dire foolishness.

Dire foolishness indeed.

CHAPTER FOURTEEN

Fortunately for the king's peace and my life expectancy, Hyperia was on hand at the rubbing-down house. Wickley paced as if delivering a third-act soliloquy at high volume, Tenneby and Hyperia watched him, and grooms and horses coming and going from the building seemed intent on ignoring the whole performance.

"Golden should have won," Wickley said. "By God, that colt should have won. He was gaining on Moonglow, and that his victory was snatched from him by subterfuge is the most unsporting thing I have ever seen."

"No," I said, "it isn't. You might have lost a few thousand pounds on the match—money you can afford to lose—but at Epsom, you saw Tenneby lose *twenty-eight thousand* pounds to the same sort of mischief, and that result was his near ruin. Cease your yelling now, and let's see what we can learn from the victim himself."

Wickley looked at me as if I'd sprouted a tail, horns, and cloven hooves. "Go away. On second, thought, don't move. You were behind the starting line and behaving very familiarly with my horse. Explain yourself."

Viginti, undeviginti, duodeviginti... "You yourself heard Miss

West ask me to lend a hand when your colt was behaving badly. You heard her with your own ears, Wickley. You held my drink while I succeeded in settling your horse, and you made off with my punch, I might add. If you require further explanations, I am happy to make them, but not here. Two more races are to be run today, and half of creation has its field glasses trained on us at this moment. Sir Albertus has already made quite the scene, and my patience is fast eroding."

"Your patience!" Tenneby came to life like a cuckoo clock chiming the hour. "Your patience! This is *my* race meeting, my chance to redeem the family fortunes, and twice now, a horse in top condition has been barely able to complete the course, much less prevail as predicted. This is worse than I could have imagined, Lord Julian, and your one purpose here, your one reason for attending, was to ensure that this exact problem did not arise."

What a convenient and inaccurate sense of recall he enjoyed. "Tenneby, you arguably insult my intended. Please clarify: Are you asking me to leave?" Now that I probably should quit the scene, I didn't want to. Somebody was making a fool of me, fleecing a lot of popinjays, and foiling Tenneby's grand scheme to gallop his way to solvency. That was all quite depressing and annoying, et cetera and so forth.

But what about Golden, a good young fellow who'd tried his heart out, and for all I knew, today's performance would see him trotted off to the knacker's yard. Juliet might fare no better, though as Bean had pointed out, she was a lovely creature with many fine qualities.

Excalibur would be the next horse to suffer ill usage, I was nearly certain of it. He'd already been sent home in disgrace once for losing a battle he hadn't been equipped to fight. That Tenneby, Miss Tenneby, and an entire household of servants would share the next disgrace bothered me, but the disrespect to the horses, the manipulation of them as if they were nothing more than chattel to be rearranged on a whim, offended me sorely.

Hyperia ceased rummaging in her reticule and took the place

beside me. "His lordship has asked after your continued hospitality, Mr. Tenneby. A reasonable question, when it was you and you alone who prevailed upon his lordship to come in the first place. I flatter myself that my Lord Julian sought some pleasant time in my company, but his efforts since arriving have been bent upon keeping the races honest."

Denton emerged from the rubbing-down house, a wet, weary Golden Sovereign on the lead line behind him.

"Let's have a look at the horse," I said, because time was of the essence. "If he's been drugged, the sooner he's examined, the more likely we are to see the symptoms. Caleb Bean's opinion should be sought immediately."

"Bean?" Tenneby said. "My farrier?"

"And part-time horse doctor. Wickley, look him over. Listen to his gut sounds, make sure his pupils contract when you shade them with your hand—it takes longer than you think, but the reflex should manifest. Pull his tail either direction and see if he staggers." These were basic diagnostics any senior groom knew to undertake when a horse turned up listless or off his feed.

"Please do," Hyperia said. "We might learn something of value. His lordship served among cavalry officers who worshipped all things equine." She extracted her fan from her reticule, unfolded it, and began a languid motion beneath her chin.

The voice of reason was apparently audible to Wickley when the words came from a sensible female. He set about examining his horse, Denton murmured to another lad to fetch Bean, and I stood back, trying not to be furious with Tenneby.

He was more loyal to his horses than he was to somebody trying to prevent disaster from parking on his damned doorstep.

Wickley's examination revealed no symptoms of poisoning. Bean's slower, more formal measures reached the same result.

"Not poison," Bean said as the call went out for the runners in the second race to assemble. "Not a poison I've seen or read about, in any case. I've discussed Juliet's defeat with my wife, whose pedigree as a farrier goes back generations, and she's equally confounded. We've both heard of horses simply running out of puff, passing in a moment from all's well to barely moving, but the ailment seems to afflict only the rare coach horse, and Golden is not a coach horse."

At the mention of his name, Golden pricked his ears. He ambled over to me, Denton playing out the lead line, and nudged my pocket. Nobody could explain to the horse what had happened, and the horse couldn't give us any answers either. I scratched his ear, and he cocked his head in enjoyment.

"If he can't redeem himself next week," Wickley said, "I'll have to sell him, and at a loss, blast the luck. I thought he was the better of the two. He and Remedy are half-brothers, and their sire's progeny are all doing remarkably well. I can't afford a no-hoper in my stable, and running out of puff won't do. Won't do at all." He assayed a scowl at Denton, who ignored him, and at Tenneby, who stepped back as if slapped, and then at me.

"Have you something to say, Wickley?"

Hyperia laced her arm through mine and gave Wickley a half-bored, patient smile.

"Not in present company." He nodded to Hyperia. "Miss West, good day and… good luck." That last part was sneered and accompanied by another contemptuous perusal of my person.

Tenneby watched Wickley cross back to the throng on the other side of the course. "He insulted you, my lord. That doesn't bode well. As displeased as I am with your efforts to date—what were you thinking to insert yourself among the runners before the start?—I must warn you that Wickley can be hotheaded, as can several of the other owners present. His rivalry with Pierpont is legendary. We take our racing seriously."

No, they did not. They took their *wagering* seriously—and their vanity and their pride.

"Tenneby, it might surprise you to learn that you insulted me first by questioning my efforts before the earl. When my own host, the man who all but insisted I attend, disrespects me, then any other guest, groom, or passing mongrel is invited to do the same."

"Suppose you have a point, my lord." He craned his neck to regard the crown of the hill. "Ye gods, there goes Pierpont, rubbing it in, and Wickley trying to laugh it off. I am not up to their weight, and Evelyn tried to warn me, but Evelyn is always nattering on about this or that. What will you do next, my lord?"

"Accept your apology, provided one is tendered."

Now he was the recipient of Hyperia's patient-governess-with-a-slow-charge smile.

"I do apologize. The heat of the moment stole my manners. Most abjectly sorry. Are you staying or leaving?"

"If you send me away now, and the next few races run smoothly, everybody will conclude that you hired me to rig your meeting. You haven't lost any great sums yet, but Wickley just lost a packet, and he was among those who profited from your defeat at Epsom."

Three slow blinks. "You're saying people will think... that I... that I hired you... Oh dear."

"You cannot hire me, because I am a gentleman." I spoke slowly, exhausting the last of my forbearance. "But the rest of your conjecture is logical. Send me away if you please to. The culprit has tossed at least two lucrative races, and perhaps that's enough for him. Send me away now, and your meeting is disgraced. You and I share blame we do not deserve, and a villain, enriched by cheating, goes free to rig another meeting and fleece another upstanding member of the turf."

"Is that what you want, Mr. Tenneby?" Hyperia asked with exquisite indifference. "Or would you prefer to persist in the face of difficulties, get to the bottom of the cheating, and even recover some of the pecuniary reverses visited upon you earlier, when no investigation was attempted?"

"I am a plain mister," Tenneby said. "You try speaking reason to the Epsom stewards, to *anybody*, when half the peerage is laughing and pointing at you and smirking behind their hands whenever you pass."

I, who had been court-martialed in absentia by Mayfair hostesses and half of Horse Guards, did not howl or slap my forehead. "Very trying, I'm sure. I will leave if you ask it of me, or I will stay, but you should know that Sir Albertus is very opposed to my continued presence."

"Evelyn doesn't like him. Says he's cozening Vicar's widow just because he wanted to run Juliet. Everybody else puts the boot on the other foot, but Evelyn claims to know cozening when she sees it."

"Your sister is very astute." Hyperia continued to languidly ply her fan. "She approves of Lord Julian's presence, as do I."

Whatever else was true of Tenneby, he had the heart of a gentleman.

"I suppose that decides the matter, hmm? Stay for the nonce, my lord. If retreat is to be your fate, let it at least be an orderly retreat on another day. I'd best get to the starting line, troupe the colors, for whatever that's worth."

"Let's stay," Hyperia said when Tenneby had bustled off. "I want to see Excalibur run, and Tenneby is right that a display of calm is in order."

"A tall glass of punch is in order. Wickley means to call me out, Hyperia. I ought not to mention such a topic before a lady, but Sir Albertus has already offered me public insult, followed by a lot of blather about honor, seconds, and sorting out scoundrels."

"Julian, you didn't...?" She snapped her fan closed. "Please say you did not let that windbag in boots goad you into dueling?"

"I don't suppose you'd release me from my promise, Perry? The promise not to duel? I could pot him across the fundament, and he wouldn't sit a horse for weeks."

"The heat is affecting your humors, Julian. If you think I would stand idly by while you risked your life at gunpoint among a crowd that is clearly adept at cheating, you are much mistaken. *Much* mistaken. You survived the thirteenth circle of hell and worse on sheer stubbornness alone. To invite one of these... these dimwits to put out your lights over an accusation we know to be false would be an obscene return on the suffering you've endured. I refuse to countenance such foolishness."

She was so quietly passionate, so clear in her own mind regarding questions that bewildered me.

"Hyperia West, I do love you."

"No dueling, and don't think to wheedle and flatter your way around me on this point."

She loved me too. On that fortifying conclusion, I offered her my arm and escorted her once more unto the breach.

The last two races, a hurdle and a steeplechase, proceeded without incident. Excalibur won the steeplechase by a gentlemanly three lengths, and Tenneby was congratulated all around with apparent sincere good wishes. The colt—technically a stallion due to his age— would run again in matches later in the week, for what the owners referred to as "serious money."

Foolish money, if you'd asked me.

Tenneby had several other prospects on the cards for the upcoming races, but my concern was focused on Excalibur. This running-out-of-puff scheme had apparently been used successfully with Excalibur in the past. That made him the closest thing to a safe bet for another bad turn from the cheater.

Then too, Tenneby was likely to be betting his last groat on the horse, making for high stakes even by racing measures.

"Watch Tenneby's stallion closely," I said as Atticus hooked Atlas's final water bucket of the evening to its peg on the stall wall. "He is a truly fine animal and Tenneby's only remaining hope for avoiding ruin."

Atticus dipped his fingers into the cool water and applied them to his forehead. "Denton says Excalibur has perfect conformation. Built for speed, strength, and stamina. Piggott agreed with him, and even Hercules said the same. They all want Excalibur to win this time around. They don't say that when the owners are on hand, but they say it to each other."

Atlas dipped his nose into the water bucket and slurped noisily.

"The grooms are a congenial lot, aren't they?"

"Seem to be, until it's time to line up at the start. Denton has a temper, but I would, too, if I had to put up with Wicked and his struttin'. Pierpont's no better, but he don't order his grooms about just for the sake of making noise. They hop to do his bidding just the same."

Atlas lifted his head, his chin dripping. He watched as Excalibur was led past the stall, then went back to his slurping.

The stallion moved with feline economy and leonine power. Stubbs would have been powerless to resist his equine majesty. I was again aware that only a truly nasty soul would wish harm on a helpless equine.

"Is the well recharging?" I asked as St. George was led past. Healy's gray had the same grace and power as Excalibur, but with more muscle behind and a wider barrel. Two different varieties of excellence, at least as far as appearances went.

"The well's not coming back fast enough," Atticus replied. "Hercules worked out a roster for us so we don't all have to take our horses down to the river one by one. We take them by twos or threes. You take mine, I'll take yours. Woglemuth approved. We're getting a little more sleep, and the horses are on a schedule so nobody goes thirsty."

"And yet, you still personally bring Atlas his bucket for overnight?"

"If it was me, in this heat, I'd want to know I could have a sip now and again through the night. Bean got us a wagon from the home farm, so we fill up all the night buckets after supper and haul 'em over from the kitchen garden before we turn in. When the wagon pulls up in the stable yard, we set up a bucket line, like they do for a fire, and the whole business is done in no time."

Common horse sense and a little cooperation were making a long two weeks more bearable for the rank and file. Up at the manor house, fortunes were being wagered on a whim, potentially mortal threats flung about, and impending ruin ignored, while somebody flogged honor past all recognition.

Many an officer had claimed to envy the common soldier.

"Keep up the good work, Atticus, and keep a sharp eye out. Someone from among these hardworking stable hands took several horses out for unscheduled gallops. Denton might well have been trying to swap Cleopatra for Maybelle, Blinken was put out of the running by foul play, and you doubtless heard about Golden Sovereign's defeat this afternoon."

"Bad business, guv." Atticus peered into the bucket, which was by now half empty, and frowned. "Golden shoulda won. Yeah, the weather is hot and close, but it's hot and close for everybody. If he lost, he shoulda lost by a nose, not like some old granny who gets to wanderin' on the way home from Sunday services."

Apt description. "But he did lose, and his defeat exactly mirrored Juliet's recent defeat and Excalibur's loss from several years ago. Somebody has figured out how to tamper with a horse so it's not apparent until the creature actually falters."

"Bean says he's heard of it in coach horses, like tyin'-up, but not tyin'-up."

Tying-up referred to a serious stiffness or lameness that could come on quickly, particularly after a horse in steady work had enjoyed a deserved rest, or a horse out of condition had been asked for strenuous exertion. The reigning theory among my cavalry cohorts had been that the horse was enduring muscle cramps, because a badly afflicted animal either could not or would not take a single step.

"You are learning a lot here, aren't you, Atticus?"

"Between Denton, Woglemuth, Hercules, and Bean, I'm learning everything worth knowing. Denton says I have a good seat."

This again. "You're hacking up to the Downs every morning?"

"Aye, no gallopin', though. Me doddering old guv won't have it."

He assayed a grin as he scratched at Atlas's hairy ear. The horse craned his neck, the better to enjoy the cosseting.

"You may attempt a hand-gallop tomorrow, if one of the other grooms will pace you. Stand in the stirrups to free Atlas's back, don't let the reins go slack lest he take off at top speed, but let him stretch his legs. Grab mane if you need to. There's no shame in that if your horse is on the muscle. When Atlas has galloped off the fidgets, bring him back for a breather at the canter, then give him one more good push forward, followed by plenty of walking to cool down."

I described basic training to build speed and stamina in the horse and rider. I'd far rather have reserved the pleasure of such an outing for myself, but Atticus deserved to enjoy the challenge in the company of his temporary confreres. They—and Atlas—would school him as I could not.

And yet, Atticus was still a mere child, and I was inviting him to gallop on a warhorse without my supervision. Hyperia would disapprove, St. Just would understand, and if the boy came to harm, I would have regrets for the rest of my life.

"Pull up if Atlas forgets his manners. Haul his nose around to your knee and be firm about it. He's tried to bolt with me a time or two when my attention has wandered. He needs to know his jockey is on the job, not daydreaming about hot cross buns and lemon ices."

Atticus finished scratching Atlas's second ear. "I won't be thinkin' about no lemon ices when Atlas is flying over the Downs. You should go on up to the house, guv. Folk get to mutterin' if you hang about the stables for too long."

"Anybody muttering in particular?"

"*Everybody* gripes and moans about everything. Like singing a hymn to get the congregation settled in the pews. The weather, the nobs, the flies, the well, the sot on the throne... and the strange milord with the blue glasses who seems to be on hand when a race is rigged. Then they look at me to see if I heard 'em, which they meant me to do."

"I do wear blue glasses, that can't be helped, but for the love of fast horses, don't let those fellows rile you. Drink plenty of water yourself, Atticus. Heat is devious. It saps your strength from day to day, but you think you'll rise in the morning fit to march again, only to drop in your tracks three miles on. I've seen it happen over and over."

"Like Juliet and Golden Sovereign?"

Interesting observation. "Yes and no. The horses are not soldiers in wool uniforms, who've tramped thirty miles over hill and dale, with packs and weapons. When a soldier goes down like that, he's often stopped sweating, and he's half out of his head." Still, the boy's observation got me thinking. "Nobody is rugging these horses at night, are they?"

"Nah, too hot for that."

I patted Altas's sleek quarters and left the stall. "None of the grooms are falling asleep at odd times and places?"

Atticus followed me and took up an empty bucket. "We all fall asleep as many times and in as many places as we can manage. Lugging all this water about, getting up early for the gallops, the extra work from the races, and all the nefarious goin's-on… We're all cadging naps when we can."

"Where are you off to with that bucket?"

"To get another half measure to top up Atlas's bucket for the night. He didn't have nothing left in his bucket this morning, and you just saw him drain the thing half empty. The heat ain't gonna break for another few days at least, more's the pity."

"Amen to that. Do not fall asleep out here, Atticus. I'll come find you if you do."

"Guv, I'm tellin' ya…"

"I know. The strange lord is a suspicious character. I'll be careful, and you get up to the house when your day is through."

If suspicion was falling on me, it could all too easily fall on the boy, too, a vexing thought. We passed a knot of grooms smoking pipes under the stable's overhang. Denton, Hercules, and Corrie nodded to me, and I felt their gazes on my back as I made my way toward the house.

Lowly grooms they might be, but they doubtless took meddling with one of their charges as seriously as I'd take ill will directed at Atticus. They were kind to the boy for the nonce, but he'd fare very poorly indeed if he was tarred with the brush of suspicion already applied so liberally to me.

I was halfway up to the house when a man stepped out from the deep shadows of the privet hedges bordering the path.

"A word, my lord, and now if you please."

My first instinct was to throw a punch and sprint for the house. Battle nerves. "Bean, good evening. My tiger has been singing your praises for appropriating a wagon to haul buckets from the kitchen garden well to the stables."

He fell in step beside me. "Woglemuth is too stubborn to ask for that sort of help, but he's not stupid. If the grooms get too worn out, somebody's temper will snap, and then a substitute jockey will be drafted from the ranks and losses attributed to the understudy, sparking more pugilism. No schoolyard ever had to be as carefully managed. Pierpont's head groom sorted out a schedule for watering the horses, and there's less grumbling as a result."

"One more week, and they will all go on to the next meeting." I would go home to Caldicott Hall, and never again leave its beauteous acres for so vexing a destination as a race meeting. Unless the nefarious powers below and a quantity of rotten luck prevailed, I'd do so as a man still engaged to be married.

"Speaking of going on to the next meeting," I went on, "Rubicon's owner has apparently already decamped."

"For Town, so I'm told. A solid gentry bachelor with London connections has better things to do than mill about at horse races."

"He quit while he was ahead, I'll give him credit for that." And he'd quit before I'd had a chance to question him, blast the luck. "Any other news?"

"I have further investigated the feeding situation," Bean said.

"Nothing out of the ordinary presents itself. The runners are all fed by their own grooms on rations brought from home and tailored to that specific horse, which is typical for a race meeting. The grooms keep their stores secured, no insult intended when mice delight in undefended grain. Our lads feed our horses, and they would notice anything out of the ordinary in the oat bins. It was worth a look, but tampering with feed is not your answer."

Somebody had tampered with Blinken's saddle, tampered with the exercise routine, and possibly tried tampering with the stall assignments. What did that leave?

"I am frustrated, Bean. My theories lead everywhere in terms of suspects and nowhere in terms of answers."

"That's not the worst of your worries, my lord."

We approached the flight of stone steps that led up from the garden. Bean moved off the path to the shadow of the retaining wall that buttressed the park-facing façade of the terrace. We would not be visible from the house, though why anybody would begrudge me...

Ah. Bean did not want to be seen fraternizing with the strange lord. That, I understood.

"The worst of my worries has to do with Healy West betting the family fortune on a horse who goes like the wind at dawn and cannot be bothered to break a sweat in the afternoon. If the family finances are ruined, so are my marital prospects."

Bean's flaxen brows drew down. "One would think a lady without means would be more eager to marry a solvent bachelor."

"One would, except that's not how it works. You have bad news. I am hungry, thirsty, tired, and out of sorts. You'd best unburden yourself before I run barking mad into the woods."

His teeth gleamed in the shadows. "Take a dip in the river. Cool the humors. Take a dip with your lady, in fact."

"Bean."

"Very well. Sir Albertus has vowed to confront you for what he deems your highly questionable conduct on too many occasions. He claims that if you will not meet him honorably, then you had best be on your guard on moonlit paths after dark."

"He thinks to deliver me a beating?"

"Or worse."

"Take it from one who barely survived captivity by the French— mere beatings are proof of a lack of imagination." I had been repeatedly tormented by a man who had the most diabolical imagination ever possessed by an ostensibly human mind. The nightmares never left me for long.

"A beating is unpleasant nonetheless," Bean retorted, "and you assume you will survive Sir Albertus's boring display. He won't sully his hands personally, you understand. He'll have the local ne'er-do-wells deliver the drubbing and empty your pockets for form's sake."

"Because I will not leave. What does that suggest, Bean?"

"That Sir Albie is protesting too loudly? If so, he's protesting very convincingly, my lord. Please be careful."

"This week's contests were the cheaper races to lose, and if I were our cheater, my best disguise would be as the first victim, wouldn't it?"

Bean kicked at the dry earth and tore up a patch of brown grass. "My lady wife raised the same argument. Said Sir Albertus's loss would distract everybody from considering him as the culprit. You are not distracted."

"Nor am I convinced that all fingers should point at Sir Albertus. I will watch my back, and I appreciate the warning, but I am not about to be dissuaded by a few threats."

"I thought not. I'll bid you good evening, my lord."

He sauntered off amid the lengthening evening shadows, and I took a moment to bide on the nearest bench. Over in the home wood, the birds had begun their evening chorus, and at the edge of the park, a doe grazed on the sparse grass.

I had not yet solved the riddle of the rigged races, and not for want of trying. Somebody's scheme was working, as it had likely worked at Epsom on a grand scale several years past.

I rose wearily and directed my steps to the manor house. Had Old Scratch popped out of the ground and offered me a cool bath in exchange for my soul at that moment, the bargain would have tempted me. As it happened, I was accosted again before I had crossed the terrace, and tempting bargains did not figure in the ensuing conversation *at all*.

CHAPTER FIFTEEN

"I thought you fellows who went off to lark about in Spain would become inured to the heat," Healy West said. "You don't look very inured, my lord."

He was "my lording" me. A combination of pleading and exhorting regarding some aspect of his cork-brained scheme with St. George was doubtless to follow. I wasn't in the mood for either.

"Spain was nearly three years ago, West, and it might surprise you to know that particularly in the mountains—Spain has many— the weather can be as bitter as it is dry. If you don't mind, I'm overdue for both washing up and lying down in anticipation of the evening's socializing."

"I thought only ladies napped, Caldicott. Ladies and infants. Put off your slumbers for another moment and heed my request."

He was Hyperia's only sibling, and soon—pray heaven—to be my brother-by-marriage. I scraped together an iota of manners from the dregs of my exhausted stores.

"Let's sit, shall we? The view from the bottom of the garden is pleasant, and I trust the topic you contemplate will benefit from being aired at some distance from the house." The garden itself was going a bit droopy. The petals of the potted geraniums were brown at the edges. The tulips were listing hard to port, their greenery pale and wilted.

"Some distance...?" West eyed the house. "Oh, right. By all means, let's find a garden bench. I see Tenneby has turned off the fountain. Saving water, poor sod. This weather does not bode well for the harvest hereabouts."

The chief crop exported from the local surrounds was racehorses, but for Berkshire in general, the comment was valid. Horses needed nice big haystacks to get them through winter, and if the drought didn't break soon, haying and planting were both imperiled.

"Rain is on the way," I said, navigating the steps a bit stiffly. "That is the prognostication according to every bad knee, sore hip, and bum shoulder in the stable yard." I found a bench, sat, and placidly contemplated spending the rest of my days in that very spot. I was reaching the stage of fatigue characterized by a sort of beatific detachment that could shade into silliness or melancholy all too easily. "Speak your piece, West. I have promised your sister my company at supper."

"About my sister..."

"Who is also my affianced bride."

He sat beside me, knees spread, gaze on the crushed-shell walkway. "Hyperia, dear to both of our hearts."

Where on earth was he going with these peregrinations? "The light of my soul."

"And the best of siblings, but she does take a dim view of anything less than parsimony when it comes to investments."

Ah. He needed a loan. Of course. I had all but predicted this. "Most prudent people mind their pence and quid."

"Which is all well and good if those people are spinsters or vicars or bachelor uncles. A young man, the head of his family, a gentleman, must be allowed some daring maneuvers in his personal business."

"You refer to the extravagance that is St. George. You'll have to hire a groom who can keep him fit, you know. The fellow you've picked up for this meeting probably won't be content to muck stalls the livelong day if he can earn more at the larger jump races."

"Barrington is a good lad," Healy retorted. "Stable name Bear, and he was recommended to me by George's former owner. He'll stay the course, I'm sure."

Oh right. He'd be back to Newmarket to chortle into his beer with his coconspirator in the ongoing rig that was St. George Goes to the Races.

"West, might you get to the point? My stamina is not what it once was, and the heat is taking a toll."

"Very well, blunt speech it shall be. I've laid a few wagers with the other owners, wagers on my George. Sporting wagers, as one does. He'll run again Monday, and then he has three match races at the end of the week. Today's steeplechase was just to limber him up, of course, to let him see the countryside and put his mind on racing."

The steeplechase that Excalibur had won handily. "I wasn't aware that St. George was competing today."

"I added him at the gate, so to speak, and Bear and I agreed that today was for exercise, not for any great exertion. We're of very similar minds when it comes to training and conditioning the beast."

How much did you lose? "I did not see the finish. I trust St. George comported himself admirably?"

"Very admirably, for a fellow who wasn't asked to exert himself at all, I'd say. Sixth out of a field of fourteen."

Well out of the money. "Then you accomplished the goal for the day, didn't you? George should have his mind on racing and on winning when he competes next week."

"I'm sure he will."

I was nearly falling asleep where I sat, a talent one developed in the military if not at public school and university.

"West, whatever you have to say, please say it. I promise not to explode into vitriol—I haven't any vitriol left, at the moment—and if I did, I'd save it for whoever is rigging these races."

"Don't say that. The races are not rigged. The weather is to blame, is all. The weather and everybody who wants Tenneby to shut his mouth about what happened at Epsom."

"But it's happening again here, isn't it?"

"Julian, mind what you say. If it is happening, most people assume you are to blame. I do what I can to scotch the rumors, but at every turn, you provide more evidence to fuel their conjectures. You aren't rigging the races, are you?"

If I said yes, West would ask me to rig George's races. I knew that the way a mother knew when her darling prodigy was lying. The situation must be beyond dire for him to risk that sort of request.

"I am not rigging any races, and I won't call you out for asking. Hyperia frowns on dueling, and both Sir Albertus and Lord Wickley would cry foul if I met you over pistols when I have declined to meet them. I'm in demand as a dueling partner, you see, but I have turned away all comers. Sir Albertus is sufficiently frustrated with my unavailability that he's promised to dispense with the *Code Duello* twaddle and beat me to a pulp instead—have me beaten to a pulp, rather. That approach wants imagination on his part, but it does speak to some determination."

This oration was met with a brief silence, then West shifted on the bench. "Are you working up to one of your forgetful spells, Julian?"

"A spell of cursing, perhaps. Say what you have to say, West, before Morpheus snatches me away to the land of Nod." Mixing metaphors. Truly, I needed rest.

"Very well. I've placed a few wagers on St. George, as stated, but Wickley asked me who my backer is. Seems it's the done thing to have a guarantor for more sizable wagers, if one is new to the turf and without an established reputation. Pierpont didn't contradict Wickley or intervene in any way, so I assume this is simply a bit of holy writ I haven't come across yet. New to the business, my first runner, and so forth."

"West, you didn't." Was this Wickley's revenge upon me for another defeat?

"Well, yes, I did— discreetly, of course. I didn't name you specifi-cally. I alluded to a ducal scion with military experience and a great fondness for horses, meaning you, but not naming names. I was afforded a bit of gentlemanly discretion, because racing demands civility among the owners."

Even in my reduced state, I grasped the magnitude of this latest disaster. "You have just destroyed my repeated insistence to all and sundry that I am *disinterested* when it comes to the outcomes of the races. I am ostensibly here to enjoy Hyperia's company, not to waste a fortune on either luck or cheating. Damn you, West. I'm already the object of rumors and threats, and now you've made a liar out of me."

That last part—being held up as dishonest—bothered me sorely. The rumors and threats were merely annoying.

"You are approaching a vitriolic state, Caldicott. One must note the obvious."

"You are approaching an interview with Saint Peter, West. Your sister is already furious with you for risking funds you cannot afford to lose." *Her funds*, though I did not disclose that I knew the depths of his perfidy. "Now you add insult to foolishness and drag my name into your schemes."

"Not schemes, for pity's sake. You make it sound as if I'm doing the rigging, and I assure you I am not."

He wasn't smart enough to carry off an extended, devious scheme. But I was supposedly smart enough to foil such machi-nations.

Think, lad. The voice in my head was Harry's, who'd excelled at charming and bamboozling his way out of tight corners. He'd once told me that every problem had a solution, if one looked hard enough and long enough. I would never regard his death as a solution to the problem of captivity in French hands, but perhaps at the time, Harry had.

How I wished St. Just were still...

"I am not your backer." I pushed to my feet, which caused my ankles and hips to ache. "You must make that very clear."

West trotted along after me as I trudged toward the house. "I know that, and you know that, but I'm asking that you humor me with a very small fiction. I haven't a backer, of course, and I won't need one, because George is the best jump racer here."

"He's a ruddy morning glory, West. The whole meeting doubtless knows it, as does Hyperia. Your backer is St. Just. You will hint as loudly and often as you can that you went to St. Just because you knew I was too high a stickler to involve myself with wagering when I'd already refused to join that affray. Do you understand me?"

He stopped at the foot of the terrace steps. "Devlin St. Just?"

"Ducal scion, military experience, devoted to horses. Of course, St. Just. Could not stay to watch George compete, but knew a winner when he saw one. Repeat that until you have it memorized."

"Oh, I see. *Devlin St. Just.* Colonel St. Just, why yes, that will serve. Should have thought of it myself. The simplest thing in the world. A relief, actually, because now we needn't tell Hyperia about this slight departure from strictest fact, need we?"

I stared at the steps rising before me like the cursed slopes of Monte Perdido. "I will not lie to my intended." Hyperia sought to know even my memories, good and bad. She would sniff out prevarication at twenty paces if I even attempted such measures.

Besides, I did not want the burden, the taint, of colluding with Healy West in any regard, much less in deceiving his sister.

"Then don't lie," West said, "but don't quibble over a harmless fiction. For pity's sake, Caldicott, show some fraternal regard."

I started up the steps. There were twenty. I knew that because I'd been a reconnaissance officer, and measuring distances, heights, and travel time between locations was second nature to me.

"I will inform Hyperia regarding this harmless fiction you are perpetrating so that she will not be ambushed by gossip and innuendo. In the alternative, you may apprise her of your foolishness."

"It's not foolishness, Caldicott. George will win me a packet, and you'll have to eat your lack of faith when he does."

We gained the summit, or so it felt. "Do you tell her, or shall I?"

West sent a fulminating glance at the house, then turned his gaze on me. Oh dear. He was unhappy with me. I was beyond furious with him but too tired to ring the peal he deserved. Soon enough. St. George would bring him to ruin, and then I could ring all the peals I pleased.

"I'll tell her." His aggrieved air was worthy of the great thespian David Garrick. "You would muck up the business and put me in a bad light. I'll see you at supper, if you can remain awake that long. Do wash up, though. You are overdue for a thorough reacquaintance with soap and water."

He stalked off, and I envied him his energy. As I navigated the journey to my quarters, my temper cooled, and I sent up a prayer that St. George, for just this one meeting, could defy his reputation as a morning glory. I wanted Healy West on sound financial footing. I wanted Hyperia's settlements earning their humble way in the cent-per-cents, hale and whole.

I wanted whoever was rigging the races to go straight to hell, none of which was within my power to bring about apparently.

When I saw my bed, the covers smooth and tidy, the pillows neatly stacked, I pulled off my boots and granted myself the one boon it was within my power to grant and very nearly slept through the third dinner bell.

As the stifling Sabbath wore on, I realized that my intended was again avoiding me. Hyperia took a tray in her room at breakfast and attached herself to Pierpont on the walk to divine services and to Wickley for the stroll home. I was relegated once again to the company of Miss Cornelia Reardon, Sir Albertus's sister, who nattered on about bloodlines and broodmares until my head swam.

"Did the ladies enjoy yesterday's outing to the weekly market?" I asked.

"We're a small village, my lord. Our market is modest, but one doesn't want to sit about the house with a lot of bored males who'd rather be getting muck on their boots and draining their flasks up on the Downs. The ladies made a tactical retreat and took the occasion to appreciate the innkeeper's lemonade. Albertus is still beside himself over Juliet's loss. He had almost reconciled himself to Dasher's poor showing, and then the filly failed him too. He blames you, you know."

"He has made his suspicions clear to me as well."

"No fool like an old fool." Miss Reardon marched along, no rancor in her tone. "Juliet was coming in season, no doubt. Leave it to a man to forget the imperatives of nature. Sheer folly, housing fillies and colts in the same yard, but then, much about horse racing is folly. I don't suppose you've had a chance to look up the pedigree of Pierpont's Minerva? She's about as perfectly bred as a filly can be, and that's saying something, but then, all of Pierpont's runners are related to royalty."

Miss Reardon chattered on, like an endless artillery bombardment. When we reached the manor house, I excused myself on the pretext of minor ablutions and went in search of Hyperia.

I was informed that my darling was having a lie-down.

Instinct told me her bare feet were propped on an obliging hassock while she enjoyed a book borrowed from Tenneby's library— a book I should have been reading to her. She pleaded a megrim at the supper buffet, which was mildly worrisome. Hyperia was not prone to megrims.

Her continued absence earned me matching smirks from Wickley and Pierpont and a sympathetic smile from Miss Tenneby.

I thus rose Monday morning in a foul mood. My intended was playing least in sight. Sir Albertus was still muttering foul threats into his port. The day was, if anything, more stifling than its predecessors, and the expensive races were scheduled to start that afternoon.

The heat should have thinned the crowd, but the rumors of foul play had instead swelled the ranks. The viewing hill was a carpet of picnic baskets, gently waving fans, and gentlemen sweating under their hats.

The first race was another outing for the fillies, and it went smoothly enough. The favorite—one of Pierpont's string—won in a close finish, which the crowd appreciated loudly. In the lull before the second race, I caught sight of Hyperia strolling arm in arm with Miss Tenneby.

If Hyperia saw me, she was ignoring me. My puzzlement and concern acquired an edge of frustration.

A blast of beery fumes on the humid breeze announced Sir Albertus's presence. "You are not absolved of all suspicion just because one race delivers an expected result. My Dasher runs in the next race, and by God, he had best prevail, my lord, or you will rue the day."

He shook a riding crop at me, right there in view of the other spectators.

I stepped closer and kept my voice down. "Tell me, Sir Albertus, how exactly am I rigging these races? Caleb Bean will assure you the feed has not been tampered with. Every horse running has been marked for identification in some indelible manner. No ringers allowed. The ne'er-do-well who attempted to add midnight gallops to the program was foiled—by me, I might add. The nasty mischief perpetrated against Blinken was also exposed—by me. What possible scheme does that leave? The horses are not drugged, according to all knowledgeable sources, and the jockeys are riding honestly. Enlighten me, please, as to what, besides heat, possible overtraining, and hard terrain, is yielding all these suspicious results?"

He burped audibly. "You agree the results are suspicious! You know I'm on to you. Doubtless that little sly boots you've dispatched to the stable is in on the mischief somehow. Taking advantage of a mere child, sir, is beyond contemptible."

"You'd best see to your runner, Sir Albertus. The starters will scratch him if he's not ready to go on time."

Sir Albertus wheeled unsteadily and tottered down the hill. His bellicosity struck me as out of character. One week ago, he'd been civil, if not quite congenial, and now he was openly threatening me and overimbibing in public.

"What did he want?" Pierpont asked, a tankard of cider in his hand.

"To accuse me again of rigging the races, though he was at a loss to describe how I'm perpetrating my crimes."

"One explanation for the results we've seen is that bad luck just seems to follow Tenneby, my lord. He's a good fellow, means well, does right by his horses and grooms, but he's a slow top, for all that. He's prone to holding low cards, and the progress of this meeting thus far is not that different from what one should have expected. We'll do what we can for him when the inevitable occurs—discreetly, of course."

Down the hill, the runners for the second race had begun to assemble, though if a thunderbolt from on high had landed behind the starting line, I would not have ventured into the ensuing chaos. The starters were shouting, the jockeys cursing, and Sir Albertus was making everything worse by grabbing Dasher's bridle and delivering a sermon to the jockey despite other horses needing to get past him to the starting line.

Bad luck and heat—or something—was taking a toll on every-body's nerves.

"What can you do for a man who has raced his way to the edge of ruin?" I asked as Corrie, the groom, came up on Dasher's offside and gently tugged the horse forward. Dasher was bearing the confusion reasonably well, but then, perhaps he was growing accustomed to it.

"If Tenneby cannot swim free of his debts, we'll take his cattle off his hands, promise them good care, and try to mean it. If they were first-rate runners, Tenneby wouldn't be in the situation he's facing. We'll spare him having to watch them go for a pittance at auction, at least. We know any one of us might be the victim of bad fortune. Take this weather, for example. It's nobody's fault, and yet, the farmers will suffer for it."

"Why not let Tenneby win a race or two, if the brotherhood is that sorry for him?"

"Wouldn't be sporting, and every jockey would have to agree to the outcome beforehand. Hard to keep that sort of thing from starting rumors, and there's always one high stickler in the bunch, or one fellow who can't rate his horse closely enough to make the victory seem credible. Interesting question, though, from somebody who claims not to know a thing about horse racing."

He sauntered off on that gently accusatory note.

The starters gave the signal, the second race commenced, and I took advantage of the spectators' interest in the competition to make my way to the punchbowls.

"Lord Julian, good day." The Welsh footman who'd been so solicitous toward the old earl was serving the libation. "Gents or ladies for you, my lord?"

"Ladies, and a full pint, please. How fares the earl?"

"Heat's hard on him, sir, but the cold is worse. You might stop up and let him know how things are progressing, if you've a spare moment." He handed me my drink.

"When does his lordship receive visitors?"

"Mornings are best, sir. After breakfast, before the heat starts to build. I can pour you another if you like."

"No, thank you, this will do. I will make it a point to look in on his lordship before the meeting breaks up."

I should have taken two tankards, but that would have left me wandering the crowd, ostensibly carrying a drink for my lady, who was having no parts of me.

I sipped my drink and watched the race from the viewing platform while the crowd around me ignored my existence. To be fair, they were watching the race, but the ladies were also whispering behind their fans after glancing my direction, and the gentlemen were offering me some sort of oblique half cut—not quite acknowledging me, not quite snubbing me.

Tenneby, mine host, was outside the rubbing-down house,

lecturing a much shorter fellow who gestured grandly in the direction of the village. Hyperia and Miss Tenneby were across the course in the shade of the hedgerow, both of them using field glasses to watch the field gallop the final stretch.

As the horses thundered down the hill to the finish, Dasher was in the lead by a neck. Just as he ought to have been exerting himself to the utmost to hold his lead, he took a step out of rhythm. The colt beside him gained a few inches, and Dasher's jockey applied one smart whack of the crop.

The finish line was mere yards away when Dasher took another false step. The jockey was ready with another whack, and the finish looked to me to be Dasher by a nose. The stewards agreed, and Sir Albertus strutted into the circle where winners were congratulated at length. He bowed extravagantly, waved a handkerchief at his well-wishers, and made a general fool of himself, but one forgave him.

Dasher had likely salvaged Sir Albertus's finances by inches and, more importantly, salvaged his owner's dignity. The horse himself stood, head down, sides heaving, just as he had on the occasion of last week's defeat.

"Does that look odd to you?" Healy West appropriated my tankard, found it empty, and scowled. "I mean, aren't the horses supposed to know when they win and prance about and lord it over the other fellows?"

West, like the proverbial blind hog, had a point. "The stultifying weather is taking a terrible toll," I said. "The runners are shut in their stalls at night, and those stalls aren't nearly as cool as even a dirt paddock would be."

"The stalls aren't sweltering either. Stone barns tend not to be, according to Bear. George is running in today's steeplechase, and this time, I've told Bear to make an effort. My boy has had his sightseeing tour, and it's time to show these plowboys how to cover some ground."

"How much have you had to drink?"

"Not enough. Why?"

"You ran that horse on Friday, West."

"A practice outing, no more strenuous than a romp on the Downs, which he was spared that morning because it was race day. He'll show 'em what he's made of today, trust me, and by Friday, you will be singing a very different and more humble tune, Caldicott."

"You're running him *again* on Friday?"

"And Saturday. Match races, though I might put him in the over-fences heat as well. That is his forte, after all."

"You are asking for a bungled jump, West, and the final jumps on this course are downhill, which means you could well bungle your horse to death."

West shoved my empty tankard back at me. "You ought to be in Mr. Johnson's lexicon under the definition of spoilsport." He stomped off toward the punchbowls, where a long queue had formed.

I made my way to the rubbing-down house and met Joe Corrie leading Dasher past the brick structure.

"Congratulations. Your charge distinguished himself."

"He did, didn't he?" The groom patted the horse's sweaty neck as they walked along. "Knew he had it in him, though that was a close one."

"Was it too close?"

Corrie glanced over his shoulder and slowed his pace. The horse, still breathing heavily, slowed with him. "What's that supposed to mean? He won, and Sir Albertus is over the moon."

"He nearly did not win. He ran out of puff again and stood in the winner's enclosure like a horse ready for last rites."

"Don't say that. I mean, please don't say that, milord. He'll come right. He just had to work a bit for the finish."

"The race was rigged, Corrie. I know it, you know it, and half the spectators might be coming to the same conclusion. They expect a winner to act up amid all the congratulations and well-wishes, but Dasher has the same look about him that he had last week."

"Sir Albertus won't want me to be seen talkin' to you, milord. No disrespect. Dasher won fair and square, and there's an end to it."

We'd passed the place where Corrie had circled Blinken during our previous tête-à-tête. Corrie did not want to be seen talking to me, and I was reluctant to cause problems for the lad.

"What was different about Dasher's routine today, Corrie?"

"Nothin', and that's the truth. He had the small serving of oats that he gets on race days, and I took him to find some grass by the river, but that's what I allus do the morning before a race. Your lordship had best be getting back to the course. The steeplechase will be starting any minute. Wouldn't want to miss that, if I was you."

"Corrie, if you recall anything out of the ordinary, anything at all, no matter how small, please pass it along. You can tell Atticus, and he'll get word to me."

"I'm not to speak to him either. He said that weren't no matter. No hard feelin's. Owners can be contrary."

"I'll leave you to tend to your horse, but do not relax your vigilance. Dasher has twice been the victim of rigging, though today he was lucky."

"He were lucky, true enough. I'll be glad when we're home, I will."

Joe Corrie would have walked clear to Hampshire to get shut of me, so I returned to the rubbing-down house and stepped around to the back as if heeding nature's call. The talk from inside was desultory, not the usual banter and teasing I expected on a race day.

The grooms had reached the same conclusion I had: The rigging was still going on, not as successfully as before in Dasher's case, but successfully enough that the horse's victory was attributed much more to luck than ability.

CHAPTER SIXTEEN

The steeplechase yielded a similar result: Excalibur by a faltering nose, half the pack hot on his literal heels. St. George dawdled along with the second half of the field, apparently enjoying himself despite his jockey's liberally applied heels.

No spurs, though, which was puzzling. Not even short, blunt spurs such as were handed out to less-talented riders mostly for show. A jockey could wear spurs without applying them to the horse's sides, but a rider without spurs was forgoing an accepted means of cuing a horse to further speed.

Another puzzle, which I tossed on the growing heap along with rigged races, Hyperia's disappointing behavior, and Healy West's impending ruin.

I wandered at the back of the stragglers returning to the manor house and took the turn that led to the stable yard. I wanted to compare notes with Atticus and ask him about the morning's preparation for the races.

The usual early evening bustle was ensuing. Horses brought in from paddocks, still others turned out for the night, some led down to the river for a drink. A few of the owners wandered from stall door to stall door, but the enthusiasm and energy apparent a week ago had fled the scene.

The stone wall at my back held heat instead of blessed coolness. The grooms retrieving water buckets from the parked wagon moved wearily, and not a single good-natured insult was exchanged.

Something was off. They all knew it. The horses seemed to know it, too, but what, how, and who was responsible?

I was staring at nothing and thinking nothing, when a small, dark-haired boy approached me. The lad was on the thin side, his wrists and ankles beginning to outpace the cuffs of his sleeves and trousers. His face was dusty, his hair tousled, and his boots worn at the toes but well heeled.

Young for a stable hand, but probably born to the trade.

"Guv, you ought not be hangin' about here. I'll find you after supper. If I'm asleep, you can wake me. Tired as I'm gettin', I will go right back to sleep sure as Eclipse had a pair of balls."

What a presuming little fellow. "Pardon me, young sir, but who are you, and what in blazes inspires you to address me so familiarly?"

He blinked at me, rubbed his chin, and looked about us. "You going forgetty on me, guv?"

"Young man, you will address me as..." I reached for my own name, my station in life, a Christian name, anything, and came up blank.

The boy scanned the stable yard again, his gaze alert. "The card's in your pocket. Don't make a fuss. Read the card."

I fished in the pocket of my morning coat and produced a linen stock card on which somebody had penned several tidy lines. My name was Lord Julian Caldicott—a fine-sounding moniker, but it rang no bells—and I was prone to temporary and complete lapses of memory.

How inconvenient. "What exactly does 'temporary' mean, and who are you?"

"I'm Atticus, your tiger and dogsbody. 'Temporary' means you need a good night's sleep, and you'll be fit in the morning. Your memories come back, or they have so far." He continued to dart glances over his shoulder, as if worried somebody might overhear him.

I was uneasy taking the word of a dusty boy for something as serious as mental infirmity, and yet, I hadn't known my own name.

We were speaking English—I grasped that much—so I presumed I was in England, but we might as well have been in the wilds of America or the Antipodes, for all I truly knew.

"Can anybody corroborate your tale?" I might well have been drugged and this card slipped into my pocket as a sort of prank. Who would pull such a nasty trick and why?

"I can fetch Miss West, but it might take some time. Don't move, don't talk to anybody, and don't get into any trouble until I come back. You got that?"

For a mere boy, he had a formidable glower. "I am in some sort of trouble, aren't I?"

"You and trouble march side by side, guv. This lot,"—he jerked his chin toward the stable yard—"don't think you can be trusted. They're wrong, but they don't know that. You're safe here if you just sit quiet and keep your mouth shut."

Where was *here*? Safe from who or what? I had a thousand questions, but the boy trotted off quick time and left me to watch the end-of-day routine at what had to be the stables of a grand manor.

Or a not-so-grand manor. A gardener, for example, was due for a reprimand. Red, yellow, and white tulips occupied regularly spaced half barrels. On one side of the yard, the flowers were in fairly good trim, but on the other, most of the blooms were long overdue for watering or lifting.

The horses looked well cared for, if a bit lean, but then, how did I know even that much? Except that I did. I knew or recalled what a fit, healthy horse looked like. What else did I remember?

I was tempted to leave the bench, to wander among those horses and hope that a familiar equine face might jog my memories. The boy Atticus had been insistent that I not leave my post, and for some reason, disobeying that child was beyond me. He'd worry if I went absent without leave, and I did not want him worrying about me.

I bided on the bench and received a few curious stares, also some hostile glances.

"Julian." A pretty, curvy, little, brown-haired young lady carrying a straw hat approached my bench, the boy at her side. "Atticus says your memory has deserted you."

I rose. "Miss, you have me at a disadvantage. Might somebody provide introductions?"

"Certainly not, unless you want to attract the notice of every guest at this misbegotten gathering. Come along, I'll see that you get to your rooms and make your excuses at supper." She waved a hand at me in a preemptory, get-moving manner.

"Am I putting you in danger, miss? Your demeanor suggests that haste is imperative, not merely convenient." And who was she, to order me about so summarily?

"Julian, *let's go*, and yes, there is danger of a sort. We're at a race meeting. Talk abounds that you have rigged the races, and ill will is building against you. Today's matches achieved credible results, but only just. Please do hurry."

She slipped an arm through mine—bold little thing—and hustled me down a shady path, the boy trotting at our heels.

Atticus. His name was Atticus. My ability to recall what I'd recently heard was in working order, a slight reassurance. "Miss, I still don't know your name."

"Hyperia West. We've known each other for ages, and you are not to worry. Your memories always return, complete and accounted for, and you will remember everything about this hiatus, so don't do or say anything you'll regret."

Interesting. "Am I prone to misbehavior?" I was attired as a country gentleman, my clothing all fitting me well enough, if a bit loosely. My boots matched, my heels were newish, and my seams all tidy. Perhaps I had a wife looking after my wardrobe?

The thought felt alien and sweet, but heaven help that lady if I'd forgotten her so easily.

"You are not at all, on your most vexed day, prone to misbehavior. Just the opposite."

"I'm a high stickler?" That didn't feel right either.

She paused as we approached a half-sunken walled garden. "You are a perfect gentleman who served honorably under Wellington. We are guests at a private race meeting in Berkshire, and the heat has tempers flaring. Somebody is rigging the races, and you are determined to figure who and how."

How... bold of me. "Truly? Am I some sort of horse-racing expert?"

"No, but you were asked to help, and you felt sorry for Mr. Tenneby. You learned that I was to be among the guests and thus attended against your better judgment."

"I fancy you." I knew that much, because even in our ten-minute acquaintance, I had taken a powerful liking to her. Miss West was confident, sensible, kind, and worried about me. A lovely combination, if not exactly what a gentleman hoped to inspire in the distaff.

"You fancy me, and I—heaven help you—fancy you. We are engaged to be married, my lord, hence our strolling together unchaperoned will not be remarked. Your quarters are on the first floor, and Atticus can see you safely to them. I'll have a tray sent up and come see you in the morning."

"Are you confining me to quarters?"

A military term, as was absent without leave. I'd served under Wellington, though I had no memory of that honor.

"I am suggesting a respite, until your mind rights itself, which it always does. I'll have a tray sent up to you in the morning, too, lest you have to brave a gauntlet of questions over the breakfast buffet. I'll tell any who ask that your eyes aren't equal to all the bright sunshine."

I became abruptly aware that I was sporting spectacles.

"Keep 'em on, guv," said the boy. "They're tinted to protect your eyes. Take 'em off and you'll regret it."

"My head does ache slightly." More than slightly, in fact. "And I'm thirsty."

"Ain't we all."

Miss West took her leave of us on the back terrace of the large, handsome manor house. Watching her bustle off, I experienced a sadness that made no sense. She'd said I was safe, but I would have felt safer had she not abandoned me. Not safer... happier, more at peace.

"C'mon, your forgetful-ship. Best get you outta sight while everybody's changing for supper." Atticus explained to me how to find my quarters and decamped for the steps that would lead to the kitchen and servants' hall. I made my way to my room, aware that the boy would soon reappear with a tray.

In those few minutes of solitude, I used a basin and towel to limited good effect and changed into silk pajama trousers and silk dressing gown. I apparently liked my creature comforts. I was weary to my bones, hungry, thirsty, and missing half my mind.

For some reason, the image of the tulips insisted on intruding on my musings. Drooping tulips along one side and the barrels across the yard full of cheerier specimens.

An odd detail to fixate on, but perhaps that was my habit, to fixate on details, forget my entire history, and worse yet, fail to recognize the lovely woman to whom I was engaged to be married.

What a muddle. What a complete, spectacular muddle, and apparently, a frequent state of affairs for me.

I slept long and hard, all the windows to my suite open, the bed curtains drawn back. Soft gray light illuminated my quarters as Atticus emerged from the dressing closet and made for the door.

"Wait a bit," I said, sitting up in bed and scrubbing at my eyes.

They ached, all of me ached, but it was the ache of a body that had finally found much-needed slumber. "Are you going onto the Downs today?"

"Thought I would. You're yourself again?"

"If you mean, have my memories returned, they most assuredly have. Thank you for your quick thinking last evening. Might you find Miss West's maid and convey the message that all's well? I'd like to accompany you for the morning gallops."

The Atticus whom I'd taken into service at the Hall months ago would have protested vocally. This slightly older, more self-possessed fellow looked me up and down. "Nobody wants you up there, guv, and it might not be safe."

"I'll be safe enough. I'll remain attached to some group or other. The morning gallops are an aspect of the meeting I've neglected to study."

"Won't do you no good, but it's too early in the day to start arguin' with you." He slipped out the door, a sentry going about his rounds.

By the time he returned bearing a laden tray, I was dressed for riding and mentally reviewing the previous day's races. Rigged, but unsuccessfully. Yesterday had also seen St. George make a second undistinguished showing in the steeplechase. Hyperia, when last I'd seen her, had been notably brisk with me, and Healy's impending doom had doubtless been on her mind.

If Pierpont was to be believed, the vultures were already circling over Tenneby's stable, anticipating his ruin and prepared to all but steal his horses under the guise of pity offers.

Atticus set the tray on the sideboard.

Two racks of buttered toast. A mound of fluffy omelet, thick slices of ham. The boy was wise beyond his years. "You found Miss West's maid?" I asked, whipping my cravat into an ever-serviceable *trone d'amour*.

"Aye, she said Miss didn't sleep well. The heat and all. Tempers belowstairs gettin' ragged. Hard to do the washin' when the cistern's empty."

I wasn't accustomed to the heat either, but I was well rested and pressed by a sense of time running out. Tenneby's meeting had only two more racing days, plus some match races on the final day. Those two days were run for the highest stakes, and still, I had no idea how anybody was tampering with the runners.

I ate heartily, though I left enough on the tray for Atticus.

When we arrived at the stable, I cadged a seat beside Sir Albertus's sister in her pony trap. Atticus took Atlas out under saddle, and we were soon joining the procession up to the Downs. Polite greetings were offered to the lady, while I merited the barest nod or muttered word.

"They're all tiring," Miss Reardon said, handling the ribbons with casual expertise. "The horses, the grooms, the owners. The big money is starting to change hands, and the whole business grows serious. Albertus won't admit it, but Dasher's performance yesterday, while victorious, was disappointing. He should have romped to victory, my lord. Romped. Pretty morning, though. A pity about the weather."

She kept up the predictable patter, nattering on about to whom Juliet should be bred now that her racing peak was behind her and how Wickley's colts weren't half bad, considering their owner never listened to his jockey. Somewhere in Miss Reardon's narrative, I gleaned that it was her money supporting Sir Albertus's racing ambitions, though she enjoyed the whole business too.

I thanked her for the ride and parted from her when we arrived at the prescribed patch for morning gallops. The horses, who had been walked and then trotted along the lanes and bridle paths on the way from the stable, knew the routine. The jockeys lined up by twos and fours on a level patch at the foot of a gentle hill.

The heats were organized such that a horse having an easy day was run beside another with the same agenda. The runners due for a harder workout paced one another and so forth. Atticus on Atlas formed a third for a pair that included Golden Sovereign.

As they awaited the signal to start, Lord Pierpont joined me.

"That boy is a natural," Pierpont said, swigging from his flask.

"Has the hands. Plenty of fellows can stick in the saddle, but that lad has the hands. He listens."

"He has to listen," I replied, "because he lacks the strength to impose his will on the horse. He's also on a beast who'd plant him for a serious lapse in manners."

"A very fine beast." Pierpont put away his flask and took up the field glasses he'd slung about his neck. "Denton's gone fractious on us. Watch, he'll not keep the pace with Golden Sovereign. He'll let himself be taunted into a flat-out run. He's getting too ornery for this business."

Pierpont scanned the other parties knotted along the ridge, his focus settling on Wickley and friends.

The signal was given, and Denton did not let himself be goaded into overexerting his horse. He kept the horse to a rapid pace, rather than an all-out effort against his galloping partner.

"Heaven preserve my sanity," Pierpont muttered, looking away from his field glasses briefly. "Here comes poor Mr. West's wonder horse. Such a pity the creature hasn't any heart for the win."

George, easily distinguished by his gray coat, streaked into view. If he'd been assigned a partner, that horse was far behind as George pounded up the hill, no slackening in his speed. His gait was poetically efficient, every muscle and sinew moving in synchrony to produce the most speed with the least effort.

He'd not looked like that on the steeplechase courses.

"He is fast," I said. Very, very fast and superbly fit. No wonder Healy had been enchanted.

"He needs to put that speed to use in competition," Pierpont said, once again studying Lord Wickley's group. "West ought not to allow him to sprint like that, not on this hard ground and not with the biggest races still to go."

The horse blazed past us, his jockey not even trying to check him.

"Handsome devil," Pierpont muttered. "Wrong temperament for a runner, though. Excellent form over a jump too. A pity."

The gallops were boring. Horses running this way, horses

cantering that way. Pierpont was clearly absorbed studying his human rival, while I was increasingly aware of the owners glaring daggers at me. Sir Albertus was consulting his flask regularly, while Wickley was lifting his chin in my direction while haranguing Tenneby.

"One gathers your presence is unwelcome," Pierpont said. "Take my horse back to the manor. I'll jaunt along with Denton on foot. Anything to annoy Wickley, especially now that the betting is becoming lively."

I wasn't intimidated by the dirty looks, but neither was my presence productive. I'd seen what I wanted to see, found nothing enlightening save for the degree of speed George could produce, and was growing uncomfortably warm standing around in the morning sun.

"Obliging of you," I said. "Which horse is yours?"

"The chestnut with the black saddle. Hercules insists my personal mount be allowed to loiter in the shade. No nurserymaid was more protective of her charges, I vow."

Pierpont had his field glasses pressed to his eyes again—Wickley was still holding forth, though the breeze snatched his words away— so I thanked Pierpont, climbed aboard my borrowed mount, and returned to the manor. I had hoped to find Hyperia in her quarters, but had no luck. Her maid was not to be located either, and no helpful note awaited me in my own chambers.

"I will just pay the call on my own," I muttered to my reflection as I dragged a brush through my hair. My locks were still too pale about my face—I was not meant to be blond—and too long, but not the snow-white tresses I'd acquired in France.

I did not look like myself, and I did not feel like myself. Surrounded by ill will, unable to quit the investigatory field, romantically frustrated, and craving some cold, sweet meadow tea.

That last, I could do something about. I troubled a passing footman with my request and took myself to the earl's suite at the far end of the family wing.

"Is Temmington receiving?" I asked the Welsh footman.

"On the balcony, my lord. He's grown quiet in the past few days. A visitor will cheer him up."

"I've asked for a tray from the kitchen. Might you send it out when it arrives?"

"Of course, sir."

The footman produced the understated good cheer of the seasoned retainer, but I saw worry in his eyes and heard a hint of forced jollity in his voice. The race meeting was not going according to plan, and the whole staff knew it.

"Temmington, good day." I bowed formally to my host of record. "A pretty morning."

"Too damned hot," he said, gesturing to a wicker chair beside his own. "Too dry, but we're to have rain. My bursitis declares it so, and so it must be. Tenneby's in the doldrums. His stallion won yesterday, but only by a nose. Wickley's seething. Pierpont had some luck, but word among the grooms is, that was not luck at all, but rather, somebody meddling with Albertus's mare. So much intrigue reminds me of the French court back in the day."

"You spent time in France?" I disliked even saying the word.

"One made the grand tour ages ago. I was among the last to enjoy that outing, I'm sure, and yes, I made my bow to Louis. His court was rife with intrigue, each noble maneuvering to do the other out of this or that royal favor. Say what you will about our royals, but they are church wardens compared to that lot. One almost pities the French now. Their nobility is like weeds, growing back more greedy and spoiled for having been scythed."

A change of subject was in order. "Tenneby's finances are likely to be pruned by this meeting. His stallion isn't performing well enough, and the rumors of rigging abound."

"All your fault?" the earl asked, his rheumy eyes twinkling.

"According to some, yes. I've been in the wrong places at the wrong times, and I am not of the turf brotherhood. I daren't leave, or I'd be proving my guilt."

"Unless you leave and the last few races are also thrown, eh? That's where the real coin changes hands, my boy. The early days are for assessing the competition and learning the terrain. The later matches are serious business, and I do mean 'business' in the financial sense."

He paused while a tray bearing tall glasses of meadow tea and two plates of biscuits was brought out.

I sipped and saluted. "To Excalibur's upcoming victories."

"To his upcoming crop of foals. Early indications are he's passing on both speed and strength." The earl sampled his tea. "Oh, marvelous. Was this your idea, my boy? Well done. The mint revives the spirits as nothing else."

The tea was good. Not as ambrosial as Mrs. Gwinnett's recipe at Caldicott Hall, but refreshing.

"We can't really blame Tenneby for what's gone amiss, can we?" the earl mused. "He meant well, but he lacks the *strut* to carry off a meeting like this. Evelyn would have managed matters more effectively, but the failing is on the sire side. Haven't much strut or prance myself, come to that. Neither did my brother. Our side throws a pleasant nature and common sense. Not bad traits, generally, but an impecunious aristocrat needs some arrogance to carry off his poverty."

"Does everything come down to bloodlines and athletic propensities?"

"In racehorses, yes. All vices are forgiven if the speed be sufficient. Eclipse had terrible form and a considerable temper, you know. Humans are more complicated, alas for us. Much is overlooked if one has breeding, but coin of the realm increasingly defines a man's standing, doesn't it? We call them beer barons and encroaching mushrooms, then rejoice when they marry our daughters."

I could have downed a gallon of the meadow tea. The biscuits were fast disappearing too. "Do you foresee Evelyn in such a match?"

The earl considered his tea. "Evelyn is too loyal to her brother. She keeps all the records for the stable and maintains the ledgers for the whole estate. She chooses the mares Excalibur services, too, and her judgment has been vindicated by the results. If ruin is Tenneby's lot, Evelyn will endure it with him and make it as bearable as she can. That girl should have been the earl, but here we are. Not enough strut on the sire side. A common failing among many an old respected family. This tea is wonderful. Tell Jones I'd like a supply of it while this heat torments us. Much cheaper than that stuff from Cathay."

I sensed that I'd both tired and saddened the old fellow, which had not been my aim. I'd saddened myself as well. To be referred to as *my boy* by an elder entitled to treat me so familiarly was a comfort I might seldom know again.

After a few more pleasantries, I took my leave, relaying the message to Jones as requested.

When I returned to my quarters, I sat out on my own balcony, watching lady guests play battledore on the lawn beside the walled garden. Competition was desultory, until Evelyn Tenneby took up a racket and put some strategy into the volleys. Laughter and shouts soon ensued, and the whole undertaking became livelier.

If only Tenneby could have married into some banker's family, and Evelyn could have...

A wisp of an idea floated by on the humid breeze. I closed my eyes and let the idea drift closer. *Strut* on the sire side. Excalibur, Dasher, Sovereign Remedy, Golden Sovereign, and Juliet... Four colts and a filly. Five colts, rather, if I included Blinken.

And Juliet had lost to Minerva, whose owner, Pierpont, raced only fillies.

The wisp of an idea lighted on my imagination and sprouted into a theory. While I sat, eyes closed, mind racing, the theory became a hypothesis that explained a great deal of the meeting's racing results. A great deal.

"It all goes back to Eclipse," I murmured as the ladies gathered up their effects and daundered toward the manor.

If I was right, then I knew who was rigging the races, and I knew why. I was not yet certain about the how, and without that, my theories would earn me only more ridicule. I needed to solve the central conundrum—*how* were the races rigged?—with convincing evidence, or watch Tenneby, his household, and his horses suffer social, financial, and practical disaster.

I was growing concerned that Hyperia was avoiding me at a time when my welfare might have been of heightened concern to her. True, I'd sent her word of my recovered memories, but still... Hyperia's efforts had often proven integral to the success of my investigations, so much so that I would not undertake one if the subject matter could not be shared with her.

I wanted to let her know of George's magnificent speed, wanted to air my who-and-why theory before her keen analytical eye.

I wanted to know that she was well, if not exactly having a grand time.

An under-chambermaid admitted to seeing Miss West exit the manor from the library, cross the terrace, and descend into the park. Hyperia had carried a small parcel and a parasol, but hadn't bothered to open the parasol. Upon questioning, the maid opined that the young lady had been wearing boots.

The parcel might well have been a book, possibly carried for show when the lady wanted a quiet hour to herself. Another quiet hour to herself.

I found my intended in the gazebo by the river. I approached quietly, quiet being second nature to a reconnaissance officer, and studied her. A book did indeed lay open on her lap. The closed parasol sat on the bench to her right. To her left, a straw hat was upside down, a pair of gloves folded into the crown.

Hyperia stared at the water, a handkerchief clutched in her hand.

I tossed a pebble into the sluggish stream. "Good morning."

"Julian." She closed the book and set it aside. "How long have you been spying on me?" Her tone was unwelcoming, not quite acerbic.

The tension between us had been building as steadily as the heat. Granted, Hyperia was fretting over her funds, and her concern was real. I was fretting, too, because whatever our current difference, I loved this woman and longed to marry her.

"Spying, Perry? Do I deserve that?" Rather than approach the gazebo, I stood several yards off on the path along the river.

"No. I do apologize. I'm out of sorts. I take it you're feeling better?"

Still no invitation to join her. "My memories are back in order, and I joined the outing to the morning gallops. I watched George go, and he's exceedingly, wondrously fast, Perry. Goes like lightning even without another horse to challenge him."

She rose and perched a hip on the gazebo's railing. The picture was lovely—young lady by the river in spring—but her mood was prickly.

"Then Healy fell for a true morning glory. Miss Tenneby says there's not much that can be done with a horse of that temperament. They don't understand the need to exert themselves later in the day."

"At least George is capable of speed. He might do well in the hunt field." Though riding to hounds was more a matter of stamina and a good clean jump than speed.

"Can George chase a fox well enough to replenish my settlements?"

Now, we came to the heart of the matter. "Might I join you?"

She gestured to the steps, and I took that for an invitation.

"I have a theory," I said, ascending into the gazebo, "regarding who is rigging the races and why, but I'm still at a loss to know how the mischief is being perpetrated. The matter wants more thought."

"Is it Wickley? He hasn't been at the game long enough to know how to properly train any given horse, but he boasts about knowing the dirty tricks."

"He also won't listen to Denton, who has been at the game

forever. What motive would Wickley have, though, when Pierpont's Minerva was one of the less likely victors?"

Hyperia pushed away from the railing and resumed her place on the bench. "Arrogance. Minerva might have been gifted with a win to set her up for greater failure this week. Anything to prove to the world that the Earl of Wickley is a true blueblood and Lord Pierpont a mere presuming courtesy lord."

"Anything except sticking it out at Newmarket where the real fanatics congregate? Anything except listening to Denton or promoting Denton to a training role? Wickley has all the motive in the world to win, but I have a harder time seeing him as a cheater. He's too mindful of his standing, too... fastidious about his reputation."

Though Hyperia was making me consider Wickley more seriously than I had, and that was all to the good.

She folded her wrinkled handkerchief and tucked it into her sleeve. "Wickley is very mindful of his standing, isn't he? And a reputation is an impossible thing to rehabilitate. What of Sir Albertus?"

I was abruptly weary of the subject of race rigging. My intended, the woman I hoped to spend the rest of my life with, wasn't even inviting me to sit beside her.

"Perry, what's wrong? You have been avoiding me, which is your right, but you've also been crying. Now when we ought to be fortifying ourselves with a moment of affection, you can't even meet my gaze. I know Healy's situation is vexing and that you refuse to come to the altar without your settlements, but that doesn't justify an estrangement."

"We're having a private discussion in a secluded gazebo, my lord. What variety of estrangement is that?"

Her *tone* was evidence of estrangement, as was her fascination with the slow-moving water.

"Hyperia West, we have been through much together, and you have shown me great patience and loyalty. You have also honored me with your trust, and I have done my best to reciprocate those gifts in every regard. I admit my efforts have been halting and inadequate on occasion, but I defy you to doubt my devotion. I don't give a ruddy damn for your settlements, and if need be, we can enjoy an eternal engagement. I am mortally concerned, though, that if you cannot confide in me—you, who demand to know my worst memories and greatest fears—then we are at an impasse that has little to do with your bumbling brother."

I stopped myself from delivering an ultimatum, but the temptation to invite her to cry off was great.

I gathered up the frayed ends of my patience and marched onward. "I understand, Perry, that you do not want to be wed out of pity. *Neither do I,* and the fear that your sentiments toward me tend toward pity rather than esteem haunts me. Perhaps you do pity me. Perhaps I no longer have your trust. You are shutting me out. You did not think to tell me you were coming to this meeting. You did not share Healy's latest folly until the need was beyond pressing. You kept the situation with your settlements from me until I had puzzled it out for myself. This will not do."

She was on her feet, hands fisted at her sides. "Marry *you* out of pity? You are a ducal heir, comely, in your prime, and lavishly solvent."

Utterly beside the point. "*I forget my own name*, and you don't turn a hair. Society shuns me, and I return the favor. Some label me a traitor. Others consider me daft. My eyes, even my hair... I am no prize, and I can admit that honestly. You, by contrast, are a pearl of great price."

She sniffled. "I am plain, I am old, and now I'm poor."

That was momentary defeat talking and more balderdash. "You are younger than I and gorgeous in your purposely understated way. You are formidably intelligent, kind, forbearing, and honorable. Perry..." I moved closer and bedamned to anybody who saw us. "I love you. I cannot offer you perfection in myself. Why on earth would you think I deserve it or even want it in return? I could not bear a perfect companion in this life. Harry was nearly perfect, and it drove me daft."

"*Him.*"

"And Arthur is a perfect duke, and Atlas is a perfect horse, but you... you are perfect *for me* in a world where I don't fit in. You break my heart when you push me away."

Plainer than that, I could not be, and if Hyperia was determined to chart a course away from me, nothing that I, Wellington with all his forces, or the heavenly intercessors could do would stop her.

The nightingale was serenading the morning, his song lovely, lonely, and poignant. The fellow sang his heart out in hopes of winning a mate, and he sang for us both.

Hyperia stood very tall, and all my dreams sank into an abyss of despair. I knew her, and I knew she was searching for the kind, honest words that would part me from her.

"Perry, please." *I love you.* To say those words now would be to beg. "Please talk to me."

She sighed, then, by slow degrees, listed into me.

I waited, and the bird caroled on.

CHAPTER SEVENTEEN

"I hate my brother, Jules. I hate him, and I mean that. He's a bad brother, and I am tired of being his sister."

I produced my handkerchief. "I'm plenty vexed with Healy myself."

Hyperia took my linen and dabbed at her nose, then turned her face against my shoulder and indulged in some protracted lachrymosity.

I'd been vexed with Healy before. I was ready to thrash him to kingdom come before Hyperia had gained her composure. By that point, we were sitting hip to hip on the bench.

"He t-told me I should set my cap for Wickley." Hyperia's voice was low from crying and bitterness. "Wickley would forgive even debts of honor from a brother-by-marriage. Healy tried to make a joke of it—I reminded him that I am engaged to you—but, Julian, I am tempted to allow you to meet him. My brother is incorrigible, and now my funds are gone, and all Healy can think is that I should marry to ease his debts."

Her funds could be replaced. Her willingness to repose her confidences in me was a more delicate matter. I squeezed her shoulder—

she was in my close embrace and making no move to leave—and took
a gamble.

"When I first stumbled down the mountains into France, I was
out of my mind. I had a knife and cloak. I could hunt, I could build
fires, I could fashion a shelter, and I was safe enough, but I was raving
mad. The first time I encountered another person, just some fellow
pausing by a stream, I was terrified. I lit off up the slope like the
hounds of hell were pursuing me. Got about twenty yards and
collapsed in a quivering heap."

"You were in a bad way."

"I was deranged with fear. I was afraid of sounds, light, shadows,
movement... I was the personification of dread. That you are suffering
something similar, something that makes you want to withdraw from
all life and joy and even from me, is intolerable."

My disclosure was met with silence and then, softly, "Oh."

The nature of that single syllable was encouraging. Hyperia had
uttered an *oh* that portended insight, that bore a hint of understanding. My hope had been to establish common ground with her, to put
us on the same footing. I knew what it was to feel destroyed, and she
was devastated by her brother's betrayal.

His most recent betrayal.

"Jules, I don't know what to do. I want to marry you, of course,
but Healy has stolen all I had."

"He hasn't stolen me. One challenge from my perspective is how
to restore your settlements, but the more pressing problem is how to
restore your trust in *us*. I consider myself bound to you, Hyperia,
whether we are wed or not, whether we ever wed. Healy's perfidy
doesn't change my loyalties."

She relaxed against me. "I do love you."

I hugged her lest I insist we have the banns cried.

"And I'm sorry, Jules. I did not mean to hurt you, but if we are
to cry off, if *I* am to cry off, then a cooling in our relations would
lend credibility to the decision. Especially if the cooling was clearly
one-sided. I am ashamed of Healy, ashamed I could not better

manage him. You are right about that too. I want to hide away and take long naps and not wake up until... until Healy isn't a problem."

"He is not your fault, Perry. He's simply a natural-born dunderhead. I often felt the same way about Harry, and he frequently told me I was the bane of his earthly sojourn."

This earned me a careful perusal. "Did he mean it?"

"At the time, I'm sure he did. I would be angrier with Healy, too, except that today I saw George run. The beast's speed is breathtaking."

"But fleeting, as it were."

We sat upon the bench, my arm around her shoulders, her arm about my waist. My heart was lighter, my mood sweeter. We had not solved the problems facing us, but I hoped we'd made progress on the problems that had lain *between* us.

"Jules, are the match races always held in the afternoon?"

Hyperia had leaped to one of those obvious-in-hindsight shifts in perspective. "Match races are agreed upon by the owners involved. The length of the course, terrain covered, weights, jumps, and so forth are all a matter of agreement. Healy cannot insist on a match first thing in the day. Pierpont at least knows of George's morning-glory tendencies."

"So does Wickley, but I gather Tenneby did not, and he's fairly well informed about the horses. Healy cannot move the races to the morning, but could I? Could I plead the heat and a lady's delicate constitution?"

Whatever else was true of the owners gathered for the meeting, they regarded themselves as gentlemen. "The cooler morning air would benefit the horses too. What if you enlisted Miss Tenneby's aid as hostess of this event, speaking for all the ladies? She could ask for the match races to be held in the morning."

"She'd do it. This could work, Jules."

Or not. George was allowed to run flat out in his morning gallops, nothing saved back for race days. Perhaps he was better conditioned as a result, but perhaps he'd be completely knackered by week's end too.

But one had to try, even for a serial bungler like Healy. "I saw Evelyn leading a group of ladies into the house following some after-breakfast battledore. They're likely in the conservatory or library. Would you like an escort?"

Hyperia sat up, smoothed a hand over her hair, and reached for her hat. "Yes, please. I am all at sixes and sevens."

"Battle nerves. The artillery has ceased its pounding, but the enemy is out there, and the infantry must yet deal with him. Patience, Hyperia, and steady on."

I could have waxed symbolic about forming an infantry square of two, but the image failed to inspire. I gathered up Hyperia's book and parasol instead and offered her my hand.

"What will you do with the rest of the morning?" she asked as we emerged from the trees along the river.

"I'm returning to the stable. The horses are fed, groomed, and housed there. The jockeys, grooms, and owners congregate there. The stable must be where the tampering occurs, and if I observe closely enough for long enough, the answer will come to me."

"Julian, you aren't welcome in the stable."

A towering understatement, and, in truth, I'd have less than a full day for my reconnaissance. "I will be careful."

We walked across the park, the grass dry beneath our boots. "You'll disguise yourself?"

"Atticus himself won't know I'm on hand."

"He's enjoying this meeting, isn't he?"

"Very much. Too much, I fear. Fancies becoming a jockey."

"Julian..."

"I know. Broken bones, never a decent meal, out in all weather. I'm trying to let the likes of Denton, Woglemuth, and Hercules make the argument for me."

We approached the garden, and on the terrace, footmen were

setting out some sort of pavilion along with the ubiquitous punchbowls.

"The conservatory must be too warm," Hyperia said, taking the book and parasol from me. "The heat really is oppressive."

I bowed. "Rain is on the way."

Hyperia hugged me, and I all but danced up to my room. That hug, beneath any number of windows and in plain sight of gawking footmen, restored all hope and vigor to my heart. I had only to catch a cheat, expose his methods, and heavily back George on his morning contests, and all would come right.

Or so I hoped.

The art of the disguise had become necessary to my work in Spain, and the old skills were in fine working order. With the help of some cosmetics borrowed from Hyperia's vanity and rice powder pinched from the old earl's stores, along with clothing provided by the Welsh footman and ashes from my own hearth, I became a grumbling geriatric gardener whose accent suggested Yorkshire origins.

Not that I said much beyond, *G'day to thee*, or *Must spuddle t' thistles afore they take hold*.

The last of the morning gallops were over, the sun baked the cobbles, and any groom stirring about did so slowly.

Pushing a wooden barrow appropriated from the kitchen gardens, I moved from one barrel of tulips to the next, inspecting as I went. My spectacles had been sacrificed for the sake of effective deception. The queue of hair trailing from my battered hat was gray. My attire was worn, patched, and quite loose, though my boots were sturdy.

"Poor mites," I muttered, examining one of the pots of tulips faring the worst. The soil was so much caked dust, the foliage a wilted memory on a pale stalk. Long past due for lifting.

I inspected and grumbled and inspected, pausing between every few barrels to consult the sun, wipe my brow, and—twice—to remove a boot and dump imaginary pebbles from inside. This went on until I could credibly repair to the shade for a protracted one-eyed nap, and then I resumed when the noon hour had passed.

"Hey, old man." Atticus had emerged from the shadows of the barn. "You'll miss nuncheon in the hall. Hadn't you best grab a bite before Cook puts the food away?"

"Thankee, lad. Thankee, but I'll bide awhile yet. Posies is done for, poor things." I hefted my barrow and moved to the next barrel.

Hercules Smith emerged and stood beside Atlas, hands on hips. "What are you about, old man?"

"He's tending to the flowers," Atticus said. "Such as they is."

"The flowers are past tendin'," Hercules retorted. "Get you back to the gardener's shed, old man, take a nap, and call it a day."

He would say that. "Stable boy does not tell gardener what to do. That lot,"—I used my elbow to point to the colts' side of the yard—"are faring well enough. This lot,"—I nodded to the fillies' side—"mostly want lifting."

"Then tend to your work and be gone with you. I don't want you underfoot when the evening work begins." He squinted balefully at the westering sun and stalked back into the barn.

"Best do as he says," Atticus added. "The grooms are short-tempered of late."

The tulips on the different sides of the yard were indeed faring differently. I had noticed before that some pots were holding their own against the heat, while others—fewer in number and mostly on the fillies' side—were past salvation.

The earl's comments about the sire line being problematic for the Tennebys came back to me, as did Hercules's ill will. The fillies' side... the dam line. The colts' side... the sire line.

A cool sensation washed over me, part insight, part surprise. "I know how they're doing it."

Atticus stepped closer. "*Guv?*"

"I know how he's rigging the races, and I know why. We've got him."

"Got who?"

"Our culprit. Can you get me a copy of the watering schedule?"

Atticus dug around in his pockets and produced a much-folded, grimy piece of paper. "Hercules set it up. Saves a lot of work."

"I'm sure it does. Is Corrie about?"

"Napping out back. Hard to sleep in the carriage house, with the nights so hot."

"Please tell him Caleb Bean would like a word with him at the smithy, and, Atticus?"

"Guv?"

"Mind your back. Things could soon grow lively." I collected my barrow and mentally thanked the flowers for their assistance. I would see the spent bulbs lifted and the survivors regularly watered if I had to lug the buckets from the kitchen garden myself.

By the time Corrie presented himself at the forge, I was again wearing my blue spectacles and gentlemanly attire. I'd brushed the powder and ash from my hair and taken out the braid, my boots were freshly shined, and I was keen to interview my witness.

"You." Corrie frowned, but he was too polite to simply turn and leave. "What does milord want with me now?"

"I want answers, and they had best be honest. Dasher won by a nose when that race was supposed to be his by lengths. Explain his morning routine on race day to me. What was different?"

Corrie glanced about, but the smithy and its yard were deserted— by design.

"I did the same as I allus do. No galloping. Half a ration of oats, a good grooming, then I took him out for some hand-grazing. The only decent grass is down by the river, and even that's getting sparse."

"His water bucket was empty?"

"Most of 'em are, come morning. Nights aren't coolin' off like they should."

And that misery had been very convenient for the cheater. "You let Dasher have a good long drink from the river, didn't you?"

Corrie looked like he was about to bolt.

"You did," I went on, "and that isn't part of the routine for this meeting, and you are worried that such a nice, long drink is why he was nearly defeated."

"How do you know that? Nobody saw me, and I kept trying to tug his head up, but he were desperate for that water. A thirsty horse can colic, and I know racin' with a bellyful of water is stupid, but the races were hours off, and... I didn't mean to slow him down."

"Joseph Corrie, listen to me: A thirsty horse can *die*. He can stumble on course and break a leg. He can fall and get his jockey injured or killed. Watering your horse probably saved his life, because for a certainty, he would have lost the race otherwise. He drank like a sailor arriving in his home port because the poor beast was absolutely parched."

Corrie studied me, honest blue eyes searching my face. "The buckets are almost always empty in the morning. You tellin' me somebody is dumpin' 'em? That's vile, that is."

The situation was worse even than that. "The flowers on the colts' side are thriving. Whoever is dumping the buckets is pouring the water into the flowers rather than risking wetting down the cobbles. The fillies are faring better because those races don't bring as much money, and it's the colts our cheater is after."

"What about Juliet?"

"I have a few theories regarding Juliet, but you've confirmed that the cheating is being done by withholding water from the favorites. I must confer with Mr. Tenneby, since this is his race meeting, and ask you to say nothing. I expect the matter will be resolved before tomorrow's races."

"Dumpin' the buckets. That's the work of a right varmint."

"A clever, determined cheat, in any case. Give no hint that you're on to him, but do see that Dasher, Juliet, and Blinken are amply supplied with water. Take them out hand-grazing by the river at the odd hour, but be casual about the whole business."

"I can do that." He paced off, then turned back. "Dasher won anyway, dint he? Won when he were parched. My old lad ran his heart out, and he won."

"He ran his heart out, he has the world's most devoted groom, and he did win against stacked odds."

To my discerning eye, the boy's walk had acquired a hint of confidence as he departed from the stable yard. He'd hold his tongue, for now, but nobody would stop him from singing Dasher's deserved praises when the race meeting was over.

That assumed, of course, that Tenneby listened to me when I explained to him who had been sabotaging the meeting, how, and why.

"If you insist, I will provide you a demonstration tomorrow before noon, when the Downs are deserted. I will use my own horse, my own jockey, and prove that I know how the races are being rigged."

Atlas might forgive me for that rash offer. Atticus never would.

Tenneby stared hard past my right shoulder at the neatly copied racing cards stacked on his desk. "But if you're the fellow running the rig, of course you'd know that."

"Tenneby, I am not the fellow running the rig. This rig cannot be run without the cooperation of the grooms, most of whom already hold me in considerable suspicion. Pierpont's grooms are in the best position to deny the horses their water."

"Right. I'd forgotten that part. Not a detail. This is all quite awful, my lord. You're sure Lord Pierpont Chandler is our villain?"

"I would bet what remains of my reputation on it."

Pierpont was charming, competitive, at ease among the fraternity, and even admired for his determination to win. He'd been clever and ruthless, first sabotaging poor Blinken, then putting his grooms up to galloping the best colts to exhaustion. His next scheme—denying water to the favorites during a hot spell—was truly diabolical.

When I'd examined Wickley's horse for signs of drugging, it hadn't occurred to me to do the simple tests that indicated serious dehydration. When a horse has been adequately watered, a finger pressed against his gums then released should result in a patch of skin gone momentarily white, then quickly restored to pink. The pink would come back much more slowly if the horse was seriously thirsty.

Even simpler would have been to take a fold of the beast's skin, pinch it together and watch how quickly the skin resumed its previous contour when released. A parched horse's skin would return to a smooth contour only slowly.

Simple tests, and neither I nor anybody else had thought to try them on the defeated favorites. If I did not stop Pierpont now, he'd just keep cheating the honest owners and mistreating the four-footed competitors.

The topic was grim. Tenneby's sitting room, by contrast, was lovely, in a horse-saturated way. The scheme was green, brown, and white, the furniture comfortably upholstered, the windows open to admit a humid breeze. Periodicals concerned with racing adorned the low table and the couch cushions, and a portrait of Excalibur held pride of place over the mantel.

Framed sketches had been arranged on the opposite walls, every one featuring an equine subject, and a pair of worn riding boots sat airing by the open balcony door. A leather crop lay on the mantel, and a pair of braided reins had been curled on the sideboard.

"One hardly knows what to do," Tenneby said. "For years, I've told myself I was fleeced at Epsom. Made a laughingstock before the whole fraternity. Now you explain the how of it—so simple, really—and one can hardly... I should call the blighter out."

"To graze his lordly arse with a bullet would offer considerable satisfaction, I'm sure, but he's a cheater, Tenneby. He has been running these schemes for years, probably even before you lost all that money at Epsom. He's good at it, though my guess is, your private meeting has seen him raise his dark art to new heights."

"Denying a horse water in this weather is heinous," Tenneby said. "I should at least plant him a facer."

I could not tell Tenneby what to do, though his situation was analogous to Hyperia's frustration with Healy. She wanted her settlements returned, down to the penny, and Tenneby needed coin far more than he needed to risk his life teaching Pierpont a lesson.

"If you could choose," I said, "between having the swindled funds restored to you or winging Pierpont in a duel, which would you choose?"

Tenneby paced to the balcony door, picked up a boot, and sniffed the interior. "I am supposed to say I'd rather put a bullet in him, rather see honor satisfied over pistols at dawn. An earl would say that. Wickley would say that and sound dashing." He put the boot down beside its mate.

"You would rather have the money. That speaks well of you."

"Does it?" He peered at me. "How? Isn't money supposed to be beneath me?"

"Your household is on the brink of ruin that has been coming closer for generations. Your sister is yet unwed. The old earl will soon go to his reward knowing he has failed his family. You getting your lights blown out under scandalous conditions makes life considerably more difficult for all who depend on you."

"Good point. Mustn't shirk. The trades must be paid. Uncle Temmie did the best he could and backed me for the win, as it were, when I am the long shot. Evelyn deserves to set up her nursery, if that's her desire."

He brightened, and then the slow-top, certifiably plodding, not-very-bright-about-anything-other-than-horses fellow said something kind, wise, and nearly shrewd.

"I know what to do. We'll ask Evvie for her views. She's overdue to get back a bit of her own from Pierpont, and she owns the family's whole complement of cleverness. Evelyn Tenneby will sort the whole business out, and Pierpont will rue the day."

His demeanor had become that of the scholar who'd come up with the obscure, difficult, *right* answer, and, in fact, he had. Seek help, rely on loved ones. *Pull together.*

"What of the earl?" I asked. "Do we tell him? The meeting is on his property, and the guests are swilling his brandy."

Tenneby's smile dimmed. "You think I ought to? I've brought scandal to the house when I meant to win us some time with the creditors."

I thought of Hyperia, trying to carry the whole burden of Healy's betrayal on her own. Of me, stumbling around on frigid mountain slopes, unable to tolerate even a greeting from another human being.

"Temmington is your family, Tenneby. Yours and Evelyn's. He wants to see you succeed, and he's nobody's fool when it comes to horse races. He is your backer. Trust him to take your part as you trust Evelyn."

"He is a dear old thing..." Tenneby's gaze fell on the painting of Excalibur, a magnificent creature who had already been the butt of an expensive, avaricious swindle, thanks to Pierpont. "We will tell his lordship and Evelyn, then. Pierpont has behaved very badly. You will explain matters to the others for me?"

In the interests of time saved, I would, but also because Tenneby was on the battlefield with only a very small square of supporters around him. He was right about this, too—one mustn't shirk. I had agreed to take up his fight, and I wanted to see him achieve the victory he deserved.

"Might Miss West join us? I believe she has a few matters to discuss with Miss Tenneby that relate to the races yet to be run."

"Miss West is clever. Evelyn likes her. I like her too. Bring her along, then, and we'll see what the ladies have to say."

He marched off, head up, shoulders back, ready for a council of war and looking every inch the heir to an old and respected title. He also looked like a man who'd been given hope for the first time in years.

I silently saluted him as he retreated.

Perhaps the valiant nightingale had been singing for Tenneby too.

"A dehydrated horse can't run," the old earl said. "We forget that. We're always worried that they mustn't be waterlogged at the starting line. Mustn't be allowed to guzzle the whole bucket when cooling out. We forget that withholding water can be just as bad. A putrid, unsporting trick."

"A *lucrative*, putrid, unsporting trick," Evelyn murmured from the sofa she shared with Hyperia.

We were assembled in the earl's sitting room, an airy space still adorned in the elegant, graceful style of the previous century. The carpet was faded Axminster, the walls sported faded blue silk, and the slightly worn upholstery matched the walls. Time had stolen the glory from the appointments, and yet, not a speck of dust or cobweb was to be found in the whole chamber.

Gilt frames and gleaming vases caught the light, though the sole bouquet was a dozen tulips on the sideboard in the red, yellow, and white theme of the stable.

A jarring note—also cheerful.

Tenneby propped an elbow against the mantel. "Won't do to call Pierpont out. He's a cheater, and I am not yet ready to take up my harp and wings."

"No duels." The ladies had spoken in very firm unison.

"No duels," I said, "but honor demands that Pierpont be held accountable. He stole victory from Sir Albertus and Wickley at least, and he was likely behind the mischief at Epsom three years ago. He was prepared to turn this race meeting into the scandal that hastened

Tenneby's ruin. For that, Pierpont deserves a severe comeuppance. The question is, by what means?"

We conferred, drinking a gallon of meadow tea between us. We sorted and tested and theorized and pondered. In the end, the ladies fashioned a plan whereby Pierpont would rethink and regret his great scheme to cheat his way to victory in the sport of kings.

"What of the bets already placed?" Hyperia asked. "Pierpont won a packet by defeating Juliet, but not a fortune."

"Less said the better," the earl observed. "Racing is a chancy sport. The risks aren't supposed to include cheating, but the unusual weather, hard terrain, and unfamiliar location all weigh against certainty. Sir Albertus recovered his losses with Dasher's victory. Excalibur held his own despite the tampering. Let the wagers stand."

I could not blame the old earl for his reticence. Temmington had an eye on the family reputation, and if Pierpont's mischief became widely known, the Acres would be recalled as the scene of a horrendous racing scandal. Hardly a legacy to bequeath to one's heirs.

"I agree," Evelyn added. "The results have been credible thus far and most of the wagers modest. But we put an end to Pierpont's cheating here and now, once and for all."

I was dispatched to fetch his lordship, whom I found lounging in the library, reading some publication out of Newmarket that reported racing results.

"Lord Julian, good day. You know a meeting has gone on too long when you're reduced to reading week-old results. Newmarket needs rain, too, apparently."

"My lord." I offered a quick bow. "The Earl of Temmington would appreciate the courtesy of a call. If you can tear yourself away from the results, he's receiving now."

Pierpont rose languidly. "Suppose I should observe the courtesies. Poor old boy doubtless wants for company. He's kept the house up fairly well, but one wonders how much longer Tenneby will be able to do likewise."

Tenneby would manage splendidly. "The family will contrive, I'm sure."

We made our way up to the earl's suite in silence, though a fresher breeze was whipping through the house, and the quality of the natural light suggested clouds might be moving in.

"I don't suppose you've considered placing any bets on these last few races?" Pierpont asked as we reached Temmington's door. "One can make a tidy sum in a very short time if one knows which horse to back."

"And you'd be willing to advise me?"

He smiled. "With pleasure, though you might be surprised at some of my choices. I have an eye for the unappreciated gem, you know."

Charlatan. Varlet. Swindler. Cad... "I will continue to keep my coin in my pocket, thank you just the same."

We were shown into the sitting room. The earl in his Bath chair sat near the empty hearth, the ladies were on their couch, and Tenneby stood by the sideboard. The footman hovered near the door by arrangement.

"A gathering, I see." Pierpont bowed to the ladies. "How pleasant. I sense we're in for a change of the weather. That will be pleasant, too, I daresay."

Evelyn gestured to a wing chair opposite the earl's perch. "Please have a seat, my lord, and before you begin to work your way around to offering for Excalibur, you should know that we're on to your scheme, and I swear on the bones of Eclipse, you will be made to pay for your trickery."

Pierpont eyed the door.

I smiled at him and gestured to the indicated chair. The race was on, and Lord Pierpont was no longer the favorite.

CHAPTER EIGHTEEN

"Why would I offer for a horse," Pierpont began, "who, despite all efforts and breeding to the contrary, could barely eke out one victory on home terrain? Tenneby's aging stallion is an object of pity in the stable yard, and one does so hate to see a proud man made a fool of. Epsom three years ago was bad enough, but really, Tenneby, you need to sell that horse and get what you can for him."

"Sell him to you?" Tenneby asked.

"I would take him off your hands, provided the transaction was handled discreetly. One doesn't want to be known as a bleeding heart in this business. I'm sure you understand."

I gave Pierpont credit for steady nerves, but then, a man whose fortunes were built on chicanery needed a criminal's brand of fortitude.

"One doesn't want to be known as a cheat either," I said, "and you deserve that reputation many times over."

Pierpont studied his manicured nails, then aimed a pitying look at me. "*One hears* that you do not deal well with excessive heat, Caldicott. One hears that Spain robbed you of your wits and, clearly, your common sense too. Perhaps you'd like to retract that last, nigh laughable accusation?"

"I'd rather back it up with facts. The horses at this meeting who have inexplicably lost their wind just short of the finish line exhibit the very symptoms of equines deprived of water. They make a fine start, run hard, and hit the end of their tethers just short of victory. Caleb Bean agrees with my deductions, and I've offered to demonstrate the technique for Tenneby—for the whole meeting—if necessary."

Pierpont crossed his legs at the knee, which a gentleman wasn't supposed to do before ladies in proper company.

"An imaginative conjecture, I grant you. I especially like the appeal to the stalwart blacksmith, but I run mares, Caldicott, and but for Minerva's victory, the distaff have been unaffected by this lack of wind. Minerva was the second favorite, after all."

"You tampered with Juliet," Miss Tenneby said. "Your grooms did, rather. Probably a little test of the terrain and a sort of joke, on the whole meeting, to put some needed cash in your pockets. Even a cheater needs stakes money. By the time the fillies ran, your Hercules had convinced the other grooms to cooperate with his leading-horses-to-water scheme. The drought has been a godsend for your ambitions, my lord, but you weren't clever enough."

"My dear,"—Pierpont smiled with exquisite condescension—"at the risk of appearing ungentlemanly, might you not be viewing the situation from the perspective of—one hesitates, but must be firm in all matters of reputation—a woman scorned?"

Evelyn beamed back at him. "More like a woman who feels pity for a bumbler and doesn't want to see him hanged."

Pierpont rose abruptly. "I refuse to listen to such pure nonsense. The Tenneby family is on the brink of ruin, and wild accusations such as that will only hasten their downfall. I must in all good faith caution you lot to hold your tongues lest there be repercussions you regret. I've been more than tolerant, but this clumsy attempt to ambush me is at an end."

He was fortunate that the ladies were not in possession of their parasols.

"Pierpont, sit down," I said. "The particulars are as follows: You buy only fillies, claiming they keep their value after their racing careers because they can become broodmares. You buy the best bloodlines you can afford, and your reasoning makes sense up to a point."

"Of course it makes sense." He sat. "I am nobody's fool."

Anybody could become a fool for love. "Beyond that point, it's very odd thinking. The fillies' purses are smaller than the colts', and yet, the females cost just as much to house, train, and feed as their brothers. Then too, the fillies have no hope of becoming broodmares without the cooperation of a first-rate stud to service them. Ladies, my apologies for blunt speech."

"None needed," Evelyn snapped. "You were after the colts, Pierpont. You fixed races that made Golden Sovereign, Dasher, Blinken, and Excalibur all perform poorly. Excalibur and Dasher pulled out victories, but not the easy wins they deserved. Your next move would have been to make pity offers on the disgraced colts, all of whom are also descended from Thoroughbred royalty."

"Three or four years from now,"—I took up the narrative—"you'd have the most impressive crop of youngsters in the realm, a fortune in horseflesh, just like old Richard Tattersall made with his Highflyer and the daughters of Eclipse."

Pierpont's mouth opened, then closed.

"Don't make it worse," the old earl put in. "I know your papa, you scurrilous young jackanapes, and he'll be none too pleased to hear of this."

For the first time, Pierpont's lordly demeanor faltered. "You'd carry tales supported by nothing more than conjecture and coincidence?"

Enough of this. "Sir Albertus's groom allowed Dasher a protracted drink of water—which the horse was desperate to have— the morning before the race, which is how Dasher snatched victory from the jaws of your scheme. Excalibur outran your villainy on the strength of sheer determination. The stronger case comes from the flowers, Pierpont."

He glowered at me. "What flowers? I've not sent anybody flowers."

"The flowers," Tenneby said, "that Evelyn insisted we set out to decorate the stable yard. The tulips in my stable colors. On the fillies' side, the flowers are wilting and dying. The grooms and gardeners were all given orders to conserve what water we have for the household and the horses. All of the stable yard flowers should have been casualties of the drought."

Pierpont was on his feet again. "What has that to do—?"

Tenneby mustered an expression that even I found intimidating. Thunderous, righteous, and very, very determined. Pierpont sank back into his chair.

"On the colts' side," Tenneby went on, "the flowers are doing much better. Why? Because your grooms, in addition to not watering those colts at the river as they agreed to do, dumped out the buckets hung in those stalls for the horses to drink from through the night. Any one of those gallant young equines could have expired in an agony of colic thanks to you, Pierpont. I am certain that, if questioned, your grooms will admit to the orders you forced upon them."

"They won't have to," I said. "My tiger was dispatched to follow Hercules on this morning's watering rounds. Atticus will confirm that Hercules led Sovereign Remedy away from the stable yard, but stopped short of the river without allowing the horse to drink. Remedy is scheduled to run for considerable money tomorrow."

"That is..." Pierpont shot his cuffs. "That is Hercules's affair and nothing to do with me. Grooms are prone to jealousies, and..."

I let him run out of puff, as it were.

"I have committed no crime," he said at length. "Betting on the horses is a matter of honor. No court would convict me of anything based on these, these... spiteful conjectures. I will take my mares and leave, and this is the last you will ever see of me at one of your slipshod private meetings, Tenneby. I wish you the best, but fear you and your stables will be very poorly received at any competition worth the name."

Threats. Pierpont was going down swinging.

"Pierpont," I said, "I will explain the whole of your very bad behavior to every owner at this meeting unless you cease denying the obvious. The flowers don't lie. I doubt Hercules will lie for you. He's a horseman at heart, and what you've asked of him goes against the grain of his very soul."

The threat of exposure to his titled father had bothered him, but the thought of revealing his unscrupulousness to his racing cronies caused Pierpont to go pale.

"Very unsporting of you, my lord, and your own reputation among the other guests is less than pristine. Far less. For your own sake, you must not spread such vicious rumors. I could easily point a finger at Tenneby too. He's bleated for three straight years that he was cheated at Epsom, and if that's not a motive to throw his own race meeting, nothing is. I suggest you exercise great caution."

I would exercise caution, but not in the direction of Pierpont's choosing. Before I could embellish further, Hyperia rose.

"I've heard enough," she said. "Lord Pierpont, if you have any sense, you will resolve this matter to Lord Julian's satisfaction. Do that, and I will forget the entirety of this discussion. Perhaps the rest of the company will join me on the terrace for a glass of punch? Lord Temmington, you must come too. You've been least in sight for too long, and I'm sure you have stories from past meetings that the guests would love to hear."

Every inch the duchess, that was my Perry. The room cleared. The footman stepped out into the corridor and closed the door, leaving me alone with Pierpont.

Time for the gallop to the finish, and I did not intend to lose to a cheating scoundrel.

~

"The quality of fillies you've purchased come dear," I said. "As a fourth son, one without a wife or independent wealth, you needed means to acquire your future broodmares. Fixing races provided you those means. Don't bother to deny it."

"I haven't admitted anything."

Stubborn, which would serve him no longer. "You won't have to. The facts already stated convict you. Your grooms graciously inveigled the whole meeting into their cooperative schedule for watering horses. You grew too ambitious, Pierpont. At Epsom, probably at half the courses where your mares competed, you simply had Hercules step into some promising favorite's stall and dump out the water bucket two or three times prior to that horse's scheduled races. Hercules is well-liked and a familiar sight. If asked, he could say he was kindly refilling the bucket, not emptying it."

Pierpont went to the sideboard and helped himself to a brandy. "You can't prove that."

"You can't disprove it. Tenneby was probably your first big swindle. He was cheated out of twenty-eight thousand pounds, money he very much needed, that should have been won by a colt the likes of which England hasn't seen in years. The next Herod or Highflyer, maybe the next Eclipse, but you sent Excalibur back to Berkshire in disgrace."

"Every horse has an off day."

"Pierpont, I will tell *Wickley*. You even turned your dastardly machinations against him, and then you had the nerve, the absolute gall, to throw accusations of unrequited love at Miss Tenneby."

The hand holding Pierpont's drink began to tremble. He set the glass down without tasting the brandy. "I beg your pardon."

"For the esteem in which you hold Lord Wickley, you should not have to beg anything of anybody, but for the damage you have done to countless good horses and honest owners, you should be covered in shame."

He braced a hand on the sideboard as if assailed by a paroxysm.

"The race is over, Pierpont. Give it up. Your personal life is private, but the cheating has come to an end."

He drew in a breath and let it out slowly. Then another. From the terrace below, laughter floated up—Wickley's distinctive merriment —and the murmur of friendly conversations. The sound seemed to penetrate Pierpont's awareness as all my admonitions had not.

"You cannot say a word. Caldicott, it's worth my life. I beg you, be silent."

He was contemptible in his self-pity and arrogance. A creeping, posturing, lying insult to the racing fraternity, a scoundrel and a swindler, et cetera and so forth.

He was also a man with a broken heart and no hope, no sliver of a miraculous possibility, that he would ever see that heart healed. His brothers with their burgeoning nurseries and cheerful Society marriages had what Pierpont never would and couldn't even bring himself to want. Wickley, in all his golden, lordly strutting and bumbling, would never know the blows he'd dealt Pierpont under the guise of either rivalry or casual bonhomie.

"Tenneby is decent to his bones," I said. "Miss Evelyn wants her family's fortunes restored, though you had best give her a wide berth going forward. She proposes the following resolution: You will pay for Excalibur's stud services and pay handsomely. You will send the first three foals to Tenneby when they are ready for training and sign them over to Miss Tenneby."

He nodded, took a shaky sip, and nodded again. "I can do that."

"You will bet heavily against Excalibur in the final race. The details I leave to you and Tenneby. He isn't looking for the full twenty-eight thousand pounds with interest, but you stole a fortune from him and knew that he'd never be able to hold you accountable. Worse yet, you put his reputation at risk when you know him to be a man above reproach."

"I don't have... That is... I'll need some time."

"You will need to sell off some of your mares, once they are in foal to Excalibur, just as you planned to do, but only with Tenneby's prior permission. The majority of the proceeds will go toward the wagering debt you incur at this meeting."

"You assume Excalibur will win?"

"We both know he will if he's allowed to run a fair race. Otherwise, what was this whole debacle in aid of?"

Pierpont sipped his drink again, his hand steady. "I didn't really want Blinken or Dasher, but Sir Albertus does get on one's nerves. I contented myself with disgracing Juliet. Won a tidy sum. I would have been content with Golden Sovereign or Sovereign Remedy. They aren't quite in Excalibur's class, nobody is, but they belonged to *him*. My allowance stops when I turn thirty, and I have only a few more years to establish myself. The horses take every groat I have, but Wickley is turf mad, ergo... The plan seemed so sensible when I first concocted it, and it would have worked splendidly in another few years."

The racing obsession would have provided the bond, however competitive, that was better than nothing, and the scheming would have provided the means to continue racing.

"Does Wickley suspect you of holding him in particular regard?"

Pierpont shook his head. "Of course not. He'd be horrified. You doubtless are too."

"A ruthless cheat is a horrifying prospect, but where your affections lie is your business. I told the others that I was certain I could bring you around to atoning for the harm you've caused—some of the harm. I did not tell them how I would convince you to see reason."

"You will hold your tongue?"

This was what Arthur faced every waking day. Anybody who knew the true nature of his love for Banter could see him disgraced and hanged.

I could do better than simply holding my tongue. "You have my word that should anybody within my hearing speculate on the nature of your regard for Wickley, I will dismiss their dangerous and unkind gossip with all the lordly disdain I can muster, which is considerable when I'm in good form."

He nodded again. "One appreciates... That is to say, you have my thanks."

"None needed. Try to show the colors at lunch, and go easy on the brandy. You face a gauntlet of your own making. Should I ever hear that you're up to your old tricks, or that you're not keeping the bargain with Tenneby, I shall wax eloquent about courtesy lords who cheat at the races."

"I understand." He finished his drink. "How did you know, Caldicott? I've been endlessly discreet. That is, I've never even hinted... but you knew."

"I suspected. Up on the Downs, you didn't watch your own horses on the gallops. You did not watch your competitors' mares. You watched only Wickley. You have a fine pair of field glasses and you kept them trained on Wickley."

Pierpont nodded. "But that was only a suspicion."

"Nobody else took note of your behavior, Pierpont. You needn't worry. Wickley's laughter is meant to attract notice, after all. My suspicion bloomed into a hunch when I recalled that you had approached me about keeping my eye on Wickley. You didn't quite point a finger at him—you in fact described him as honorable—but you hoped that I might be distracted from watching you."

A cleverly timed ploy, given the opening set-to between Paddy Denton and Josiah Woglemuth, and Wickley's possible involvement in it.

"You watched me anyway, damn the luck."

"I considered what I knew of you, and it was ancient history that confirmed my theory. Three years ago, you purposely caught Miss Tenneby's eye. Her brother was not yet the heir, such that she'd have been considered an acceptable match for a marquess's son. You had already devised a scheme for ensuring that Excalibur was disgraced, and you had any number of informants among the racing set. You did not need to winkle any of Tenneby's racing secrets from her. You had no *apparent* reason to pretend to court the lady."

"Except," Pierpont said, "that Wickley was taken with her.

Evelyn knows all about racing, she wouldn't mind a few rough edges on a newly fledged peer, and she is clever. Wickley adores cleverness."

"To be quite blunt, you did not want to lose Wickley to Miss Tenneby. She might have discouraged his rivalry with you, or worse, seen the situation for what it was. She is clever, but she's also kind. She has proposed a solution that allows you to survive with your reputation and your racing stable intact, and that should matter to you."

I resisted the urge to sermonize on the point.

"I will offer her a sincere and overdue apology. You have the right of it. I was not thinking clearly, and... I expected him to fight for her. He truly is mad for the turf."

Easier perhaps, to lose the contest to a lot of galloping horses than to a clever lady or unkind fate.

"Which means as long as you run your mares, you and he will cross paths." Would that be consolation or torment? None of my business.

"So we will." Pierpont stuck out a hand. "You've been spectacularly decent, Caldicott."

I did not want to shake. He was a swindler and a thief. He'd put horses and jockeys at risk of death for his financial gain. He was selfish and nasty and a thousand other contemptible things.

He was also a man cheated in love and so very, very lonely. Given his standing in Society and his abruptly reduced financial prospects, he likely always would be.

I shook, we bowed briefly, and I absented myself, leaving him to the dubious consolation of Lord Temmington's brandy and—call me a fool—an unburdened conscience.

Twelve hours of steady, pattering rain pushed the next set of races back a day, to give the ground time to absorb the moisture. The old earl had made that suggestion, and the owners had been too polite to gainsay him. Since leaving his apartment at Hyperia's insistence, he'd hardly returned to it. Wickley in particular wanted to hear every tale, myth, and memory Temmington had from his racing days, and Miss Evelyn goaded her uncle shamelessly to share them all.

In the stable yard, Woglemuth had declared that, given the rain, grooms would resume taking their own horses, and only their own horses, down to the river for watering, lest a tendon sprained on the muddy riverbank become an excuse for brawling.

His proclamation was met with an odd sort of relief, suggesting that at least some suspicions had been swirling over Hercules's cooperative watering schedule.

The horses were thus given time to recover from any tampering, and Tenneby and Pierpont had an interval during which to agree on the specifics of reparation.

I left them to it. I'd successfully completed my mission, my intended strolled at my side, and the only lingering issue was the match race St. George was about to run on this lovely spring morning.

"You brought up Wickley?" Hyperia asked as we passed the viewing pavilion.

"I might have mentioned that Wickley would be especially disappointed to learn of Pierpont's scheming."

She nodded to Miss Evelyn, who had said earl firmly by the arm some yards away. "That must have been an awkward exchange."

Hyperia and I had not discussed this aspect of the situation privately. I'd given Pierpont my word, and I intended to keep it.

"The confrontation as a whole seemed to come as a relief to Pierpont. He'd probably begun his mischief out of a younger son's need for some quick cash and realized he'd happened onto a means of establishing himself among the racing brethren, where he dearly longed to be. He became more ambitious the longer he kept at it, though all the while, he knew better. He's not a scoundrel at heart, and now he will mend his ways."

We walked along among the crowd on the viewing hill, the mood around us cheerful in part thanks to the rain and in part thanks to a plan announced by Pierpont and Tenneby to partner in the brood-mare venture. Excalibur's spectacular win the previous day had occasioned vociferous congratulations to both and protracted discussions between Tenneby and several other owners.

Including the Earl of Wickley.

"Wickley will offer for Miss Tenneby," Hyperia said. "He told me so, but he doesn't think it appropriate to ask a lady's permission to pay her his addresses at a race meet."

"Miss Evelyn might view the matter differently."

"Jules?"

"Hmm?" The horses were at the starting line, which at this early hour was still in shade, as was much of the course. St. George was on his mettle, and well he should be. The match race had attracted other entries, given the cooler early hour, and the wagering was fierce.

"Even if George loses, we will still be engaged."

"Utterly correct, Miss West." But what was she implying?

"You meant it when you said that your devotion to me does not rest on marriage vows now or ever."

"Truer words and all that. Healy looks nervous. I find that encouraging." I kept my tone light, though I wished the crowd around us to perdition and longed to take Hyperia's hand.

"Well, my devotion to you should not rest on having settlements, and while I'm on the subject, I have no right to demand that you share your memories or nightmares or imaginings with me. I was wrong to insist, and I'm sorry for presuming."

I did take her hand—to blazes with the milling crowd. They should all be watching the start anyway.

"You were not wrong to ask, Perry. You were not wrong to inform me that you felt rejected and belittled by the way I guarded my privacy. I was not wrong to need that privacy, just as your desire to manage Healy without creating any fuss wasn't wrong either. If we are truly devoted, we will have failed missions. We will consult inaccurate maps. We will make fallacious assumptions. But we'll discuss our difficulties like the allies we are. Agreed?"

She squeezed my hand. "Agreed. I do hope George wins, for Healy's sake."

She smiled up at me, and I was helpless not to smile at her like the most fatuous, besotted, hopeless gudgeon ever to make sheep's eyes at his beloved.

"With respect to Healy..." I put Hyperia's hand on my arm and resumed our progress.

"Julian?"

"I hedged my bets."

"But you aren't wagering."

"Not on the horses. I mentioned to Healy that I knew what he was about, buying a racehorse, bumbling his way into a private meeting. I suggested that his next play will be a satire set in the racing world and that this whole outing was undertaken by him in the way of researching his topic."

"A play? A stage play? About racing?"

"He seemed to like the notion. He went off muttering and rubbing his chin, and I saw him an hour later scribbling furiously in the library, cuffs turned back, a full tea tray sitting ignored at his elbow."

"He was still there last night. I went down to return a book, and he didn't even look up when I walked in. Julian, I love you, and sometimes I also adore you."

What did a fellow say to that? I patted her hand. "Then I have work to do. Nothing less than constant adoration shall become my fixed goal."

She discreetly elbowed me in the ribs, and all the joy in the universe filled my heart.

The horses ran splendidly. St. George beat the lot by five easy and excessively lucrative lengths. In the general applause that greeted the victor, I kissed my beloved, and she kissed me right back.

Healy won a considerable fortune. Tenneby was beaming more

brightly than the sun. Wickley sauntered about in a besotted daze, and Miss Evelyn exuded great good cheer. But the true winner at that long, hot, difficult race meeting was my humble self. The investigation had been successful, and more significantly, Hyperia and I were firmly in each other's good graces.

All that mattered was right with my world.

And as it happened, Healy's play was hilarious and quite successful. My next investigation was far from hilarious—felony crimes seldom are—and, for most of the undertaking, I and my cohorts were far from successful.

But that is a tale for another time!